Letting Go

Debby Fowler

A Felicity Paradise crime novel

ISBN – **978 185022 206 4**

Published by Truran, Goonance, Water Lane, St Agnes,
Cornwall TR5 0RA
www.truranbooks.co.uk

Truran is an imprint of Truran Books Ltd

Text © Debby Fowler 2006, reprinted 2011
Cover photograph © The publishers

Printed and bound in Cornwall by R. Booth Ltd,
The Praze, Penryn, TR10 8AA

Acknowledgements
I would particularly like to thank Jo Pearce who turned my
appalling writing into something readable, to Sally Gilbert
and Winnie Pollard for being such reliable and long suffering
couriers, to Tony Stevens for sharing his knowledge of all
things maritime, to Nigel Stevens for his computer skills, to
Ivan and Heather for their huge help and encouragement and,
as always, to my husband and children for enduring the
inevitable mood swings and erratic catering, which
unfortunately seem to accompany my writing efforts.
Bless you all

For Michael, Charlie and Deets

PROLOGUE

1st May 2002, 6.15 a.m., Warwick College, Oxford

Harold Rose had been a porter at Warwick College for over forty years and he loved his work. The succession of students who had passed through the lodge, year after year, would have been astonished to know just how much he revelled in their exploits, for his apparent disapproval of all student excesses was legendary. No one could ever recall having seen him smile.

The girl was in a state: her boyfriend would not respond to her increasingly frantic knocking on the door of his room; they would miss the May morning celebrations at Magdalen Bridge. Could he help? He could, and with a resigned expression and an audible sigh, he reached for his keys.

The smell of vomit was the first thing that assailed Harold's experienced nose as he cautiously opened the door. Oliver Colhoun enjoyed the privilege of his father's old room in the oldest part of the college, overlooking the quad. It was a

1

beautifully proportioned room, but the squalid scene that confronted Harold obliterated any traces of its rich and glamorous history. The boy was half on the bed, half on the floor, his head in a pile of sick. He appeared to have vomited in several places. There were beer bottles littered about, a half-finished takeaway, the food dried hard in its foil dish ... and an empty syringe on the rumpled duvet. Peering over Harold's shoulder, the girl screamed.

'Is he OK?'

Harold stepped into the room and went through the motions of feeling for the boy's pulse, but it was just a gesture for the poor girl's sake. He had been in Korea and he had seen a great deal of action. He knew immediately that the boy was quite dead.

1

The last words Felicity Paradise said to her husband, Charlie, were spoken in anger.

Now their argument seemed so trivial. At the time, it had fitted into a pattern of bickering, which had begun when Charlie agreed to take on the Colhoun case. It had developed into a kind of ghastly game between them, and seemed to erupt every time they were alone.

'I'll be very late tonight,' he'd called as he opened the front door.

'You can't be. The Fergusons are coming to dinner.'

'Sorry, nothing I can do, I'm afraid. I have the preliminary hearing next Wednesday – there's a mass still to do. Anyway, I can't stand the Fergusons, as you well know. They're your friends, not mine; you'll have a much better time without me.'

'You could consider cutting down on the lunchtime sessions in the Lamb and Flag – that would get you home several hours earlier.' She could hear the unattractive bitter note to her voice.

'Fizzy, I can't get home until late tonight and

that's all there is to be said.'

'Sometimes Charlie, you're such a selfish pig.'

That was it, the end of twenty-six years of marriage. The next time Felicity saw him was to identify his body.

They had done their best with his appearance, she could see that, but his head had a kind of caved-in look on one side. Apparently, the car had thrown him up into the air and his head had slammed down on the edge of the kerb, destroying his clever brain and breaking his neck. Death was instantaneous, they kept telling her. No pain, no fear. There simply had not been time. Felicity didn't believe them. She imagined that journey, Charlie's final journey, from being struck by the car to seeing the pavement rushing up to meet him. It must have seemed like a long time, certainly enough time to feel fear.

In the mind-numbing days following his death, Felicity had performed surprisingly well. She had comforted her two grown-up children and little grandsons and had insisted on going back to work part-time the day after the funeral. She replied to the hundreds of letters of condolence and had done her best to answer patiently and unemotionally the rather intrusive questions of the police. Even the return of Charlie's poor broken bicycle had not moved her, had not prompted the storm of tears the young and hesitant policeman had obviously expected. The look of a frightened rabbit turned to one of undisguised relief when she calmly thanked him, but asked him if he would dispose of it for her. It seemed that nothing going on around her could touch her, it was unreal, as if she were seeing life through a gauze curtain – distant, removed, and absolutely nothing to do with her. Yet, endlessly in her head, her final conversation with Charlie played and replayed, like some awful looped tape.

Even now, four months later, sitting in the early autumn sunshine on the harbour wall, she felt no better, no clearer, still in a land of fog. It frightened her that to the outside world, she appeared to be functioning so well – 'you're marvellous, Fizzy, the way you've coped' – while inside she was a mess, a nightmare casserole of guilt, anger and downright misery. It was odd that a perfect stranger in the form of her landlady at the slightly eccentric B & B at which she was staying, seemed to sense something was seriously wrong and was treating her as if she were an invalid. Annie Trethewey had been a daughter, a sister and a wife to fishermen, all now dead. She herself was elderly, bent and apparently frail but Felicity could sense the strength in this little woman. At a time in life when retirement seemed appropriate she was running a highly successful business from the pair of cottages just off the harbour where she had herself been born and where she had raised her children.

'It's not the money I do it for,' she confided to Felicity. 'I do it for the company; I like having people about the house. Now, take your coffee and go and sit on the harbour wall. There's a nice bit of sunshine out there, that'll do you good, my girl.'

Felicity, doing as she was told, sipped her coffee and smiled. 'Some girl,' she thought.

She gazed around her appreciatively. It was a beautiful, colourful scene which managed to appear both relaxed and busy at the same time. The tide was coming in fast and two fishing boats were being prepared to leave harbour, decks scrubbed, lobster pots loaded. Beside her, little hire boats were being run down the slipway and secured on moorings. There were few visitors around as yet, but up and down the Wharf, shops were opening, awnings unfurled, pavements swept. The area outside the Sloop Inn was being hosed down and tables wiped. There was a sense of purpose, of industry, of calm routine and all set against the magnificent backdrop of St Ives Bay with its translucent blue-green water, white sand and, today, the sun riding high in a clear blue sky as if it was midsummer. Felicity could already feel its heat. She envied this little town its sense of community as it prepared for the day ahead.

This was a very different visit to St Ives from the ones she had made with Charlie in the past. With Charlie they had always stayed in the big hotel just outside town. Charlie liked plush hotel life and would have been appalled by the intimacy of Mrs Trethewey's Cormorant Cottage. For some reason, it suited Felicity very well just at the moment. She had a tiny bedroom, sparse but clean, looking over a back courtyard with no view of the sea, but its simplicity was pleasing. The only other guests were a couple of energetic walkers, probably a few years older than Felicity herself, she judged, who left early and

6

returned late, flushed, exhausted and very self-contained. Mercifully, they seemed to require nothing socially from Felicity at all.

It had been a sudden decision to come to St Ives. For some weeks now both her children and her best friend, Gilla, had been urging her to take a holiday, had even all offered to come too. She knew, however, that she needed to be alone – alone to reconcile the person she was on the outside with the emotional mess inside.

Charlie Paradise had been a very well-known character around Oxford. He was a moderately successful barrister but it was rather more his flamboyant, larger-than-life personality, which made him such a memorable figure. An extraordinarily good-looking young man, he had matured well. Latterly, he had put on too much weight but had maintained his shock of hair, which had gone seamlessly from glorious blond to a fetching white. His dress – ancient tweeds, combined with a series of flamboyant bow ties – coupled with his preferred mode of transport, an old 'sit up and beg' bicycle, had firmly established him as one of Oxford's landmarks. He had been born and brought up in North Oxford, schooled at Eton and then on to Magdalen College to read law. Felicity often felt that he would have been more suited to life as an academic than a lawyer, for he had adored college life and had regularly enjoyed the hospitality of several of the Masters of various colleges. Theirs had been a predominantly happy marriage, particularly when the children were small, but Felicity knew that once their children had left home, some of the glue that cemented her and Charlie together had come unstuck. He had been right about the Fergusons. They had known the family for years, having met originally at the school gate, but they were not Charlie's sort of people. They were too North Oxford, too alternative, too anti-establishment. By contrast Charlie's friends tended to be academic, upper middle class, conservative and very like him. Initially, in the early days of their marriage, these differences had been stimulating and had spawned some very lively dinner parties round their kitchen table. Recently they had proved irritating. Still as couples go, they were compatible enough or indeed had been until Charlie had agreed to take the Colhoun case.

Oliver Colhoun aged twenty, student of Warwick College, had died in his own vomit in the early hours of May Day from a particularly pure and lethal dose of heroin. Not unusual, certainly not unusual in Oxford in 2002, but it had made instant headlines because Oliver was the son of a High Court judge in the Family Division – a very moral but rather pompous man who had strong views on family values and degenerate youth. The press had adored it. Within a short time a young man named Ben Carver had been arrested by the police and charged with supplying the heroin which had caused havoc on the streets of Oxford. While it had killed no one but Oliver Colhoun, the particularly powerful mix had kept the stomach pumps at the John Radcliffe Hospital working around the clock.

Ben Carver was a victim himself. Born in Blackbird Lees, the rough end of Oxford, his family was classically dysfunctional. His father was a drunk and his mother augmented the family income by frequently crossing Magdalen Bridge for an evening of prostitution. Ben had a history of truancy from school, a string of convictions for petty crime and had been a habitual drug user since he was ten years old. No one wanted to take his case; he was a loser, a no-hoper, best behind bars for his own sake as well as that of society. Yet, something about the lad must have touched a nerve in Charlie. He wanted the case even before meeting the boy, yet his interest seemed extraordinary. He rarely defended: he was at his best as a prosecution barrister, but more importantly Charlie, represented establishment in every way – how he lived, worked, his friends. Normally, he would have considered poor Ben Carver to be no more than pond life yet after his first interview with Ben he had become his instant champion, utterly convinced in his own mind that Ben was as much a victim as Oliver, that the police had got it wrong and that there were bigger fish to fry. The case had caused considerable interest in Oxford. The Colhoun family, like Charlie's, were Oxfordshire people. Oliver had enjoyed a privileged education before taking up his place at Warwick College. The case highlighted the extraordinary divide that exists in Oxford between town and gown – two young men, one with every possible privilege, the other with absolutely nothing at all, linked together for all eternity.

Felicity had raged at Charlie. 'How can you

possibly defend a drug pusher? We were so lucky with our children. You should get down on your knees every night and thank God they got through their adolescence without becoming hooked on something. These people are evil, preying on young lives and destroying them. What about the boys, what about your grandchildren, what will they think – it's like you condone drug abuse?'

'The boys are far too young to take the slightest interest in what I'm doing,' Charlie replied, smoothly, which, of course, was irritatingly true.

Still, though, however much Charlie protested, however plausible his arguments, his taking the case made no sense. Oliver Colhoun was Charlie's sort of person. Ben Carver was not. In different circumstances, Felicity would have applauded Charlie's defending the underdog for once, but not a drug pusher. Their friends were outraged. It was not as if Charlie was ever short of a brief and yet he had chosen to defend someone who in their eyes was beyond contempt. The battle between Felicity and Charlie had raged on: Charlie stoutly defending his position, Felicity weak with frustration at his blinkered view of the case, which seemed to become all-consuming. He had been working late in the evenings and at the weekends until that fateful night. Biking home from work very late, Charlie had been hit by a speeding car. The driver did not stop, there were no witnesses. Charlie had lain alone and dead for some minutes before he was found.

Felicity drained her coffee mug and stretched;

the whole day lay ahead of her. Although the sun was warm and the sky cloudless, there was definitely a hint of autumn in the air. It was not a beach day. The cliff path to Zennor, she thought, would do her good, yet the prospect of a solitary walk did not appeal. In the days before he had become overweight and a workaholic, Charlie had loved to walk. 'The perfect way to exercise mind and body,' he used to say and Felicity agreed with him. Walking alone with one's thoughts tended to be a melancholy affair, while tramping along with an engaging companion was splendid. She stood up slowly, reached for her empty mug and with a reluctant backward glance at the harbour, started up the hill towards Cormorant Cottage.

Felicity knew, of course, why she was so reluctant to commit herself to hours of her own company with little chance of interruption. She would be forced to face the niggle that was growing larger and larger in the back of her mind, threatening to engulf even her sense of guilt. It had started two weeks ago and was now a growing conviction which simply would not go away. It was why she had made the snap decision to come to Cornwall, to try and shake herself free of what was becoming something of an obsession. For with every passing day, however hard she tried to deny it, she became increasingly certain that Charlie's death was no accident. She was by now quite sure that he had been killed deliberately and that somehow his murder was linked to the Colhoun case.

2

That day, two weeks before, had begun innocently enough. She had agreed to meet Gilla, her best girlfriend, at the Pancake House in North Parade. Normally they would have met at Brown's restaurant on the Woodstock Road but as she slammed the front door behind her, she realised they would probably never meet there again. It was only yards from where Charlie had died. Glancing at her watch, Felicity knew that she was leaving rather early for her lunch with Gilla. It was a pleasant enough day and she began ambling down the Banbury Road, towards St Giles, when a thought struck her. She had been studiously avoiding the place where Charlie had died. Perhaps today, when shortly she would have the support of her best friend, it was time to make the pilgrimage. She tried to remember what the police had told her – between the Radcliffe Infirmary and the little newsagent's but on the opposite side of the road. Having made her decision, she reached the spot far too quickly for her vulnerable emotions to cope. She felt sick, and guilt, her constant companion these days, was at her shoulder. She should have laid flowers, it was what people did, naff perhaps but it would have been a caring gesture. She stared down at the kerb. There were no visible signs of the accident. It was an absurd notion of course; what was she expecting – blood and bits of bicycle?

She looked left and right, up and down the Woodstock Road, trying to imagine what Charlie had seen in his final moments of life. It would have been dark, of course, but the road was always well lit ... and then ... the road before her darkened, the people around her melted away. Coming towards her from the opposite side of the road was Charlie on his bicycle. He slowed before crossing, wobbling slightly. There was no visible traffic and then ... out of nowhere, a car came hurtling down the Woodstock Road. Seeing it, Charlie began peddling frantically to avoid it, but the car aimed straight for him. It caught him – the bike went one way, Charlie the other. As he was thrown into the air just feet in front of Felicity, the vision faded. She must have screamed, for a cluster of people were all round her.

'What is it, what's wrong, love?' An elderly man was holding her arm. 'Come and sit on the wall.' She did as she was asked. People drifted away, losing interest, but a kindly couple persisted. 'Can we call someone? Are you ill, where do you live?'

Eventually, Felicity rallied. 'No honestly I'm fine, truly. I'll just sit here a moment.' Reluctantly they left, too.

All her life, all her conscious life, Felicity had suffered from what her mother referred to as 'Fizzy's little moments'. It was something she never sought out, nor was it something over which she appeared to have any control. She was not clairvoyant, she never saw the future. Just sometimes, scenes flashed before her, sometimes bizarre, sometimes worrying, but never before as terrifying or as vivid as this. She had tried on occasion to make herself 'see' things, like when her cat went missing, to find what had happened to her, like when she had been spectacularly dumped by a boy called Tom, she had wanted to check if he was with someone else. Nothing. It was this lack of control which had made Felicity never take her 'visions' very seriously ... at least not until now.

Despite her reassurances to the couple who had helped her, she felt faint, her heart still beating wildly. She knew without doubt what she had seen. She had just witnessed her husband being killed. It was clearly no accident; the car had actually accelerated towards him. It seemed so obvious to her now. How could it have been an accident? How could Charlie have not seen the car coming before crossing the road? The road was wide, enough for three, even four, cars to pass one another, plenty of room to take avoiding action for both motorist and cyclist. Visibility in both directions had been perfect. Her mind, until that moment numbed with pain and shock, slowly galvanised itself into action. It was clearly not an accident; the driver had deliberately driven at Charlie. Why had he done so – it had to be linked to the Colhoun case, all her instincts told her so. Maybe Charlie had been right, maybe there was more to the case than the police would acknowledge. Maybe someone didn't want Charlie encouraging Ben Carver to talk. From that moment an obsession was born.

Turning on her heel, without a backward look at where her husband had died, Felicity hurriedly retraced her steps to North Parade. She walked unsteadily, still deeply shocked, but there were no tears, just a grim determination.

Gilla had already secured a table in the window. Felicity could see her wild red curls, standing out like a Belisha beacon, from halfway down the road. She burst into the restaurant. Gilla had a bottle of champagne on ice and two glasses. Despite their long and close friendship, as the two women embraced, Gilla looked anxious and faintly embarrassed.

'You probably think the champagne is in unbelievably poor taste,' she said. 'It's just you've survived your first three months without Charlie and it seemed right somehow that we should mark the occasion.'

'No, that's fine,' replied Felicity distractedly, her mind still swirling around what she had seen.

'What is it, what's wrong?' said Gilla, instantly aware of Felicity's preoccupation. 'Oh look, I'm sorry. I've upset you, haven't I? This was a completely crass gesture on my part.'

'No, no,' said Felicity, 'pour away, it's just that I've, I've seen something, realised something.'

'What?' Gilla asked, as she began pouring the champagne.

'That Charlie was almost certainly killed.'

Gilla glanced at her sharply, a bewildered expression on her face. 'Well, we all know that, old love,' she said, gently.

Felicity smiled. 'I'm not going bonkers, Gilla. I mean killed, as in murdered. It was a hit and run, yes, but it wasn't an accident, it was deliberate.'

Gilla handed Felicity a glass; they both sipped appreciatively, in silence for a moment.

'What on earth makes you think so and why now?' Gilla asked gently. Felicity unfolded her theory – the well lit road, the good visibility and the sinister nature of the Colhoun case. Gilla listened in silence. When Felicity had finished, she leant across and took her hand. 'It sounds a bit Inspector Morse to me, Fizzy.'

'Maybe,' said Felicity 'but the thing is, Gilla, I've also just seen it happen.'

Gilla winced. 'You mean one of your funny turns?' There was no ridicule in her voice. They had known each other long enough for Gilla to be very familiar with Felicity's strange visions. She noted Felicity's high colour, the look of animation back in her eyes. This might have been a horrible shock, she thought to herself, but at least it's woken her up a little. With her unusual combination of fair hair and brown eyes, if not stunning, Felicity had always been good to look at, in the healthy, clear-skinned way of someone who loved fresh air and exercise. What really lit her up though, what transformed her sometimes from being merely nice-looking to almost beautiful, was her vibrant personality. Old Fizzy was one of nature's enthusiasts, her cup was always half full, her energy breathtaking. So, in recent years, her blonde hair had faded, her girlish figure had thickened a little, but the dynamism of her personality had remained undiminished. Until now, until she had lost her lifetime's companion and she had become an empty shell. Gilla took a deep breath to steady herself. Felicity was playing with the cutlery, turning it over and over, her eyes averted. 'It must have been awful – seeing it happen,' Gilla ventured.

'Yes, it was.' The animation left her face as quickly as it had come. 'It's not real though, you know, you can't do anything to intervene. It's like watching a film – horrible but not to be confused with real life. I saw the car, saw it hit Charlie; they meant to kill him.' Her voice trailed away.

There was a lengthy silence. At last Gilla said, 'What are you going to do about this?'

'That's what I've been wondering,' Felicity said. 'The obvious people to tell are the police, of course, but I suspect they lost interest in Charlie's death weeks ago. Admittedly, the inquest has been adjourned to allow them to "pursue their enquiries", whatever that means, so they must have considered it worth investigating. Still, if I tell them I saw it happen, they'll just think I'm barmy.' She hesitated, noting that Gilla did not contradict her. 'I think my starting point should be Will McPherson.'

'Will McPherson,' said Gilla, 'now that's a name I haven't heard in a long time. Whatever happened to him?'

'He's the senior consultant at the Path Lab now,' Felicity replied. 'He's got a bit stuffy actually, well very stuffy, if the truth be known. He married into the landed gentry – Lady Pamela something or other, and he's become terribly posh. They have a great stone pile and thousands of acres somewhere out beyond Bicester, masses of children, ponies and Labradors, you know the sort of thing.'

'Dear God!' said Gilla, 'so he fell on his feet? I wonder what attracted the Lady Pamela. Rather an ugly little chap as I remember – all sandy, freckly, generally puny and deathly white – weak handshake, silly laugh – yuk!'

'Oh, don't be so mean,' Felicity smiled, wanly, 'he's very bright, and has a natural instinct for the job, so I'm told.'

'Exactly,' said Gilla. 'I rest my case, a natural instinct for dead bodies. So how do you think the odious little Will can help? Are you still in touch with him then?'

'Not really,' said Felicity. 'As I say, he's become a bit posh for us, but he and Charlie were students together.' Felicity hesitated; looking down at her hands, she began fiddling with the pepper mill.

'What is it?' asked Gilla.

'Well, when Charlie died, as you know, I had to identify the body. I didn't want the children involved, or even anyone close, like you. It was private somehow. At the time I wondered about contacting Will, for sort of unemotional moral support, but in the end ...' Her voice trailed away and she fumbled for a handkerchief.

'Oh, Fizzy,' said Gilla, 'this doesn't get any easier for you, does it, and after this morning, God, actually seeing the accident, what you must be going through, I just can't imagine?'

'No sympathy please,' said Felicity, blowing her nose heartily. 'It only makes me worse, you know it does.'

'Have you been sent a pathology report?' Gilla asked.

'No, but I wondered whether it was worth ringing Will and asking him about it. Maybe there is something in there which would indicate it wasn't an accident.'

'I can't imagine what,' said Gilla.

'Well, neither can I, but you asked me where I should start and Will McPherson seemed to be the right place.'

'If you don't want to talk to him,' Gilla said, 'you could always get Josh to do it for you.'

'Josh wouldn't ask the right questions.'

'Yes, he would,' said Gilla. 'Lawyers are dealing with pathology reports all the time.'

'He won't be persistent enough,' Felicity said. 'I know he won't. He'll just say my idea is a half-baked theory, and not worth pursuing. Even before I thought it could be murder, I kept asking Josh to hassle the police, to try and find who was responsible for killing Charlie, but he won't. He says usually hit and run drivers get caught in the end because sooner or later they take their car to a garage.' Felicity hesitated and blew her nose again. 'In the case of Charlie, Josh reckons, the car must have been quite a mess.'

The two women were silent for a moment, the thought making them both queasy.

'Ah, the gorgeous Josh!' said Gilla, as much to

break the tension as anything else. Josh was Charlie's partner, younger by nine years, and unfairly attractive. He had been married once in his early twenties, divorced soon after, and since then had been an absolute menace to female society throughout Oxfordshire, and beyond.

'I think talking through your new theory with Josh Buchanan would be too much of a strain for you, Fizzy. I think you should leave it to me.' Gilla reached across the table and placed a conciliatory hand on Felicity's arm. Her voice was gentle and sympathetic, but her eyes were wickedly bright.

Felicity looked at her quizzically for a moment and then burst into laughter. It was a good sound. 'You're incorrigible, Gilla. Any excuse – Josh is immune to marriage, you know that.'

'Who's talking about marriage?' said Gilla. 'I'm quite happy to settle for a hectic and lustful affair.'

'You're a very bad example to Ellie,' Felicity said severely. Ellie was Gilla's fifteen-year-old daughter, the product of a brief and unsuccessful marriage at a time when Gilla was in her early thirties and suffering from a slight hiatus in her otherwise colourful love life – a hiatus which lasted long enough to make her feel so insecure that she had agreed to marry the first person who asked her. Simon Carter was a banker, an attractive pleasant man in his late thirties who had spent far too much of his youth carving his career. He was completely bowled over by the red-haired bombshell that was Gilla. He was not a bore, but he was deeply traditional and set in his ways and perhaps not exactly exciting. He returned from work early one day, when Ellie was just two years old, to find a strange young man in bed with his wife. Not surprisingly, it was more than he could bear. Within a week he had a job in Hong Kong. In keeping with his very correct nature, he punctiliously sent Gilla maintenance cheques for his daughter, but he had seen neither of them since the day he had left, nor had he remarried.

Only very occasionally, usually when drunk, Gilla did admit to moments of remorse. Had she ruined Simon Carter's life? Very probably, Felicity would say. Since her husband's departure, there had been a string of discreet affairs, with deference to Ellie, but Gilla's confidence was seriously dented. Felicity was also very conscious of the fact that no attempt had been made on either Simon's part, or Gilla's, to instigate divorce proceedings. She secretly entertained the fantasy that one day they would get together again.

Felicity looked fondly across the table at her friend. At forty-eight, Gilla could have passed for thirty, with her bright red curls, her cat-like green eyes and her beautiful unlined creamy complexion. She had maintained the figure of a girl and the enthusiasm, too. Gilla never did anything by halves, yet, for all her erratic ways, she was a true and loyal friend. That first terrible night, the night Charlie had been killed, Gilla had been there for her, of course.

'Talking of Ellie,' said Gilla, cutting through Felicity's thoughts, 'I don't know what I am going to do about her. She's gone completely monosyllabic on me. All she ever does is grunt and she wears such terrible clothes. She's in what she calls her "Goth" period.'

'Ah,' said Felicity 'I know a bit about that, Oxfam overcoats and big black lace-up boots.'

'Heavens,' said Gilla, 'you are well informed. I don't remember Goths in Jamie and Mel's day!' She hesitated. 'The thing is, Fizzy, do you think I'm going wrong with her in some way?'

It was a difficult question to answer. The real problem, Felicity suspected, lay in the fact that Ellie was not now, nor ever would be, anything as attractive as her mother. She had a heavy frame and slightly jowled look about the face, which was not attractive on an adolescent girl. She had also inherited her mother's beautiful colouring but at the moment her hair was long, unkempt and dulled by infrequent washing. Felicity suspected Ellie had a fine brain but Gilla had never much rated any form of academia and so did nothing to encourage her daughter. Gilla owned and ran a small art gallery in Woodstock, selling mediocre paintings and upmarket tat to tourists visiting Blenheim Palace. Hers was a frivolous world. She had style and flair and a mass of friends. A grumpy fifteen-year-old was a bore, yet for all her sullen ways, without doubt Ellie was currently very vulnerable and needed support. As Ellie's godmother, Felicity knew she should do more. She studied her friend in silence for a moment. She felt guilty but right now she knew she couldn't cope with Ellie's problems. 'No, I don't think you're going wrong with Ellie, it's just a stage, a rite of passage. She'll snap out of it soon, they all do. Mel was a nightmare at fifteen, so rude and aggressive. It passes, I promise.' Felicity felt mean and spineless, but what could she do? There were just no reserves left to cope with Ellie.

Gilla, as if sensing her thoughts, said quickly, 'Look, the last thing we should be talking about at the moment is my grotty teenager. Now, are you sorted as to what you're going to do – you'll get hold of Will?'

'I think so,' said Felicity. 'That's the starting point anyway.'

'You seem so much better today,' said Gilla, anxious to steer the conversation away from Charlie too directly, 'so much more positive, focused, somehow – perhaps it's the champagne.'

'Talking of which, we ought to be eating something or I'll be flat on my back in a minute.'

'I ordered us pizzas,' said Gilla, 'they'll be here any second and a salad to share. I hope that's OK.'

'Perfect. Oh, Gilla, look, umbrellas!' Felicity was pointing in the direction of the bar.

'I am more than happy to pander to your every whim, dear heart, but why do you want a cocktail umbrella in your champagne?'

'I'm working on this huge nursery découpage – it's a toy box, a vast affair. I need some suns – two, maybe three – those yellow umbrellas would be perfect opened up and taken off their sticks.'

'Your wish is my command. I need the loo anyway.'

In a moment Gilla was gone and returned triumphantly with a fist full of umbrellas. 'Here, quick, put them in your handbag.'

'Gilla, I can't, it's theft.'

'Oh, don't be so wet, Fizzy. The profit they're making on this champagne is outrageous. Besides, it will be really embarrassing if we get caught now.'

Felicity grinned and did as she was told. 'I wonder how many times you've done that for me over the years.'

'What, filched stuff for your ghastly art projects? More times than I care to remember.'

The two friends smiled at one another in comfortable silence for a moment, the years slipping away.

'Gilla, about what I saw ...' said Felicity, suddenly, snapping them back to reality.

'Now what?' Gilla asked, not unkindly.

'Seeing Charlie's accident, you won't tell anyone, anyone at all, will you Gilla?'

'Oh come off it, Fizzy, of course not. I just feel so awful for you, it must have been dreadful.'

'Yes, but in an odd way, it's a relief.'

'Why?' Gilla asked, incredulously.

'Well, as you know, Charlie was working on a case which I believed was fundamentally and morally wrong for him to take. He was working all hours of the day and night and shutting me out completely. Then biking home from work, he's so tired, he gets himself killed. He had been putting his work ahead of everything, including me, and as well as feeling guilty, I also felt angry with him. If he was murdered, then while the guilt persists, the anger's gone. He was right to take the case because if someone wanted him dead then his instincts were spot on. There has to be more to it than simply defending Ben Carver. Is this making any sense?'

Gilla nodded. 'I understand completely. I felt exactly the same when Mum died.'

Gilla's mother had died of cancer when Felicity and Gilla were in the last year of the sixth form. Gilla's "A"-Levels had been a wash-out as a result.

'You never said so at the time' said Felicity.

'Well, I wasn't as brave as you, couldn't put it into words. In any case, I was so young I probably wasn't capable of analysing my feelings. However, I do remember being bewildered at how angry I felt, that there she was dying when I still needed her, when I was trying to sit my "A"-Levels. So, don't worry Fizzy, you may be a selfish, self-centred cow, but at least you're in good company.'

On the day following her lunch with Gilla, Felicity had rung the Pathology Department at the John Radcliffe Hospital.

'Could I speak to Mr McPherson please?'

Moments later she heard the rather prim Edinburgh accent of Will McPherson.

'Is that you, Felicity?'

'Yes, Will, yes it is.'

'How are you? I'm so sorry about Charlie. What an awful thing to happen. How are you bearing up?'

'Well, you know,' Felicity replied, 'coping. Look, Will, I want to ask you a favour. Were you involved in Charlie's case?'

'No,' Will said, in a hesitant voice, 'not personally, anyway, though strangely enough, I signed the pathology report only yesterday. It'll be on the way to your solicitor now.'

'So you've read it?'

'Yes.' Again a reluctance to be drawn out further.

'I just wondered if I could come and talk to you about it.'

There was a long silence. 'Well, I don't think that is quite right Felicity, the police are involved, it is a potentially criminal matter; ethics, you must understand.'

'I'm his wife, for God's sake,' Felicity burst out. 'I'm going to see the report anyway and surely, as a friend, you can spare me enough time just to talk it through. My husband is dead, Will, and I need your help.'

'I don't think it would be appropriate to meet here,' he said, his voice very impersonal. 'I suppose I could come round to your home, this evening after work, about six-thirty?'

'Thank you,' said Felicity. 'I'll see you then.'

Time had not been kind to Will McPherson. His haircut was unnecessarily expensive, given what was left of his hair; his suit, tie and shoes had clearly cost a bomb, but he had a pinched and wizened look. His haughty manner seemed ridiculous on a spare little man of barely five foot. Felicity tried very hard not to be irritated, offered him a drink, which he refused because he was driving, and launched straight into her theory, being careful to stick to the facts – no question of second sight, or weird feelings. Will had a scientific background: he would think her mad if she told him what she thought had really happened.

'I don't know what you want me to say?' Will said when she had finished. 'I'm afraid I can't help you at all. Charlie was hit by a car, travelling at speed. It was a metallic blue car, the type of paint used on many makes, though most likely a Citroën or a Renault. The impact threw him into the air and when he landed on the edge of the kerb, his neck was broken, causing instant death.' He gave her what could pass as a kind smile. 'The extent of his brain damage probably would have killed him anyway; there was a great deal of bleeding in the brain. Mercifully, the broken neck ensured the agony was not prolonged – for either of you.'

'But, surely the car must have been travelling terribly fast to have thrown him up into the air high enough for the impact to have broken his neck when he hit the ground?' She spoke calmly but her irritation was mounting.

'Certainly it was travelling fast. The police reckon somewhere between seventy and eighty mph, and I agree with them.'

'On the Woodstock Road?' said Felicity, incredulously. 'Nobody travels at that speed.'

'They do if they're drunk, or on drugs,' said Will. 'You should see some of the injuries we get in. There is no more lethal weapon than a car, particularly in the hands of a young drunk or drug addict.'

'Will, I don't need a lecture on degenerate youth,' Felicity said.

The patronising smile wavered. 'Yes, of course, I'm sorry.'

'So there's nothing you can do to help me with my suspicions?'

'Nothing at all, my dear, I'm afraid. Oh, there was just one thing.'

'What?' Felicity's eyes lit up.

'No, no, nothing to help you, I'm afraid, but something perhaps, as a friend, I should warn you about. Charlie had been drinking, not heavily, not like the kind of cases we normally see, but he would have failed a drink-driving test.' Will's expression was smug. Felicity wanted to poke his eyes out.

And that, essentially, had been that. Once the pathology report had become common knowledge, everyone lost interest, including the police. Charlie was tired; he'd had one too many whiskies at the office and had clearly misjudged the speed of the car as he was cycling across the road. The car, admittedly, was travelling much too fast but Charlie's tiredness and intake of alcohol had made him careless.

'Be logical, old girl,' Josh had said, kindly, as one would to a slightly dim child. 'No hit and run driver is going to come forward of his own volition. As for the well lit road and good visibility, if he was driving much too fast and was drunk, even if Charlie had tried to take avoiding action, it could well be that the driver was not capable of responding. Your chum, Will is right. Statistically, hit and runs are usually the work of drunks. That's why they don't stop, because they know they'll be breathalysed.'

In the meantime the Colhoun case had come and gone. Josh had gone through the motions of representing Ben Carver on Charlie's behalf. The boy had been convicted and sentenced for both possessing and dealing in heroin, and for causing the accidental death of Oliver Colhoun. Despite his miserable background being paraded before the judge, Ben had been sent down for a fifteen-year stretch – in other words, even with remission, for the whole of the rest of his youth. Ben had stuck resolutely to his story, that his supplier had come from Plymouth, that he didn't know his name nor what he looked like since the transaction had taken place in the dark and that he was operating on no one else's behalf. The police and the press seemed completely satisfied that the buck stopped with Ben and that, apparently, was the end of it. Felicity felt so powerless. Everyone was kind to her, humoured her, listened to what she had to say with sympathy and understanding in their eyes, but she knew nobody was taking her seriously. Charlie's death and the Colhoun case were totally unconnected in absolutely everyone's mind but her own.

She wondered whether she should confide in her children. Jamie, the eldest, married with two little sons, was the obvious choice, but much as she loved him, Felicity recognised that her only son was not a strong character and would be distressed by his mother's theory, without being able to reassure and comfort either himself or her. Charlie had not been an easy man to have as a father, even for the most confident and outgoing of boys. Jamie had been neither. He was a painfully shy child and young man, totally eclipsed by a flamboyant father and a noisy, confident, brilliant little sister. No wonder, he had walked straight into the arms of his wife, Trish, a brash, kindly Australian girl, who was in total control of their marriage and made all the decisions. Poor Jamie, Felicity always felt she had failed him.

There was Mel of course. Mel had adored her father but had coped surprisingly well with his death. It was part of her tough, resilient nature, which she had inherited from him. After reading law at Leeds, Mel was now in her second year of Articles with a top law firm in the Temple, frantically busy and preoccupied. Her father had put in a word on the old boy network to help her obtain such prestigious Articles. Privately, though, Felicity believed Mel would have made it without her father's help – she was so driven, always had been, even as a tiny girl. No, Mel was not likely to provide a sympathetic ear, she hadn't the time. Although her children were so different, Felicity felt the same about Mel as she did about Jamie. She should not be burdened with this extra dimension to her father's death.

So there was really no one else to talk to, no other avenues to explore, just a flash of insight, which increasingly seemed too fragile to confide in to anyone else. Even Gilla, confronted with the pathology report, no longer seemed to support Felicity's theory and firmly believed her friend should move on. Felicity had pleaded with Josh to check out everything connected with the Colhoun case and in deference to her concerns, he had a clerk

30

go through every one of Charlie's notes, both in the Colhoun file and on his laptop. There was nothing to suggest that he had established a shred of evidence to support his theory that Ben was fronting for someone else, taking the rap perhaps, because he was afraid for his own safety or that of his family.

When the day of the inquest into Charlie Paradise's death finally dawned – ironically it was only a week after the conclusion of the Colhoun case – Felicity tried to feel a shred of hope. Perhaps the conclusion of the inquest would bring closure in her head. Charlie was dead. Finding out who had killed him, and why, was not going to change the only thing that mattered. 'Best left' – if Felicity heard those words once more, she thought she would scream. Both her children offered to accompany her, but Felicity persuaded them against it. She had Josh and it was enough coping with her own feelings without worrying about how her children felt. As things turned out, it was a very good decision.

The moment the coroner concluded his findings, Felicity left Court Number 1 at a run, pursued by a worried-looking Josh. She just made it as far as the Ladies, where she was extremely sick. Josh was waiting for her when she came out.

'Are you alright, old girl? I'm sorry, it was a bit gruesome.'

Felicity looked far from alright. She was deathly pale, except for her eyes, which were over-bright and red. 'I was expecting it to be gruesome,' she burst out. 'What I couldn't bear was Charlie being branded a drunk.'

31

'He wasn't,' said Josh soothingly, 'they simply stated that he had some alcohol in his bloodstream.'

'And,' said Felicity, spitting out the words, 'by inference, it was the alcohol which probably caused the accident.'

'The coroner did not say that, Felicity.' Josh was starting to look exasperated. 'He read the details of the pathology report, and having heard medical and police evidence, he signed the death certificate as "accidental death". There was nothing else he could have done.'

'It was a very convenient conclusion, wasn't it? The easy answer, all tidied away.'

People sitting in the small foyer that fed the courts of Oxford were starting to stare at them. Felicity was almost shouting, oblivious of the attention she was attracting. The old building had been witness to every extreme of emotion over the years – for today's visitors, as they waited to be summoned, a diversion from their own troubles was most welcome and captivating.

'Enough now, come along,' said Josh briskly, taking her arm. 'I've booked us a table at the Elizabeth. We can talk on the way.'

Felicity shook off his arm and began to walk towards the exit stairs, suddenly desperate to get out of the building. They went down the stairs together in silence but as soon as they reached the entrance lobby below, she stopped abruptly and stared up at Josh.

'You were supposed to be his best friend, as well as his partner. Why didn't you say something, why didn't you say he was not a drinking man?'

'Because it wasn't relevant to the cause of death, which was all that was of interest to the coroner,' said Josh, patience ebbing. 'Look, we have always kept a bottle of Scotch in the stationery cupboard, for when we were working late. It was a very democratic arrangement – we took it in turns to replace the bottle when it was empty. As a matter of fact, Charlie had insisted on buying the last one although it wasn't his turn, because he had been slugging into it a bit with the stress of the Colhoun case. If I had said he was not a drinking man, it would have served no purpose, and the coroner would have thought I'd gone nuts. In fact, if anything, it would have drawn attention to Charlie's alcohol level, which as I say was simply not relevant today.'

'A fine friend you've turned out to be,' said Felicity, viciously. 'I don't want to have lunch with you. I just can't believe you let this happen.'

She was through the doors and out onto the pavement. A small knot of men and women stood outside, as if waiting for her. For a moment she couldn't think what was going on, such was the degree of her anger and distress.

'Mrs Paradise, how do you feel about the outcome of the inquest?' said a young woman, thrusting a microphone in front of her. 'Do you accept that everything has been done to find the hit and run driver who killed your husband?'

Beside her, a faded-looking man stood, pencil poised. Reporters, of course – a sudden recklessness seized her. 'No, I don't,' said Felicity. 'As far as I'm concerned, the law is a complete ass.'

The group, restless, only half paying attention to

her seconds before, was suddenly silent and completely focused on her. She felt a rush of adrenalin. This was her chance. Josh, red-faced with exertion and anger, elbowed his way to her side.

'Mrs Paradise has absolutely no further comment.'

'Rubbish,' Felicity said to the assembled crowd, 'Mrs Paradise does have a comment and it is this.'

'Fizzy, no,' said Josh.

'Shut up, Josh,' she said and launched into her theory, sparing no detail. The press, starved of a story, were desperate with gratitude. There was absolutely nothing of any interest going on in the courts that day – just the usual dreary round of divorces and petty crimes. The woman was probably deluded – she believed her husband had been murdered and that both the police and the court were taking the easy option of branding him a drunk – but it was good copy. When she had finished, the crowd respectfully parted, allowing her to leave. There was nothing more to ask her – she had covered everything. They were grateful. Josh, mute with fury and frustration, followed in her wake.

Throughout her tirade, Felicity could not help noticing a small man of middle years, staring at her intently. It was the intensity of his concentration upon her that drew her attention to him, that and the fact he appeared nervous and apparently desperate to hear what she was saying. He was singularly nondescript in every way, except one. He had a small mean-looking face, eyes too close together, mouth pinched, thin and cruel. He wore a brown mohair overcoat, which was too big for him, and reminded Felicity, fleetingly, of a child wearing an oversized school uniform bought to grow into. His one distinguishing feature was his very dark, over-long hair, swept back from his forehead, through which ran a pure white streak – like a skunk, Felicity thought. As the crowd parted to let her through, Felicity felt she could not ignore his scrutiny; his anxiety was almost palpable.

'Which paper are you from?' she asked.

'No paper,' he murmured, 'just interested in what you had to say.' In contrast to his unpleasant appearance, his voice had a soft West Country burr. He clearly was just an inquisitive onlooker. Felicity dismissed him from her mind instantly.

'Fizzy, come on,' said Josh urgently, 'for God's sake, let's get out of here.'

They crossed the High together, heading for the city centre. 'What on earth possessed you?' Josh burst out, as soon as they were clear of the court. 'You have to be off your head.'

'I don't see what makes you say that, Josh. Somebody has to stand up for Charlie; somebody has to put the record straight.'

'Felicity, there's no record to put straight,' said Josh. He put his hand on her arm; she was walking so quickly he could barely keep up with her. 'Look at me, stop a moment. I'm sorry, it's my fault, I should have taken you through the inquest in advance, but the fact remains, there were no witnesses and no one knows what happened, nor ever will, I suspect. You must accept the situation, Fizzy, you really must.'

'I don't need any more lectures, Josh!'

'I'm aware of that,' said Josh, 'I'm just saying, I'm sorry, I should have prepared you. Nevertheless there is no question of putting the record straight, because there *is* no record, that's the whole point. Your theory that someone killed Charlie, is no more than that – a theory, and it was so irresponsible to start talking to the press as though you had any evidence to support your claims.'

'I just know something odd happened that night,' Felicity said. 'I feel it in my bones.'

'Exactly,' said Josh. 'I couldn't have put it better myself. Feel it in your bones – what possible place does that have in a court of law, Fizzy? Come on, get real.'

'Oh, go to Hell,' said Felicity. 'Just leave me alone, Josh.' She started striding ahead of him again.

'Where are you going?' Josh shouted after her.

'I don't know, home probably.'

'Well, enjoy the peace and quiet while you can,' he said.

'What do you mean?' said Felicity, stopping in her tracks.

'Oh, come off it, Fizzy, you can't be that naïve. You don't think this story will go away, do you? By tomorrow morning your home is going to be under siege with reporters.'

So, being careful not to think too hard about what she was doing, Felicity hurriedly packed a small bag, threw it in the back of her car, and began the long drive to St Ives.

3

'Mum, it's Mel. What on earth are you doing in Cornwall?'

The sound of Felicity's mobile phone startled her and made her jump. She was sitting on the beach leaning against the harbour wall, almost asleep in the warmth of the sun. Still, it was good to hear her daughter's voice. 'Hello, darling, I'm having a holiday,' she replied. 'It was a spur of the moment thing, I thought it might do me some good after, well you know ... everything. You've all been trying to persuade me to go away somewhere.' She finished a little lamely.

'But on your own, surely that's not a good idea? Why haven't you taken anyone with you, to cheer you up, Gilla or someone?'

'I'm best on my own at the moment.' Felicity said defensively. She was very often defensive where her daughter was concerned. 'It's lovely down here, the weather is extraordinary, really hot, I'm sitting on the beach right now.'

'Lucky you,' said Mel, 'I'm rushed off my feet here, as usual. Dad always made being a lawyer seem fun. God knows how, I literally don't have a social life anymore.'

'Dad belonged to a different generation, darling,' said Felicity, sadly. 'When we were growing up it was still permissible to have fun and carve out a good career. All this single-minded ambition can't be good for the soul, when there's no room left to play.'

'You're not going to start giving me one of your lectures about quality of life, are you?' said Mel, somewhat abrasively. 'I don't think I could take it right now.' She paused. 'Sorry, I'm just so stressed – and on top of it all, Gilla says I should be worried about you.' Mel sounded very angry, very young and oddly vulnerable, all at once.

'Why?' asked Felicity, genuinely surprised.

'She's been talking to Josh and she seems to think that you're on the verge of a nervous breakdown or something. She says you're depressed and a touch weird. Are you, Mum?'

Felicity paused, giving the question serious consideration for a moment. It was not like Gilla to have alarmed Mel unnecessarily.

'I'm sad,' she said after a moment, 'and very cross. I'm cross because your father dying like that was such a waste and I'm cross because the police haven't found who killed him and I feel …' she hesitated, 'in a kind of limbo, I don't know what to do next … and I miss him so much. But no, don't worry darling, I'm not depressed as such and I won't go mad or top myself – promise.'

'Only, it takes a lot to worry Gilla,' Mel said,

echoing Felicity's own thoughts.

Gilla was Mel's godmother, as was Felicity to Gilla's Ellie. The girls were too far apart in age ever to have been friends but it was a cosy arrangement from the mothers' point of view. They were the nearest thing either of them would ever have to a sister.

'Gilla's fussing,' said Felicity, firmly.

'Gilla doesn't fuss,' Mel replied truthfully. 'How long are you staying down there anyway, Mum?'

'I don't know,' Felicity said, 'another week perhaps.'

'Another week! But why?'

'Why not?' said Felicity, with false cheerfulness.

They chatted idly for a few moments longer, including their customary bitch about Jamie's wife, Trish. It was unfair, they both knew, because she was a good wife to their rather difficult respective son and brother, but they enjoyed it.

Then the call finished and Felicity returned her mobile to the bottom of her bag and leant back against the harbour wall. What was Gilla up to worrying Mel like that and what was there to worry about? She had done a sensible thing. She had run away from the publicity that Josh had said was inevitable and at the same time given herself a break. She had not been irresponsible in her departure – she had rung the school where she taught art to the juniors, and they had been very supportive in giving her compassionate leave from her job, she had made sure that the house was locked up, the fridge emptied and a neighbour organised to feed the cat. Not the actions of someone on the verge of a nervous breakdown, surely? It was true that the thought of returning to Oxford depressed her, indeed, the thought of going anywhere other than remaining cocooned in this balmy St Ives Indian summer seemed unattractive. She was just so tired all the time. She had hardly started the book she had brought with her and as for her sketchbook, she had not attempted a single drawing. She had to admit that this lack of activity was very out of character.

The sun disappeared suddenly. Felicity opened her eyes and squinted upwards. A great thick mass of cloud had come from nowhere. She shivered; without the sun, it felt decidedly autumnal. She stood up, stretched her cramped limbs and looked at her watch – 12.20 – what to do now? She glanced across the road to the Sloop Inn. Perhaps a glass of wine and an early lunch, then a siesta, then yet another walk. For most people a delicious prospect, she knew, but for some reason she suddenly found the whole idea rather lonely and sad. It was Mel's fault, or rather Gilla's. She would have been fine if they had just left her alone, hadn't reminded her of why she was here.

The pub was dark after the brightness of the day and virtually empty. Felicity ordered a fish pie and took a glass of wine to a corner table, intent on reading her newspaper. She settled herself down and glanced at the headlines: the same old stuff, nothing much to attract her attention. She glanced about her. Two men were sitting at a table opposite her, just a few feet away. There was nothing special about them and she would have ignored them but for the fact that they seemed to be behaving in such an odd way. They were clearly angry with one another but their entire dialogue was being conducted in hoarse whispers. Felicity was about to look away, anxious not to be seen to be intruding, when she found herself staring at the smaller of the two men and almost gasped out loud. She had seen him before and she knew exactly where. On such a warm day, he was not wearing the huge brown overcoat she remembered but there was no mistaking him. The white streak starting at his forehead in stark contrast to the rest of his hair which was almost black, was instantly recognisable – skunk-like, she remembered thinking. This was the man who she had spoken to outside Oxford County Court, she was absolutely sure of it. Her heart began to pound. What was he doing here? Had he followed her?

Under the intensity of her gaze, the man glanced up; their eyes met and Felicity hurriedly looked away, staring with unseeing eyes at the newspaper. When she looked up again, he had returned to his conversation. Her instincts told her that he could not have seen her clearly enough in her dark corner to recognise her, but what was he doing here? She remembered his voice, a West Country accent. It was just some strange coincidence, had to be, it was the only logical explanation.

Ostentatiously, she refolded her paper, making a great play of finding it fascinating reading, but she kept glancing at the two men. Their argument appeared to be reaching some sort of climax. Suddenly, the 'Skunk' stood up and with one final whispered word of abuse stormed out of the pub, leaving his drink untouched. His companion appeared unruffled. He drained his beer glass, and then casually leant across and took the 'Skunk''s untouched glass and began drinking that. He was very different from his companion, Felicity noted: a big man with a florid complexion and suntanned beyond anything that could have been acquired during an English summer. He was well-dressed in a sports jacket and trousers, checked shirt and neatly knotted woollen tie – a country gentleman, or posing as one certainly. It was hard to imagine what on earth he had in common with the scruffy little 'Skunk'. He was good-looking in a large rather coarse sort of way. There was an arrogance about him, and aggression too – not a pleasant character, Felicity decided. Abruptly he stood up, making her jump. He drained the 'Skunk''s glass, slammed it down on the table and left without a word to the barman. At that moment Felicity's fish pie arrived. She looked at it without interest, her mind still churning. It had been a shock seeing the 'Skunk'; it brought everything back, completing the return of reality which had begun with Mel's call.

An hour later, Felicity was striding along the cliff path towards Clodgy Point, as though the hounds of hell were after her. The 'Skunk' was somehow connected to Charlie's death, she was sure of it. Why, she had no idea. If he was not a journalist, what was he doing outside the court apparently so interested in the case, which surely was of no relevance to anyone unless they were involved? She marched on trying to escape the returning frustration from which she thought she had freed herself. She stumbled along the rocky cliff path, almost oblivious to where she was going and certainly of the gathering clouds. She was almost half way to Zennor when the storm broke and she was totally unprepared, dressed in nothing but an old fleece, jeans and a pair of trainers. It was hard to believe the morning had been so beautiful. She started back towards St Ives, muttering about the extremes of the Cornish weather and her own stupidity in walking so far. However, despite being soaked to the skin and lashed by a surprisingly strong wind which appeared to have come out of nowhere, the violent exercise had made her feel better.

By the time she reached Cormorant Cottage and the inevitable stiff lecture from Annie Trethewey, a sense of calm was restored. Somehow, she had to find a way to be less obsessive about how and why Charlie had died, she thought as she lay in a hot bath, thankfully bringing warmth back to her chilled bones. While she remained so hung up on who had killed Charlie, assuming anyone had, she recognised she would never be able to move on, never grieve properly for her lost husband and never rejoin the real world. Was this what Charlie would have wanted? She was sure it was not. Despite their differences, particularly in the latter months of his life, he had loved her in his way; she knew that. Finding out how and why he died was not going to bring him back.

She needed a plan, she thought, as she massaged shampoo into her hair. It was Tuesday; she had already told Annie that she would like to keep her room until the end of the week. She would go home on Sunday, thus avoiding the normal changeover traffic of Friday and Saturday. That would give her four whole days to pull herself together. She would walk, relax, sleep and fix her mind firmly on the future. It was time to start letting go.

Several hours later and just a short walk up Fore Street from Cormorant Cottage. Detective Inspector Keith Penrose was running late for dinner with his wife, Barbara. The occasion was their twenty-ninth wedding anniversary but by the time he reached their table, more than a little breathless, there seemed little chance of salvaging any sense of occasion. All summer, Keith had been promising his wife an autumn break, a week away somewhere – the Lake District was her favourite. He had a ready-made excuse for not going away in the summer because the population of Cornwall more than doubled in the summer months and so did the trouble that went with it. Now, however, he was running out of excuses and Barbara would not let the subject rest. Barbara had her own career to consider and, as she never tired of telling Keith, the decisions she made would have a lasting impact on the Duchy in the way his never would. If she could find the time, then so could he.

When their children had reached secondary school, Barbara had begun serving on the District

Council. This had led in time to becoming an elected member of the County Council, with special responsibility for planning matters. Keith had no time for local government and believed that Barbara's position had been responsible for making her more than a little power-crazed. She had her own pet hobby horses and Keith resented the way these personally-held views seemed to influence her public decisions. It was a long time though since he had been able to summon the energy to voice his opinion on the matter.

By the time they reached coffee, there was no avoiding the holiday issue any longer. Barbara fixed her husband with a look which was painfully familiar. It was strange, he often thought, how in his day-to-day working life, he was constantly dealing with violent, desperate, sometimes downright evil people. There had been uncomfortable times, dangerous times, sometimes even life-threatening, but he had never met anyone who could undermine his confidence the way his own wife did.

'Have you got your diary with you, Keith?' He nodded, and began feeling in his breast pocket.

'I don't know why you have to look so gloomy about it,' Barbara said. 'All I'm suggesting is that we have a week's holiday together. That's not asking too much after twenty-nine years of marriage, is it?'

'No, of course not,' Keith agreed.

She had been pretty once, he remembered that much, with a lovely figure, soft brown, wavy hair and kind grey eyes. Now, she was abrasive in manner, cold and unsympathetic, at any rate towards him.

Despite her obsession with her job and two happy, healthy, grown-up children, of whom she should be extremely proud, her features had become hardened with discontent. Was that his fault? He supposed it was.

'I was thinking about next week,' she said. 'I can clear my meetings for the week.'

'Impossible,' Keith replied, bravely, 'that's too short notice for the team.'

'It's no good leaving it until the end of October, that's half-term week, it'll be crowded and I'm certainly not going up to the Lakes in November – it will be raining all the time, and cold. You owe me a decent break, Keith, you really do.'

Keith suppressed a sigh. 'What about the third week in October, then? I could pencil it in anyway.'

'You'd better do more than pencil it in. I'm going to book it tomorrow.'

They always stayed at the same hotel on the edge of Lake Windermere. It was pleasant enough, and extremely well run. Keith supposed he would have enjoyed it if they could have gone walking together, but Barbara, an appalling snob, spent her entire time trying to cultivate friendships among the 'right sort' of fellow guests. They seemed to move from lounge to bar to dining room, the days merging one into the other with the same monotonous routine.

'Right, that's settled then,' he said with false jollity. 'I'll just go and pay the bill. We're the only ones left, I expect they want to close.'

'If you'd been on time, we'd be home in bed by now. I have a committee meeting at 9.30 tomorrow and I need my wits about me for that, I can tell you.'

Keith rose hurriedly from the table, afraid she was going to do just that – tell him the mind-numbing details of tomorrow's meeting. There was a buzz of excitement behind the counter when he reached it.

'Where's your car parked?' the waitress asked, as she began totting up the bill.

'Up at Barnoon,' Keith replied.

'You may not be able to get it out. There's a bit of trouble up there at the moment, the news is all over town.'

Keith felt an absurd sense of relief – suddenly he was the policeman again, not merely an unsatisfactory husband. 'What sort of trouble?' he asked.

'I don't know exactly, something about a car on fire.'

'A car on fire in St Ives?'

'I know what you mean,' the waitress said, smiling at him. '"Up Country", burning cars are two a penny, but it's not the sort of thing that happens down here, is it?'

'Would it be alright to leave my wife here for a few minutes while I find out what's going on? If that's OK, you could just add another coffee to the bill.'

'No problem, it takes us at least half an hour to clear up.'

The climb up to the car park was a steep one. Barbara would have objected to it in any event.

'I don't want you leaving me here half the night,' Barbara had said, when he explained the position and handed her the coffee.

'I won't be long,' he'd promised, 'only, it's stupid you walking all the way up there and ending up standing around because we can't get to our car.'

'You're a detective inspector,' she'd said, 'you can do what you like.'

Her voice had been overloud and the waitress had glanced in their direction. Keith was embarrassed. 'I certainly can't do what I like,' he said hastily, 'but I'll be as quick as I can.'

Keith was fit for his age. He took his fitness very seriously, seeing it as his duty to do so. Of course, he could no longer give chase like he used to in the old days. As a young copper he had represented Cornwall in cross-country running and there were very few villains who could outrun him. Keith was not a tall man and slightly on the stocky side, but there was no hint of a beer belly. He worked out in the gym three times a week to ensure that. In the old days he would have sprinted up the steps to the car park. He walked briskly now, and by the time he reached the top of the steps he was definitely out of breath. He paused for a moment, gazing out over the tranquil beauty of St Ives Bay, and then to his left, he saw a thick column of black smoke rising from Barnoon. He hurried on, ignoring his laboured breathing.

The scene before him was a mess. The fire engine had extinguished the flames and there was foam everywhere. Groups of people were standing around, much too close to the car. What were they thinking of? A lethal combination – petrol, fire, an overheated car – it was like an unexploded bomb. He hurried towards the scene. A figure detached itself from the throng. 'Good evening, Sir. What are you doing here?'

He recognised Sergeant Paul Davies, from the local force. 'Who's in charge?' Keith asked, without preamble.

'I am, sir.'

'Well, for heaven's sake, Davies, get everyone away from here. That car could go up at any moment.'

'Apparently not, sir,' said Sergeant Davies. 'The fire brigade are quite satisfied that it's stable.' He was deferential still but a little smug.

'Well, let's just hope they're right,' said Keith, grudgingly. 'Was there anyone in the car?'

'No, it was empty. I expect it was just some kids thinking they were having a laugh.'

Keith stared at him, a little quizzically. 'Do you really think so? It's not the sort of thing that normally happens around here.'

'Well, most of "Up Country's" bad habits are starting to filter down, aren't they, sir?'

Keith walked over to the smouldering shell. The windows had blown out with the force of the heat, the paintwork entirely blackened. It was difficult to tell what sort of car it had been, but it looked vaguely like a Renault.

'And no one saw anything, I suppose? How long ago did it happen?'

'About half-an-hour ago, sir. The local fire

brigade were very quick on the scene.'

Keith gazed at the wreck. 'Has anyone checked the boot?'

Paul Davies looked crestfallen. 'Well, no, sir. There hasn't really been time; it's only just been safe to approach the vehicle.'

Keith looked down regretfully at his own immaculate suit, a requirement of the anniversary dinner. Paul by contrast was wearing a sensible police flak jacket. 'Can I borrow your jacket a moment, Sergeant? The metal will still be very hot.'

Taking the jacket from Sergeant Davies, Keith used it to cover his hands and attempt to depress the button on the boot. Nothing happened – he punched it, but it was firmly stuck.

'Either it's locked, or the metal has corroded in the heat. Get one of the firemen to come and jemmy it open for us, would you?'

'Can't it wait until we've towed the vehicle away?' Sergeant Davies asked, 'when everything has cooled down a bit, sir?'

'Always examine as much as you can at the scene,' Keith said, 'you know that, Davies. Now get a fireman over here double quick.'

A fireman was with them in seconds, a big cheery lad. 'I'll have this open for you in a moment, sir,' he said.

He inserted a metal wrench into the bottom right hand corner of the boot. For a moment his muscles bulged and there was resistance, then, suddenly, the boot sprang open. Keith and Sergeant Davies stepped forward. Although the sea below them was inky black, the lights from the car park and the fire engine lit the scene well.

'Shit!' said Sergeant Davies.

There was total silence for a moment, but for the sound of crashing surf. A body lay in the boot. It was a man, clearly from his clothes, but the skin on his face and hands was split and peeling from the heat. Hehad beenquite literally pot-roasted.

'All one can hope,' said Keith Penrose, after a pause, 'is that the poor bugger was already dead when this lot went up.'

4

Things were not improving for Felicity, in fact quite
the contrary. The few extra days holiday, which were
supposed to calm and settle her, seemed to be having
the opposite effect. She was finding it increasingly
difficult to get out of bed in the morning and having
done so, all she could think about was how quickly
she could go back there again. Her energy and
concentration seemed to be dwindling by the day. On
Thursday, after a prolonged siesta, when she lay in
bed not reading, not sleeping, not doing anything at
all, she decided she simply did not have the energy to
get up to go and find herself some supper. At eight
o'clock there was a gentle knock on the door and in
came Annie, carrying a tray on which there was a
steaming bowl of soup and a hunk of bread.

'If you won't look after yourself, my bird,
someone's clearly got to do it for you,' she said with
a smile.

Felicity was flustered. She felt a mess, her hair
was all over the place and she was wearing an ancient
pair of pyjamas, which had once belonged to Charlie
in his slimmer days. She struggled to sit up in the

bed.

'That's so kind of you,' she said, 'but you shouldn't have bothered. I only stayed in bed because I wasn't very hungry; I'm not ill or anything …'

'You're depressed,' Annie interrupted her, 'that's what is wrong with you. If you could just give in to your grief, you'd feel a lot better. You're trying to carry on as if nothing has happened.'

'I'm fine,' Felicity replied. 'Everyone keeps telling me I'm depressed, but I'm really not, I'm just tired.'

'You're more than just tired,' said Annie firmly, perching on the edge of Felicity's bed like a little sparrow on a telegraph wire. 'Is something worrying you especially – apart from losing your husband, of course?'

Felicity shook her head. Tears were not far away and she was determined not to make a fool of herself in front of Annie. It was always the same when someone was being kind. 'No,' she said, hesitantly, 'not really, but I think I would find it easier to cope if I knew who had killed him.'

'You mean, who was driving the car that knocked him down?' Annie asked.

'Yes,' said Felicity, uncertainly. Just for a moment she was tempted to tell Annie about her momentary sighting of the accident but she was always afraid of ridicule when it came to describing her flashes of second sight.

'Leave the police to do their job and you concentrate on yours, which is making yourself better, so that you don't worry your children.' Annie patted her hand and stood up. 'Now, drink that soup, I made it myself, it's full of goodness. Don't you worry, my lovely, things will look better in the morning, they always do.'

The next day wasn't any better, however. In fact, it was worse. It took all Felicity's strength to get out of bed at all. Her hair needed washing but she could not face it. She picked at breakfast and then had to force herself upstairs to fetch a thick coat, for the weather had broken. In town, blasts of wind blew down the little streets and alleyways, the sand from the harbour stung her face, making her eyes water and fellow visitors scurried past her, heads bowed against the weather. She just wanted to be in bed, but was afraid of what Annie Trethewey would say if she went back to Cormorant Cottage so soon. She found herself in the café at the Tate Gallery, but even in there, she still felt cold and wretched. She cradled a cup of coffee and stared out at the seething Atlantic below her. Despite the greyness of the day and the positively leaden sky, the sea was still a mass of colour – silver, green, navy, the tips of the huge breakers an extraordinary pale turquoise – nowhere but in St Ives could such colours exist on so dismal a day, she thought, the artist in her momentarily stirred. Yet although the view was breathtaking this morning, for Felicity there was no joy in it. Was it possible that they were all right – Mel, Gilla and Annie? Certainly she had never felt like this in her life. When she thought about the days and weeks ahead, alone without Charlie, she could simply see no point in them. She tried to focus on her children for a moment and on Sam and Harry, her grandchildren. She thought of the moment four years ago when she and Charlie had visited Jamie and Trish, just after the birth of their first-born, Sam. She remembered holding him for the first time, that precious baby smell, and then handing him to Charlie. Charlie was a natural with babies and children; he maintained it was because he himself had never really grown up and was still on their level. Tears welled into her eyes and began to pour down her cheeks; it was all such a waste. She put down her coffee cup and scrabbled in her pocket for her handkerchief. This had to stop, action was needed; she would have to take another interminable walk. She blew her nose firmly, stood up, and began walking over to the counter to pay for her coffee.

As Felicity crossed the restaurant, she glanced at a discarded newspaper on one of the tables. What she saw made her gasp aloud. She picked up the paper and stared at it. It was a copy of the *St Ives Times & Echo* and staring out from the front page was a photograph of … the 'Skunk'.

The body of a man had been found in Barnoon car park two days before in the boot of a burnt-out car. He had been identified as Ronald Baxter, a resident of Plymouth. There then followed a lengthy passage about how inappropriate it was to have both burnt-out cars and dead bodies in St Ives and it ended by saying that the case was being handled by Detective Inspector Keith Penrose of Truro CID.

'Are you alright, love?' A disembodied voice

floated across the restaurant. Was someone speaking to her? Felicity glanced up, distractedly. A pleasant looking middle-aged woman was coming out from behind the counter.

'Are you alright, love?' she repeated, speaking more slowly, as if she imagined Felicity was deaf.

'Yes,' said Felicity, 'yes, fine, thank you.'

'Only you went as white as a sheet just then, I thought you were going to faint.'

'No, I'm perfectly alright, thank you,' said Felicity. 'Does this paper belong to you?'

'No,' the woman smiled, 'a customer must have left it. You're very welcome to it, if you want. Dreadful business isn't it, that body at Barnoon. Can't believe it could happen down here.'

Felicity agreed, smiled, thanked the woman again and left. She needed to be alone to think this through and walking back through the Gallery she found an empty seat and sat down, re-reading the scant details and examining the photograph again. There was absolutely no question about it. It was definitely the 'Skunk', and he had died on the same day that she had last seen him – alive at lunchtime, dead by supper – she shivered. What did it all mean? She sifted through the facts in her mind – very little really. She still felt sure that the 'Skunk' was connected to Charlie's death, but how and why? Firstly, there was his inappropriate appearance outside the court, then there was his obvious argument with the aggressive, burly-looking man in the pub ... and now he was dead – like Charlie. What was she trying to prove? Suddenly, she wondered about the car. If the 'Skunk' had died in his own car and if the 'Skunk' was responsible for Charlie's death, could the burnt-out wreck be the car that killed Charlie? She frowned with concentration at the newsprint. Detective Inspector Keith Penrose in Truro was in charge of the case – there was only one way she was going to find out. She stood up and started for the door and as she did so, she realised it felt as though a great weight had been lifted from her shoulders. The awful despair of the last few days seemed to have completely vanished. Twenty minutes before she had almost shuffled into the Tate; now she strode out – a woman with a purpose.

It would have been far easier to have made an appointment with God, Felicity thought, as she sat on the uncomfortably hard stacking chair in a rather draughty corridor. She had been at the police station in Truro for over an hour and her refusal to talk to anyone but Penrose appeared to have annoyed the junior ranks – she suspected she was being sidelined as a punishment. She had been told he was in the building. Perhaps he was some kind of power freak who actually enjoyed keeping people waiting. She would give it another ten minutes and then she would go back to the reception desk and try again. She had made an effort with her appearance and on the journey to Truro had rehearsed her story several times, with the result that she had entered the police station feeling relatively confident. Now that confidence had ebbed and she was starting to wonder whether she was making an unnecessary fuss.

'Mrs Paradise?' A young policewoman was standing in front of her. As usual, the curse of Charlie's surname prompted obvious amusement. 'Detective Inspector Penrose can see you now, Mrs Paradise, if you would like to follow me.'

Moments later Felicity was shown into a drab-looking office, not much larger than a broom cupboard. A desk dominated the room – partly because there was space for little else and partly because it was groaning with papers and files. So much for high-tech policing, Felicity thought. A man emerged from behind the files and extended a hand towards her.

'Keith Penrose, Mrs Paradise. How can I help you?'

Felicity met his steady gaze and liked what she saw. Although a man in his fifties, there was an immediate energy and enthusiasm about Keith Penrose which belied his age. He was not particularly tall for a policeman, but thick-set and dependable – his handshake was firm, his smile appeared genuinely warm, a good man in a crisis. His colouring was typically Cornish, bright blue eyes, a fresh complexion and a rather unruly mass of dark hair, just starting to turn grey. His hair immediately amused Felicity – it was more like a schoolboy's than a senior policeman in his middle years. She smiled in return as Keith gestured her to sit down.

Keith studied his visitor with interest. It wasn't often that someone was so insistent to see him personally, and an attractive woman, at that. She was in her mid-forties, he supposed, small of stature, her blonde hair, streaked with the odd strand of grey. Her eyes were deep brown, kind but challenging. She wore a very determined expression and he sensed that, despite the friendly smile, there was a tension about her. Her clothes amused him – a brightly-coloured, baggy sweater over jeans and hectic green suede boots – not the normal dress code he associated with a women in her middle years.

Keith Penrose said nothing; it was his way and it never failed. The less he said the more his interviewees felt compelled to fill the silence. Amazingly though, in this case it didn't work. Mrs Paradise regarded him with interest but also remained silent. The silence between them grew until, much to his surprise, Keith found himself breaking his own rule. 'So, Mrs Paradise, I gather you want to see me about the Baxter case – the body we found in Barnoon car park.'

Felicity felt herself relax a little; this man was clearly no fool and he was prepared to listen which was more than anybody else had done in some long time. 'I've met him,' Felicity said, without preamble. 'Ronald Baxter. Twice in fact – once in St Ives on the day of his death and once in Oxford.'

'In Oxford?'

She had got his attention, she could see that. 'Yes, I'd probably better start at the beginning. My husband was killed by a hit and run driver just over four months ago.'

'I'm sorry,' said Keith, immediately. That explained it of course, the strain around her eyes.

'Thank you,' said Felicity. 'Charlie, my

husband, was a lawyer. He was working on a drug-related case and although nobody else agrees with me, I feel sure that his death was connected to the case he was working on.'

'Are you saying you believe the hit and run was deliberate – murder in effect?' Keith asked, his heart sinking. It was a familiar scenario. Sometimes, with the loss of a loved one, the pain could be eased by inventing more significance surrounding the death than was warranted. Giving the death some sort of status seemed to help; senseless death often could not be endured.

'Yes, I believe he was murdered,' Felicity continued gamely.

'And do the Thames Valley Police agree with you? I assume this accident occurred in Oxford?'

'Yes it did and no they don't,' said Felicity.

Oh God, thought Keith, why did I agree to see her? 'And how is all this connected with Ronald Baxter?' he asked, not really wanting to know the answer.

'There was an inquest, of course,' said Felicity, 'and after the inquest I'm afraid I rather lost my temper and started talking to the press outside the court. As I was leaving, I noticed this man. He was watching me very intently and I asked him which newspaper he belonged to and he told me none.'

'What else did he say?' Keith asked.

'Well, nothing actually. My husband's partner was very anxious to get me away from the press to stop me venting my spleen any more.'

Keith could picture the scene and allowed

himself a trace of a smile. 'I'm not surprised,' he said. 'So this man – I am presuming he was Ronald Baxter – really said nothing to you at all except to deny that he was a reporter.'

Felicity nodded, now beginning to feel more than a little stupid. 'I dismissed him from my mind completely, until last Tuesday. I was having lunch in the Sloop in St Ives. Do you know it?' Keith nodded. 'There were two men arguing at a table close to me and suddenly I realised that one of them was the "Skunk".'

'The "Skunk"?' Keith asked, perplexed.

'Sorry, sorry, it's what I call him because of that white streak through his hair.'

Keith's face remained impassive, so Felicity hurried on. 'I couldn't hear what they were saying, they were whispering but they were clearly very angry with one another. I was a little scared to start with; I thought perhaps he had followed me to Cornwall.'

'Why should he do that?' Keith asked.

Felicity met his eyes and saw she was losing him. This was her last chance. 'I know it was an irrational thought, but it was just so unexpected to see him again. That morning in court was very traumatic, as you can imagine … ' her voice trailed away. 'Anyway,' she continued after a moment when it was clear Penrose was going to say nothing, 'after about five or six minutes, I suppose, the "Skunk" – Baxter, left. His companion finished his own drink, then Baxter's and left too. It's not a very pleasant thought that he was to be dead in just a few hours.'

'No,' Keith conceded. 'Tell me, would you recognise Baxter's companion again if you saw him?'

'Oh yes,' said Felicity. 'I'm sure I would.'

'Baxter had a criminal record so it is well possible that his companion has one too. Looking through some files could be helpful.'

'Oh, I don't think his companion has a police record.'

Keith smiled. 'Why on earth not, Mrs Paradise?'

'Well,' said Felicity, embarrassed, 'he just didn't look the type, definitely a country gentleman, obviously wealthy, and not, well, sort of low life, not sleazy the way Ronald Baxter was.'

'Believe me, Mrs Paradise, villains come in all shapes and sizes and from every social background.'

Felicity felt instantly stupid. 'Yes, of course,' she said. 'I'm sorry.' She hung her head and in doing so, caught sight of something shiny in the inspector's overflowing wastepaper basket. She leaned forward and picked it up. It was the silver paper from a cigarette packet. 'Brilliant, can I have this, Inspector?'

Inspector Penrose looked justifiably bemused. 'I suppose so,' he said.

'I collect silver paper for art projects. It makes excellent ponds and rivers,' said Felicity, by way of an explanation. She fixed Inspector Penrose with a killer stare. 'You shouldn't be smoking, Inspector, a man in your position. You should be setting an example.'

'I don't smoke,' said Keith with studied patience. 'It's my Chief Superintendent who smokes.

It's his secret vice. I caught him out one day so now he comes to my office when he needs a cigarette but can't leave the building. I encourage him – it's useful to be able to bend his ear in private now and again.' Why am I telling her all this, he thought. He shook his head as if to clear it. 'Could we concentrate on the matter in hand,' he said, severely. 'What makes you think Baxter's relevant in any way to your husband's death?'

Felicity hesitated. 'Instinct,' she said, 'it made no sense that he was so interested in the court case unless he was involved in some way.'

'I see,' said Keith, 'but you have no evidence linking him to the hit and run?'

'No,' Felicity looked crestfallen, 'but I did wonder whether it might be the same car. The car that killed my husband was blue, metallic blue and probably a Renault. Does that fit in at all with the one which was burnt out in St Ives?'

'Tests are still being carried out on the car,' Keith replied, smoothly. 'Now the best way you could help us, Mrs Paradise, is to try and identify the man Baxter was with at the Sloop. Certainly, as there was a disagreement between them and it was the day of Baxter's death, this is somebody we would very much like to interview.' He stood up. 'I'm most grateful for your help.' He was around the other side of his desk in a trice and the door was opened. 'Sergeant!' he called. 'The sergeant here will run through some mug shots with you and I would be grateful if you could leave us with a contact telephone number. Thank you so much for coming in.'

The interview was over and Felicity was halfway down the corridor when she realised she had not even said goodbye. She looked over her shoulder but Keith Penrose's door was already closed. Damn, she thought, he's not going to take any notice of what I said; he just got rid of me the quickest way he knew how. He is like everyone else, just not prepared to take this seriously.

Two hours later, when she finally left the station, Felicity's sense of futility was compounded. 'Skunk''s companion was nowhere to be seen on police records. It had all been a waste of time and another dead end.

As it happened, Keith Penrose was standing at his window when Felicity walked out of the station and crossed the car park. Although he was on the third floor, Keith recognised her instantly because of the vivid nature of her sweater. Her walk was very dejected, poor woman. He already knew she had been unable to identify anyone. He wished he could have reassured her that her visit had not been in vain but experience dictated that at this stage of an inquiry it was best to tell no one more than they needed to know. Ronald Baxter's last conviction was nine years ago. He had served his time and been back on the streets for over a year. He did not appear to be short of money at the time of his death, but nor did it appear that he had ever been employed, not legitimately anyway. He had been put away for drug dealing, a nasty trade to which the participants seemed particularly loyal – once a drug dealer, always a drug dealer was Keith's experience. The car in which his body had been found was a metallic blue Renault. Keith was waiting for a telephone call from Thames Valley Police.

On the dreary, drizzly journey along the A30 back to St Ives, Felicity could feel the sense of gloom descending on her once again. The adrenalin rush, which had taken her from the Tate Gallery to her interview with Keith Penrose, had disappeared as quickly as it had arrived. The flaw in her argument was obvious – there was absolutely nothing to link the 'Skunk' to Charlie's death, except perhaps ... As soon as she reached the haven of Cormorant Cottage she told Annie that she would be checking out the next day. 'That's a bit sudden, my girl,' said Annie, staring at her with her shrewd little eyes. 'Is everything alright?'

'Yes,' said Felicity, 'and I'll be back soon, if I may. I just need to go home and see how things are.'

She was back on the A30 by seven o'clock the following morning and in Oxford by midday. It was much colder in Oxford than it had been in Cornwall. She turned up the heating and adjusted the Aga to full power, but the house still seemed cheerless. Felicity wandered from room to room. It felt as if she had been away from home for a long time, yet in reality it was less than two weeks. Alone now, with everyone gone, she could almost hear the echoes of happier times when the family was all together, her own voice calling instructions – 'suppertime, bath

time, bedtime, Jamie go back and brush your teeth' –
and Charlie's great booming laugh in response to
something the children had said which amused him.
He had taken great pleasure in his children,
particularly when they were young. Felicity took
some comfort from that.

Orlando, their cat, appeared slyly out of
nowhere and was hysterical to see her. Racked with
guilt, she collapsed into Charlie's armchair and spent
some time stroking and fussing over the ecstatic
creature. It was Orlando who grew bored first and
wandered off in search of food. He looked well fed
and cared for – she knew the neighbours could be
relied on but she wondered how much he missed
family life. Was it true that places were far more
important to cats than people? He certainly seemed
perfectly at ease with having the house to himself.

Steeling herself, she climbed the stairs to her
bedroom, *their* bedroom, hers and Charlie's. In the
rush to leave, she had taken precious few clothes
with her and for practical reasons; she needed to take
some more down to Cornwall with her, particularly
with autumn coming. She burst through the bedroom
door and in a frenzy of activity began piling clothes
on the bed. She dragged an old holdall of Charlie's
out of the top of the wardrobe, piled the clothes into
it, in a haphazard fashion, and started to rush out of
the room again. In the doorway she stopped. What
was she doing, what was she afraid of? Slowly she
turned around and surveyed the room. Her eyes were
drawn to the bed. It was here that she and Charlie had
made love for the first time, where both their children

had been conceived, where Mel, always in a hurry, had made an unscheduled and extremely hasty entrance into the world. She smiled at the memory.

She had done nothing, she realised. The room was like a shrine to their marriage, not by design, but because she had no ability to change things from the way they had always been. She remembered visiting the home of a newly-divorced friend several years before. A single column of pillows had been placed in the centre of the double bed – on her side the bedside table had been piled high with books, and on what had formerly been her husband's side, the bedside table was empty. There was no such evidence of solo living in this room. Charlie's bedside table was as he had left it. In the months before his death, he had developed a passion for the Thirties novelist, Hugh Walpole, and a pile of his books was on the table. There was an alarm clock and a little leather box, which had been his grandfather's, and in which Charlie kept his cufflinks. Felicity walked over to the table and picked up the book on top of the pile. *Judith Paris*, she read. Always careful with his books, Charlie had marked the spot he had reached with a leather bookmark. Felicity thought about the moment he had placed that bookmark in the book for the last time, not knowing that within twenty-four hours he would be dead. She clutched the book to her and determined, there and then, to take it with her to Cornwall. Perhaps reading what Charlie had last read would make her feel closer to him.

Downstairs again, she realised she was not hungry, having consumed an utterly tasteless garage sandwich somewhere on the M5. She made a cup of black coffee and continued to range around the house until after two, when she judged that most people would have returned to work after their lunch break. Oxford was always quiet at this time of year, the lull before the storm. Most of the tourists had left but the students had yet to arrive. Just after half past two, her heart beating painfully and with a profound sense of dread, she left the house and walked shakily but with purpose, to the spot on the Woodstock Road where she had seen the vivid replay of her husband's last moments of life.

Her timing was perfect, the pavement was virtually deserted. Feeling something of a fool she stopped at the place where she judged she had stood before, and waited … nothing happened. As on many occasions in the past, she silently cursed the random nature of her so-called second sight, of her total inability to have any sort of control over what and where she had her sightings. The minutes ticked by. This was awful, why was she not able to bring back the scene at will? Was it the horror of what she had witnessed, of seeing her husband being killed before her very eyes that was proving some sort of psychological barrier? It seemed a good explanation. After ten minutes of self-conscious hanging around, she realised with a heavy heart that nothing was going to happen.

In despair, Felicity finally turned her back on the road and began to walking towards the little pathway that would take her through St Giles churchyard, onto the Banbury Road and so to home.

That's odd, she thought, why is the street lamp on at this time of day? She glanced over her shoulder and realised in that instant it was suddenly night and there, sure enough, was Charlie, a little wobbly, as he slowed his bike before turning to cross the road. Dear Charlie ... she forced her eyes away from him and looked up the road towards the already speeding car. As it came towards her, she was dazzled by the headlamps and could see no detail either of the car or its occupant. Biting her lip in concentration, she kept her eyes firmly on the car as it accelerated towards its hideous impact with Charlie. As the car flew past her, the interior was lit by a street lamp from across the road. The features of the driver were blurred and shadowed but there was no mistaking the white streak of hair that stood out in stark contrast to the darkness surrounding the figure at the wheel.

It was over in a second. So focused had she been on identifying the driver that Felicity was totally unprepared for the terrible sight of her husband's battered and bleeding body lying at her feet.

5

Felicity was on the M5 again, heading south-west, and she knew she was being ridiculous. A sign flashed up – 'Tiredness can kill, take a break.' Like an obedient child, she turned off the motorway at the services, and having filled up with fuel, she bought a coffee and sat in the front seat of her car, finding surprising comfort in the hot, beige liquid. It was the first time she had stopped to think since reeling away in horror from Charlie's body. She had almost run home and once inside the front door, she knew she could not stay there. She had bundled some dirty clothes in the washing machine, picked up her bag of fresh clothes, turned the heating down again and left a note for Sally, her cleaner. Orlando had looked bemused and resentful at these goings on and clearly could not believe that she was leaving him again. His aloof independence of the morning seemed to have deserted him, but she couldn't stay, even for him. Within an hour she was out of the door and back on the road to Cornwall.

What was she doing, she asked herself now, sipping the scalding liquid. There was a rough justice in what had happened. The 'Skunk' had killed Charlie and now he, too, was dead. Surely that was the end of the story, an eye for an eye: the sensible thing to do now was to leave it at that. Everyone else had. But no, she couldn't, it simply was not an option. Like her husband before her, Felicity was hooked, sensing that there was someone and something far bigger and more powerful at work. The 'Skunk', like poor little Ben Carver, was simply a pawn in the game. While the 'Skunk' had clearly killed Charlie, she was sure he was not ultimately responsible for his death; someone else had given the orders. 'Mr Big,' she said aloud, and then smiled in amusement – she sounded like a bad Hollywood gangster movie. Was 'Mr Big' the man the 'Skunk' had been talking to in the Sloop? Certainly there was only one way to find out. She realised there was no way she could go back and talk to Keith Penrose until she had something concrete to tell him. Identifying the other man in the Sloop was clearly the top priority.

It was after nine o'clock when Felicity reached the Chiverton Cross roundabout. She glanced at the left-hand turning to Truro. Had Keith Penrose followed up their meeting in any way, she wondered? It seemed unlikely. She recognised that the only tangible connection was the car, and it seemed unlikely that a burnt-out wreck could hold any secrets which would link it to Charlie's death.

At that very moment, her thoughts were in fact running parallel with those of Keith Penrose, who sat alone in his office, long after everyone else had left.

The damage to the nearside wing of the burnt-out Renault was consistent with its having struck something substantial and at speed, but torching the car had ensured that there was no forensic evidence to link it directly to Charlie Paradise's hit-and-run. However, assuming Mrs Paradise was telling the truth, and there was no reason to assume she was not, there could be a connection. Baxter's interest in the outcome of the inquest certainly linked him to Oxford and Paradise's death, and of course, the other common denominator was drugs. He had already read up the details of the Ben Carver case and agreed with Charlie Paradise. The quality and quantity of heroin which had hit the streets of Oxford in May could not have been the work of a small-time crook like young Ben Carver. This was big-time. In the morning he would speak to Josh Buchanan, Charlie Paradise's partner, who in Keith Penrose's view, should have done more to help Mrs Paradise.

Sensibly, Felicity had rung Annie at the services, for it was after ten by the time she dropped down into St Ives. As always, the harbour lights were enchanting, giving the town a distinctly continental look. The tide was high, the fishing boats gently swayed on their moorings – the scene was soothing, familiar and oddly more like home than home, she thought. The welcome at Cormorant Cottage seemed to emphasise the point.

'Are you going to tell me what you've been up to, my bird?' Annie asked as she sat watching Felicity eat the plate of scrambled eggs she had prepared.

It was time to share her story with someone, Felicity recognised that. She needed a fresh mind to worry at the significance of what had happened in the past few days. The obvious people were either Mel or Gilla. She dismissed the idea of Mel immediately. The thought of having to tell her daughter that she had seen her father die, not once but twice, was out of the question. And Gilla: much as she loved Gilla, she suspected her to be in Josh's camp – a non-believer – and Felicity did not feel that she had the energy at this moment to try and persuade her otherwise. So it was to Annie Trethewey that Felicity poured out her story, leaving no detail untold. It was a good choice. Annie let her talk without interruption and when she had finished, Felicity looked at her quizzically. 'I expect you find the part about me seeing the accident a bit far-fetched, but it happened, truly.'

Annie smiled. 'I don't doubt it, my bird, I'm Cornish, aren't I, a Celt, I know these things happen. Did anyone else in your family have the sight?'

'My grandmother,' said Felicity, enormously relieved at this degree of understanding.

'On your mother's side?' Annie asked.

'Yes, she wasn't Cornish, though,' Felicity smiled, 'she was a Scot from the west coast.'

'Same thing,' said Annie, magnanimously, 'we're all Celts.'

'So, what do you think?' Felicity asked. 'Am I mad to pursue this?'

Annie shook her head. 'I think you have to and I think the Sloop is the right place to start. If the bar staff can't help you, speak to an old boy called Billy Jenkin. He is a friend of mine, in fact we were at school together. He's in the bar every day, you'll recognise him because he smokes an evil pipe. Talk to him. He sees everything that goes on. He misses nothing.'

'I didn't think there was anyone else in the Sloop that day,' Felicity said. 'It was early, you see.'

'I bet you Billy was there, he tucks himself into a corner so that apart from the smell of his pipe, you wouldn't have seen him. He watches, Billy, he's not one for chatting. If you talk to him, tell him that you're a friend of mine.'

'I will Annie, thanks.'

'And one other thing,' Annie said, fixing Felicity with a firm glare. 'You mustn't get too deep into this yourself. The moment you find out anything useful, you must hand it over to the police and then leave it to them.'

'A lot of use that'll be!' said Felicity. 'The police appear completely uninterested in what I've had to say so far.'

'All the same,' said Annie. 'You need to think about what happened to your Charlie, and to that "Skunk". Get too close, know too much and you could find yourself in danger.' Felicity smiled at her words, which sounded extremely melodramatic, but she was suddenly aware of the sense of unease they brought.

'Can we talk more in the morning?' Felicity asked. 'I'm just so tired.'

'Of course you can, my lovely. Your bed is turned down and I've put a hot water bottle in there.

You're in your usual room.'

Felicity felt tears prick her eyes and spontaneously she got up and gave Annie a quick hug. 'You're very good to me,' she said.

Annie looked embarrassed but pleased. 'Be off with you,' she said, 'and don't rush down for breakfast, I'll fetch you something when you wake.'

By the morning though, the impact of Annie's words had dulled. As Felicity sat up in bed with her early morning cup of tea, listening to the now familiar shriek of the gulls, she felt strangely at ease with herself. All the evidence against the 'Skunk' was still unprovable but over the years Felicity had come to trust her sightings and she had no doubt, no doubt at all, that she had seen Charlie's death exactly as it had happened. The horror of it still lay at the edges of her mind but the determination to find out exactly what Charlie himself had been trying to discover, drove her forward and away from dwelling on her pain and loss. Her mobile rang shrilly. She would have to fix that dialling tone.

'Fizzy, darling, welcome home.' It was Gilla, and Felicity was more than a little confused.

'Hello, Gilla. What do you mean?'

'There's been a sighting. You were seen in Oxford yesterday afternoon by Susie Pritchard, you know, my neighbour. Why didn't you call me last night, darling, to say you were back? I've missed you so much.'

'But I'm not back,' said Felicity, 'I'm still in Cornwall.'

'Susie Pritchard must be going bonkers then.'

'No, no, she was right. I made a flying trip up to Oxford yesterday, but I'm back here again now.'

'Good Lord!' said Gilla. 'Whatever made you do that and why didn't you give me a ring while you were here? I think I'm about to get quite cross with you.'

'Sorry, Gilla, it was such a fleeting visit, there really wasn't time.'

'So why did you come back?' Gilla asked. She was clearly not going to be put off easily.

'Well,' said Felicity. 'It's a long and complicated story which I will tell you when I'm a little further down the line.'

'You're not doing anything stupid, are you?' said Gilla.

'No, definitely not,' said Felicity, hastily. 'How are things with you, anyway?'

'A spectacular change of subject,' said Gilla. 'I wish I could come down to see you. This blasted shop is just so busy at the moment that I don't dare leave it. All those bloody Americans, still trying to prove they're related to Winston Churchill.' Gilla was notoriously unkind about the constant flow of tourists who passed through Woodstock on their way to Blenheim Palace – and, incidentally, kept her in business.

'There'll be no let-up until Christmas now,' said Felicity, with some relief. As much as she loved Gilla, she didn't want her involved at this moment.

'I tell you what,' said Gilla. 'Why don't we have a holiday together? Some bullet-proof sun in January or February. That would give us something to look forward to.'

'I'd love that,' said Felicity, genuinely.

'You do sound better,' Gilla said, grudgingly. 'I just wish I knew what you were up to.'

'Don't worry,' Felicity replied. 'Only do me a favour, would you, Gilla? Please don't go winding up Mel any more, she has enough on her plate just coping with her own life, never mind her mother's.'

'I'm sorry,' said Gilla. 'Only I was so worried about you. When will you be back in Oxford?'

'I don't know yet,' said Felicity. 'But I'll keep you posted, promise.'

At eleven o'clock sharp, Felicity was outside the Sloop. The bar appeared deserted when she entered, but a pleasant looking girl was polishing glasses.

'Good morning,' said Felicity, with what she hoped was an encouraging smile. 'I was wondering if you could help me?'

'Certainly will, if I can,' the girl returned the smile. There was no mistaking her Australian accent.

'I was in the bar for lunch last Tuesday, and I want to find out the name of somebody who was having a drink here at the same time.'

'Can't help you there, I'm afraid,' said the girl. 'I've been up in Newquay the last two weeks, I've only just got back.'

'What about the landlord?' said Felicity.

'I'm afraid he's away today, seeing the brewery. The other bar staff will be in later on, around lunchtime, they might be able to help you. The trouble is, it's always so busy here that unless they're local, it's hard to tell who is who.'

'It wasn't busy that day,' said Felicity. 'That's why I am hoping somebody might remember.'

'Sorry I can't help you.'

Felicity looked around her. From the far end of the bar in a darkened corner, a single plume of smoke rose towards the ceiling. An old man was sitting perched on a stool. He peered at her through a haze of smoke. He was dressed in an old fisherman's sweater with a cap at a jaunty angle. Despite sitting in a dark corner, presumably smoking and drinking himself to death, Felicity noted the weather-beaten face, and the far-away look in his still clear blue eyes. It left her in little doubt that he had spent his life at sea.

She walked up to him. 'Are you Billy Jenkin?' she asked, tentatively, unsure of her welcome.

'I am that, my lover, come and sit beside me and cheer up an old man.' He patted the stool beside her and she perched next to him. 'Can I get you a drink?' he asked, graciously, when she was settled.

'It's a bit early for me,' said Felicity, 'but I suppose I could manage half a cider.'

'Well done, my lover.' Drinks were ordered and Billy made a great fuss of relighting his pipe.

'My name's Felicity, Annie Trethewey suggested I came and talked to you.'

'Little Annie, God bless her. How is she? Minding everybody else's business as well as her own, I expect. No change there.'

'I don't know about that,' said Felicity, 'but she's certainly very well.'

'She was good to me,' said Billy. 'When I came

to St Ives I was just a tiny lad. I got teased something shocking at school for being foreign. Annie took me under her wing; she soon had the bullies sorted out. You don't mess with Annie Trethewey, proper job, our Annie.'

Felicity laughed. 'I imagine that's true, but I don't understand, you sound Cornish, hardly a foreigner. Where did you come from?'

The old man cracked a smile. 'Newlyn – that was foreign enough in them days. Father was lost at sea and the following winter Mother caught the 'flu. She died of a broken heart really. There was nowhere for me to go except my auntie's in St Ives. They were good to me in the main, but they were busy people with a big family of their own.' He smiled again and looked into the middle distance. 'They had no time for a little boy lost who was getting bullied at school, but Annie did, she had time.' He was silent for a moment and Felicity knew better than to interrupt his reverie. At last he fixed Felicity with a speculative gaze. 'So a friend of Annie's is a friend of mine. What can I do for you?'

'I was in here last Tuesday lunchtime.'

'I knew I'd seen you somewhere,' Billy said, with a delighted smile. 'You sat over there on your own, didn't you?' He indicated the precise table where Felicity had indeed sat. 'Looked proper miserable you did, I wondered what was wrong with you. You look better today.'

Felicity felt her spirits rise, if he could remember her, then ... 'There were two men,' she said. 'Sitting at that table there.'

'And one of them was that villain who got fried up at Barnoon.'

'That's it,' said Felicity, triumphantly. 'You remember him?'

'Well, of course I do. As soon as I saw his picture in the paper I remembered him.'

'Do you remember the man who was with him?' Felicity asked, excitement mounting. Billy nodded. 'Do you know who he is?'

'I don't know his name,' Billy replied, 'but he's in here fairly regular. Bit of an odd one, that, he looks like a country gent but seems to mix with a lot of low life.'

'Is there any particular day he comes in? Only I am really anxious to talk to him,' Felicity asked.

Billy looked at her curiously. 'Can't say there is but I could let you know next time he does.'

'Would you, would you do that?'

'Of course, my girl.'

'So, if I gave you my mobile phone number, could you call me?'

'Couldn't do that.'

'Why not?' Felicity asked.

'Don't have no use for phones, can't stand mobiles, spoil a man's peace, but I'll tell you what I'll do, the moment he comes in, I'll pop round Annie's and tell her. No doubt she can get in touch with you, and it will give me an excuse to pay a visit.'

'That would be wonderful,' said Felicity. She hesitated, not wanting to sound impatient. 'How often does he come in, I mean when are you likely to see him?'

'Can't say,' said Billy. 'But I reckon I see him most weeks.'

'Do you think anybody, the landlord, or any of the staff would know who he is?'

'Doubt it,' said Billy. 'He's not local. I'll ask around for you, though, see what I can find out.'

'Well, the least I can do, then, is to buy you a drink.'

'No, bless you, I'm alright, I'm not a drinker.' Felicity must have looked startled. 'You wonder why I sit here all day?' Billy's face cracked into a wide smile again. 'Not much else to do now I've retired. I like watching people, watching the world go by. Harmless enough, and useful sometimes, useful for you, I reckon, and I'm not such an old fool as to ask you why.'

A piece of luck at last, Felicity thought. Billy Jenkin might seem an unlikely accomplice, but he could hardly be bettered.

It was three long frustrating days before Felicity heard from Billy. It was ridiculous really; she might just as well have joined him in his daily vigil on a bar stool, for she felt unable to stray very far from Cormorant Cottage in case he came with news. Equally, though, she felt that if she kept popping into the pub to check up on his progress, she would be suggesting that he could not be relied on, which in turn might undermine his cooperation. So instead she got in Annie's way.

'It's like having a child around the place again,' Annie grumbled, good-naturedly, 'always under my feet. You'd better help me with my chutney if you've got nothing better to do.'

At this time of year, every year, it emerged, Annie made chutney – but not just the odd jar; her kitchen was transformed into a factory. She had been doing it for year, she told Felicity, and the proceeds from the sale of her jars went to the RNLI.

'It's my way of saying thank you for keeping my men safe,' she said, misty-eyed.

Felicity was impressed. 'You're just so resourceful and energetic; you make me feel completely inadequate.'

'I only do it once a year,' said Annie, 'but it raises a nice drop of money for the lifeboats and keeps me out of mischief for a day or two.'

It took them two days, and once in the swing of things, Felicity found she really enjoyed having something practical to do and, of course, she was very happy in Annie's company. They talked about every subject under the sun while they worked and it was sometime during the second morning that they began discussing how Felicity had felt seeing Charlie die.

'I just don't know how you coped with that, my bird,' said Annie.

It was such a relief to Felicity to be with somebody who clearly believed, without any doubt or hesitation, that her gift was real. 'It was awful, of course,' said Felicity, 'but, you do know, even when you're seeing it, that it's not actually happening for real. It's painful, but,' she hesitated, 'imagine you're the bereaved relative of someone famous, who is on television a lot – a politician or an actor – you turn on the television and there he or she is, although they've died. It's rather like that, I suppose.'

'Except,' said Annie, 'you had to witness the moment your husband was killed. Surely that's a bit different?'

'That's true,' Felicity said, 'but there are compensations. At the time everyone told me that he would have died instantly, but I didn't believe them, of course. Now I know it's true. He died the moment he hit the pavement, I'm sure of it. This last time, he ended up right by my feet.'

'Dear God,' said Annie. 'I can't even imagine what that must have been like.'

'I can blot it out most of the time,' Felicity admitted, 'except at night, of course.'

'I've been thinking about losing my Jim, thought about him a lot in the last couple of weeks since you've been here.'

Felicity looked up from her chopping, horrified. 'Oh, Annie, I'm so sorry.'

'No need to be sorry, my bird, he was an awkward bugger like all men, but most of the memories I have of him are happy ones. That's what I'm trying to say really. You never get over it, losing your lifetime's partner, and people who suggest you can are cracked. What you learn to do is to live with missing them. Jim's been dead for nearly eleven years now and sometimes I still turn to him to tell him something that would interest him or make him laugh and it still hurts to find he's not there. Finding a way to live with it begins by accepting the pain and recognising it's always going to be a part of you.'

Felicity put down her knife and placed her hand

on Annie's arm. 'You're a very wise old thing, aren't you?' she said affectionately, tears in her eyes.

'Less of the old, my bird, and stop that crying. I don't want you going soft on me in the middle of chutney-making.'

'It's the onions,' said Felicity, firmly.

'Well, you just get on with your chopping, that's it now.'

On the third day, they were cutting out rounds of cheerful cotton gingham to make little hats to go on the jars, when there was a knock on the door. Annie went up from the basement kitchen and Felicity, straining her ears, could only make out the muffled sound of conversation. It can't be Billy, she thought, they're taking far too long. She was extremely surprised, therefore, when two sets of footsteps came down the stairs into the kitchen and there, indeed, was Billy, for once his evil-smelling pipe tucked away in the pocket of his jacket.

'Hello, my dear,' he said, with genuine warmth. 'I see Annie's got you hard at work. You ought to let her out of here for some fresh air, you wicked woman.' He turned to Annie. 'It's a beautiful day out there, too nice to be making your old chutney.'

'I've never seen you say no to a couple of jars, Billy Jenkin, and it doesn't just make itself!' said Annie firmly.

While this exchange was going on, Felicity was weak with frustration. Clearly though, this had to be a social call, Billy was taking far too long to get to the point for there to be any news.

'Would you like a drink while you're here, Billy?' Annie asked.

'Right on,' said Billy, settling himself down at the kitchen table, beside Felicity.

'So, you haven't seen him yet?' Felicity said, frowning in concentration as she cut round the cardboard template.

'Yes, I have,' said Billy, 'that's what I've come to tell you.'

'What do you mean?' Felicity asked.

'He's there now, with another shady-looking character.'

Felicity scraped back her chair and jumped to her feet. 'Why didn't you say, he'll probably have gone by now.'

'Calm down,' said Billy, 'they've only just ordered their drinks.'

'I'd better go,' said Felicity. 'Thanks Billy,' she called as she started up the stairs.

'These young people, always in a rush.' Billy grumbled. Even in her panic, Felicity couldn't help smiling – young people, it was a long time since anybody had referred to her like that. Once outside the cottage she resisted the temptation to run, and during the five minutes it took her to reach the Sloop, she tried to compose herself and think how she should tackle the situation. It was difficult to see how she could approach 'Mr Big' direct; she could hardly go up and ask him his name. She would just have to hope that the bar staff could help. She shouldn't have left Billy at Cormorant Cottage, she should have brought him with her; he would have known other people in the pub who might have been able to help. She toyed with the idea of going back, but after a few moments of uncharacteristic dithering, she decided not to risk it and she was right, for as she turned the corner by the Sloop, there he was, with his companion, already leaving.

'Damn,' murmured Felicity, under her breath.

The two men crossed to the harbour's edge. There, parked rather ostentatiously, was what looked like a brand new Range Rover. They were in deep conversation. 'Mr Big' opened the car door. The two men did not shake hands, they simply parted, 'Mr Big' climbing into his car and his companion starting off along the harbour towards the pier. Felicity hesitated for a moment. On the side of the Range Rover there were the words 'Boswithey Gardens'. That was helpful, at least. There was clearly no point waiting by the car for 'Mr Big' to drive off, so she set off in pursuit of the other man.

Like the 'Skunk' he had a slightly down-at-heel look, but his dress – a thick navy jacket and sea boots – made it obvious he had come off a boat. He was young too, judging by the shock of hair and the speed with which he strode along the harbour. Felicity had quite a job keeping up with him. He turned abruptly onto the pier. The tide was in and his boat was moored up alongside. With hardly a break in stride, the ropes were off the bollards in seconds and he was aboard, already gunning the engine. Felicity watched, helplessly, as the boat pulled away from the harbour wall, heading out across St Ives Bay. She squinted into the sunshine.

'*Jayne Marie*,' she read. 'Plymouth.' From this distance it looked like any other regular fishing boat, but close to, even to Felicity's untrained eye, she could tell it was not a working boat. There was none of the normal paraphernalia of nets and lobster pots; it had looked altogether too tidy and uncluttered. Felicity looked around her in desperation – now what? Her eyes fell on the harbour office. A man was standing in the doorway. She dashed up to him.

'Excuse me. You see that boat going across the harbour now, the one that was just here, you don't know who it belongs to, do you?'

'I don't,' was the reply, 'but hang on a minute. I'll ask the harbour master.'

Conversation rumbled inside the office for a moment and the man reappeared.

'I'm sorry, no. No one knows. It's not a local boat, it's from Plymouth and none of us have seen it before. Up to no good though, the boys reckon.' As he was speaking, Felicity stared out across the harbour. The angle at which the pier jutted out into the harbour meant that from where she was standing she could see the Sloop very well and there, parked in front of it, was the Range Rover. 'Mr Big' must have waited to see the boat leave. As she watched, she saw the car begin to move slowly away along the harbour.

'You see that Range Rover over there,' Felicity said, pointing across the water. 'That green one. It's got ...' she hesitated 'Boswithey Gardens written on the side of it. You don't know who that belongs to, I suppose?'

There was a rumbling laugh. 'I do, as a matter of fact, but I've never known anyone ask so many questions.'

For the first time Felicity looked properly at her new companion. He was not particularly tall and, for his age, his hair was overlong, but that apart, he was one of the best-looking men she had ever seen in her life. Much to her fury she found herself blushing – blushing at forty-seven!

'I'm sorry,' she said. 'Only, it is important. Do you really know who the driver is?'

'I certainly do, I used to work for him.' The man smiled and glanced down at his watch. 'It's about time I stopped for lunch, I normally just go to the café over there,' he nodded across the harbour. 'Do you want to join me and I'll tell you what I know,' he grinned at her, 'if it's that important.'

'That's very kind,' said Felicity. 'I don't want to interrupt your lunch. I could just walk around with you.'

'As you wish. My name's Martin Tregonning, by the way.' He held out a hand, which Felicity took.

'Felicity Paradise,' she said. She waited for the inevitable quip about her name, but there was none.

'Hang on a moment,' he said. 'I'll just tell the boys I'm off.'

Moments later they were walking along the harbour edge together. If Gilla could only see me now, Felicity thought, with amusement, she would be positively green with envy.

6

In fact, at that precise moment, Gilla would not have been at all jealous of Felicity's lunchtime companion for she had one of her own. Rushing between the bank and the Post Office during her lunch break, she had bumped, quite literally, into Josh Buchanan.

'Josh, what are you doing in Woodstock?'

Josh kissed her warmly on both cheeks. 'Visiting an extremely boring client,' he said. 'It's good to see you, Gilla. Have you had lunch?'

'No,' said Gilla, triumphantly. 'In theory, I have a lot of chores to do today so I was going to have a quick sandwich back at the shop.'

'Sod the chores, come to the Feathers and have lunch with me,' said Josh, firmly.

Ten minutes later they were seated in front of a roaring log fire with a particularly delicious bottle of red wine.

'I feel better already,' said Josh. 'A glass of wine, a beautiful woman … '

'Oh, come off it, Josh, we've known each other far too long for all that rubbish,' Gilla said. They smiled at one another and raised their glasses in a silent toast.

'So,' said Josh, breaking eye contact and concentrating instead on something apparently fascinating in his glass. 'How are we feeling about Fizzy at the moment? Are we worried about her all alone in St Ives?'

'Has something happened?' asked Gilla, immediately agitated, 'is something wrong? The warm relaxed atmosphere of a moment before was gone. Gilla put her glass down on the table with a shaky hand, spilling a little.

Josh stared at her in genuine astonishment. 'No, no, nothing's wrong, what on earth makes you think there is?'

'You suddenly went shifty on me,' said Gilla. 'I'm a fool about almost everything, except men, and sadly, over the years, I've learnt to know when men are keeping something from me. You're keeping something from me now, Josh.'

'Calm down,' said Josh. 'It's nothing to get into such a fuss about. I had a telephone call yesterday from a Cornish policeman in Truro. He seems to think there's some connection between Charlie's death and a burnt-out car they found with a dead body in the boot.'

'Oh God,' said Gilla. 'Where was the car found?'

'That's the odd part,' said Josh, 'in St Ives.'

'Josh, the body wasn't … '

'No, of course not,' said Josh. 'I'm sorry, I'm not explaining myself very well, but you're so jumpy, I can't concentrate. As far as I can understand, it is purely coincidental that Fizzy happens to be staying in St Ives as well.'

'It can't be a coincidence,' said Gilla, 'and no, you're not explaining yourself very well. How on earth did this policeman track you down?'

'Fizzy went to see him,' said Josh. 'He wouldn't go into any detail – you know how policemen love to be mysterious – but apparently she alerted him to the fact that there could be some connection between the burnt-out car in St Ives and the car which killed Charlie. It seems that she is probably right.'

'Dear God,' said Gilla, after a moment, 'so her theory that Charlie was murdered is not far-fetched after all.'

'It would appear not,' said Josh.

'How awful!' Gilla said, 'and none of us really believed her, not even me.'

'Well, it seems someone believes her now,' said Josh. 'The policeman, Penrose his name is, was decidedly grumpy with me. He asked me whether I was satisfied that Thames Valley Police had done their job. When I said, how was I to know, I was just a lawyer, he started lecturing me – about the responsibilities of being Charlie's partner and surely wanting to see justice done, and about whether I was aware that Mrs Paradise was less than satisfied with the investigation into her husband's death.'

'So what did you say?' Gilla asked.

Josh shrugged his shoulders and took a sip of wine. 'Just the truth, as I see it – that I have no reason to suppose that Charlie's death was anything other than an accident. He asked me all about the Ben Carver case and I've sent him down the files, but I have to say he left me with a profound sense of inadequacy.'

'Quite right too,' said Gilla after a moment, staring into the fire.

'Thanks a bunch,' said Josh, morosely.

Gilla turned her gaze to meet his. 'Well, your Cornish policeman chum is right, isn't he? We've both let her down. Why weren't we prepared to listen to her, why didn't we take her seriously? I should have done. You know she saw the moment Charlie died in one of her episodes of second sight, one of her visions – whatever you care to call them?'

'No I didn't,' said Josh. 'I expect she thought if she told me that, it would be a step too far for me to give any credence to her story. She knows that I think her gift is simply a case of an overactive imagination – always have.'

'Charlie didn't think so,' said Gilla, quietly. 'He believed she had genuine second sight, a real gift, and for all his nonsense, you know better than anyone, Charlie Paradise was no fool.'

'No,' Josh agreed, 'no, he wasn't.'

Their food arrived and they were silent for a few moments as they began to eat. Gilla found she suddenly had very little appetite.

'He changed, you know,' Josh blurted out, after a pause.

'Who?' Gilla asked.

'Charlie, in the last few weeks of his life – well, from the moment he agreed to take on the Carver case.'

'In what way did he change?' Gilla asked, fork

poised in mid-air.

'Well, he worked a lot harder for a start and there were far fewer sessions in the pub. He also became quite secretive about the case, which was not at all how we operated within the practice. In fact, that was one of our strengths – bouncing ideas off each other. We were very different, Charlie and I, so we usually approached problems in different ways, which was tremendously helpful. We had some right old battles, but they were always valuable and productive and, in the end, of considerable benefit to the client, I think.'

'So you're saying that when he started on the Carver case, he didn't discuss it with you, and that it was a major departure from the norm.'

'That's right,' Josh agreed.

'Good God, Josh, don't you think that was something worth sharing with Fizzy and the police?'

'No, not really,' said Josh, instantly on the defensive. 'Look, I've said enough, I didn't really mean to get into this. At the time I didn't link his behaviour to the case – I just assumed that he and Fizzy were going through a bad patch.'

'What do you mean, you've said enough? Are you holding back something else, was there anything in the Carver file to indicate what could have been the problem?'

'No, absolutely not!' said Josh, angry now. 'Fizzy asked me to go through the file which I did, and Thames Valley Police went through it as well. As I told you, I've sent everything down to Cornwall now, but I have kept his laptop. I've looked at it already, but I thought I would go through it again, take it home and work on it in the evenings to see if I can find anything.'

'Charlie's been dead for four months. Don't you think this is something you should have done before, Josh?'

Josh was instantly on the defensive again. 'I don't think so, as I said, I had no reason to suppose there was anything suspicious about Charlie's death.'

'Only his widow pleading for you to listen to her!'

'OK,' said Josh, angrily. 'You've done so much better, have you, Gilla?'

'No,' said Gilla. 'That's the point, neither of us have. In fact, nobody has supported Fizzy, have they? Her children have been hopeless – Jamie is a sweet boy but terribly ineffectual and as for Mel, she's so driven by her career, she hasn't got time to think about anything else much, even when something catastrophic happens, like her father dying. I wonder about that girl sometimes.'

'It's having weird godparents, that's deranged her, I expect,' said Josh, with a trace of a smile.

Gilla returned his smile – both she and Josh were Mel's godparents and the reminder of it took the heat out of their exchange. 'It's just awful Josh, we've let them down so badly. Just think of all those wonderful meals and celebrations we've shared with the Paradise family at Norham Gardens over the years. Where would we have been without them? We're such a couple of misfits, you and I.'

'Thanks,' said Josh.

'I'm serious, Josh. Neither of us has made a success of family life but we've basked in the reflected glory of the Paradises' cosy family. Think of the generosity of Charlie's endlessly flowing wine and Fizzy's delicious casseroles. Think of the times we've sat around their kitchen table bemoaning our love lives. Think of the pleasure of reading their children bedtime stories, joining in family parties. How many Christmases would you have spent alone but for them? Who never forgot your birthday and always celebrated it with cake and balloons, like you were a kid? When Ellie was born and my marriage broke up, Ellie was just absorbed into the charmed circle. Heavens, Fizzy even bought a second-hand cot for her so that when I went to dinner, Ellie and I could stay the night and I didn't need to pay for a babysitter. Just imagine the last twenty years without the Paradises in your life, Josh – it would have been a bloody desert, wouldn't it?'

Josh looked down at his plate. 'Yes,' he mumbled.

Gilla had a sudden flash of intuition and the aggression left her as quickly as it had come. 'I bet you miss Charlie,' she said gently.

'I do,' said Josh. 'He was something of a mentor to me, not exactly a father figure, more an older brother. He was a genuine advocate of the law, but the law meted out with compassion and understanding as to the frailty of the human psyche. He was ...'

'A good man,' Gilla finished for him.

'Yes.'

'So what do we do now?' Gilla asked. 'Are we going to continue to sit on the sidelines doing nothing to help?'

'Well, as I said,' Josh replied, 'I'm going to have a good search through Charlie's laptop.'

'And what about Fizzy, aren't you worried about her, don't you think she might be getting into something that she can't handle? She was most evasive with me when I spoke to her on the phone the other day, wouldn't tell me anything about what was going on, yet she must have known all about the burnt-out car by then.'

'Why don't you go down and see her?' Josh suggested.

'The shop, you know, it's getting busy.'

'Oh, come off it,' said Josh. 'You're the one who has just been lecturing me about being a lousy friend. If you're that worried about her, surely you have an assistant who could look after the shop for a few days.'

'Yes, I do,' said Gilla, 'in fact she will be wondering where on earth I am right now, I was only popping out to the bank.' She hesitated. 'Maybe I should take Ellie down to Cornwall for a long weekend; it might kill two birds with one stone – check up on Fizzy and cheer up Ellie. God, spare me from teenagers. I sometimes think you're very lucky having no children, Josh.'

'I agree,' said Josh. 'I do dimly remember being a teenager myself and being simply frightful to everyone. It's an awful period. Poor Ellie, poor you and poor Fizzy if you're going to inflict Ellie on her.'

'Shall I do that?' Gilla asked.

'It's up to you,' said Josh. 'Fizzy is more your friend than mine, but certainly I think it would be helpful to know what's going on. As I said, the Cornish policeman didn't seem worried about her safety in any way, but it does seem rather odd that the action, such as it is, has shifted to the very town where Fizzy is on holiday.'

'You could come with us, Josh,' said Gilla, wickedly.

'I wouldn't want to come between mother and daughter on a bonding holiday,' said Josh, smoothly.

The surroundings in which Felicity was having lunch with Martin Tregonning were a far cry from the elegant comfort of the Feathers Hotel in Woodstock. The café to which Martin Tregonning had led her, had a drab, out-of-season feel about it and when the coffee had arrived, a good twenty per cent of it was in the saucer.

'Sorry,' Martin said, apologetically. 'It's not much of a place but it's quick and close by.'

'Do you work at the harbour office?' Felicity asked.

'No, I'm a coastguard, voluntary, part-time of course – it's not my proper job. I'd just popped into the office to have a chat, to be honest.' He grinned at her. 'And then, this strange woman arrived and started asking me the most incredible number of questions.'

Felicity bit her lip. 'I'm sorry,' she said. 'You must have thought I was mad.'

'A little. So are you going to tell me what this is

all about?'

'I'm not sure,' Felicity said, and then realised how rude it sounded and flushed with embarrassment.

'It's OK,' said Martin, 'I'm only teasing. You don't have to tell me anything you don't want to. In answer to your last question though, his name is Ralph Smithson and he is a thoroughly nasty piece of work. So unless you've got a very good reason to make contact with him, I wouldn't, and believe me, I know what I'm talking about.'

'The man in the Range Rover is called Ralph Smithson?' Felicity said. Martin nodded. 'And what's Boswithey Gardens?'

'That's the name of his estate,' said Martin. 'It's on the other coast, overlooking Mount's Bay, about five miles from Penzance. It's an extraordinary place, an old house perched up on top of the cliff and there are these amazing gardens which run down to the sea. They're sub-tropical and it's an absolute tragedy that they're slowly disappearing.'

'Why's that?' Felicity asked, now deeply confused.

'The sea is slowly eroding them,' said Martin. 'It's the same with the whole of that coast, though mercifully, the gardens will be around for another few years yet.'

'And you say you worked for him?' Felicity asked.

'Yes, I trained in forestry and usually I freelance – a job here and a job there – but I got married last year and Smithson offered me a permanent job. It seemed like a good idea at the time.'

'But it didn't work out?' Felicity pressed.

'No.' There was a silence between them.

'Could I ask why?'

'Not yet.' Martin gave her a shy smile. 'Supposing you just tell me why you are so interested in him.'

Felicity studied her companion in silence for a moment. He certainly was very good-looking, in a rugged sort of way. There were laughter lines around his eyes, he looked kind and Felicity suspected, from the brief time they had been together, that he was no womaniser, probably didn't even realise how attractive he was, which of course made him more so. But there was something else, a sadness, a reticence, something ... he was certainly far from carefree. Still, she thought, everyone has their secrets and if I don't start by telling him my story, I'm certainly not going to hear his. 'Well,' she said, 'if you're ready to hear something of a saga, I'll tell you why I'm interested in Ralph Smithson.'

She left nothing out, except for her moments of second sight which experience had taught her was not something she shared with new acquaintances. Martin listened in attentive silence, right up to the point where Billy had interrupted the chutney making and sent her scurrying down to the harbour.

There was a long silence when she had finished, which she took to be not very encouraging. 'So, do you think Ralph Smithson is capable of organising some sort of drugs racket and if so, would it be easy or even possible to run it from Boswithey?'

Martin's shuttered expression was in complete contrast to his response. 'I think the answer to both questions has to be yes,' he said, thoughtfully. 'He is certainly an unpleasant person. He's South African. He came over here about ten years ago so I don't know much about his background, but my judgement is he's capable of it. As for drugs at Boswithey ... well, there's certainly drug smuggling along that piece of coast.'

'Really, smuggling?' said Felicity. 'Surely not these days?'

'All you tourists see is golden sand and sparkling blue water but there is a darker side to Cornwall. There's drug smuggling all along the coast from Mullion to Penzance. It's very different from the past of course. It's "Up Country" people involved now, rather than the Cornish. There's no brandy for the parson these days, just a particularly sordid trade in human misery.'

'There's certainly nothing very romantic about drugs,' Felicity agreed.

'In reality, there wasn't anything very romantic about the brandy either,' said Martin. 'Although it was supposed to end up in London, many of the barrels that landed here never made it. They say that drunkenness in Cornwall during the eighteenth century was terrible – just a drug by another name, I suppose.'

'But not so calculated somehow,' said Felicity. 'Drug pushers today pedal death and destruction, and they know it. I would love to nail Ralph Smithson, if he is the cause of my husband's death, but I would also like to stop his filthy trade.'

'Amen to that,' said Martin, after a pause. 'I feel exactly the same. You can certainly count on me if there is anything I can do to help. Have you been to the police?'

'I have, though little good it did me. I think they thought I was wasting their time. They will be interested in the identity of the man who met the "Skunk" in the Sloop though. Is it OK if I tell them you identified him?'

'Be my guest,' said Martin.

It was nearly four o'clock by the time Felicity returned to Cormorant Cottage.

'Where have you been, my girl? Worrying me sick, you have. You weren't at the Sloop, I checked. I wondered what on earth had happened to you.' Annie looked genuinely concerned.

'Sorry, Annie. I've just met somebody who has been able to help me a great deal. He has identified "Mr Big", his name is Ralph Smithson. Do you know him?'

'Doesn't mean a thing to me,' said Annie.

'He owns Boswithey Gardens?' Felicity suggested.

'Oh, Boswithey. I know Boswithey, beautiful; I went there once with the W.I. I can't believe anybody who owns those gardens could be a bad person. Are you sure you're on the right track, my girl?'

'I hope so,' said Felicity. 'The question is whether I can convince the police. I thought I'd go to Truro tomorrow morning and see my tame policeman.'

'Why don't you just ring him, you've been doing such a lot of gadding about?' Annie said.

'No,' said Felicity, 'I think I need to see him in person if I am to persuade him to take things any further.'

7

The meeting with Keith Penrose was extremely hurried and disappointing. Felicity had arrived in Truro late morning to be told that D.I. Penrose would not be returning to the station until mid-afternoon. It was nearly five by the time he summoned her to his office. He looked tired, strained and clearly preoccupied.

'What can I do for you, Mrs Paradise?' he said, having waved her to a chair.

'I've discovered the identity of the man who was with the "Skunk", I mean Ronald Baxter, in the pub the day he was killed.'

Keith had been studying some papers on his desk but he looked up sharply at her words. 'Oh really, who is he?'

'His name is Ralph Smithson.'

Keith frowned. 'Do you know him?' Felicity asked.

'I know the name,' said Keith, 'I just can't connect it.'

'He owns Boswithey.'

'Of course,' said Keith, 'beautiful gardens. My

wife has dragged me there once or twice.' He allowed himself the ghost of a smile. 'So how did you come by this information, Mrs Paradise?'

'I spotted him again in the Sloop. He was meeting another man, not dissimilar to the "Skunk", only younger. Inspector Penrose, I really think he has something to do with both murders – both Baxter's and my husband's.'

'I don't wish to appear unkind,' said Keith Penrose, 'but, in the circumstances, isn't that rather a strong statement, Mrs Paradise?'

Felicity flushed with sudden anger. She was so tired of trying to persuade someone, anyone to take her seriously. 'Not really, surely there can be absolutely no doubt that Ronald Baxter was murdered. He didn't put himself in the car and set fire to it. I've given you the name of the man who was with him just hours before he died and, when seen, they were having a blistering argument. Only a fool would think that piece of information was of no significance.' She flushed again. 'I'm sorry, I just …'

'It's alright,' said Keith Penrose, 'I do understand how painful this whole matter is for you. I spoke to your husband's partner, incidentally.'

'Josh?' Felicity said, surprised.

'Yes, indeed. In fact he has sent me down the file on the Carver case. I have it here somewhere.' He looked a little hopelessly at his groaning desk.

Despite the frustrating circumstances, Felicity experienced a moment of amusement. There was such a contrast between the neatly dressed Detective Inspector, his presumably ordered mind and the absolute chaos of his office. 'So you *are* taking some notice of what I've said.' Felicity tried a smile and was rewarded by one in return.

'I certainly am, Mrs Paradise.'

'Can I do anything to help?'

'I don't think so. You've been most helpful in providing the name of Ronald Baxter's companion in the pub and, of course, you're right, we will need to interview him as he may well have been the last person to see Baxter alive.'

'So, you're saying that because Ralph Smithson owns Boswithey and is a well-known character in the area, he couldn't possibly be the murderer?' Felicity knew she was speaking out of turn, but she just couldn't control her anger and frustration. 'Perhaps you've had a change of heart, Inspector. I seem to remember you telling me that villains came in all shapes and sizes and from every social background.'

'And so they do, Mrs Paradise, so they do,' said D.I. Penrose, his patience clearly ebbing. 'I have an entirely open mind and I can assure you that we will continue to make all necessary enquiries. We are taking this murder very seriously indeed. We take all murders very seriously but this one was particularly unpleasant – Ronald Baxter was alive when he went into that boot.' As he spoke the words, he regretted them immediately. He saw Felicity's face blanch. What on earth had possessed him to say that? The poor woman had been through enough. She had just lost her husband in violent circumstances and this was the sort of detail she did not need.

'You mean, he was effectively burnt alive?'

He couldn't deny it. 'Yes, I'm afraid so.'

'I believe Baxter killed my husband, but I wouldn't wish a death like that on anyone. That's awful.' She regretted the words the moment she had uttered them. Shock had made her careless.

'Yes, it is,' said Penrose, regarding Felicity with interest. 'When we met last, Mrs Paradise, you gave me the impression that you believed Baxter to be in some way connected with your husband's death, but you certainly never suggested that he actually murdered your husband. What has happened to draw you to make such a conclusion?'

He didn't miss much, for all his annoying ways, Felicity thought, bitterly. Was this the moment to tell him about her second sight? He was tired, distracted, irritated – Felicity judged it was not. 'Nothing, really, just that he was in Oxford and demonstrated an interest in the inquest, which suggests he was involved in some way.'

'Why is it, Mrs Paradise that I get the feeling you are not being entirely frank with me?'

His words were spoken pleasantly enough, he was even smiling, but in that moment Felicity caught a glimpse of what it must be like to be interrogated by Inspector Penrose. For all his apparent easy going, friendly façade, Felicity spied a formidable adversary. She smiled in return. 'I really can't imagine, Inspector.'

It was quite dark by the time Felicity arrived back at Barnoon car park. Just in the last week the car park had dramatically emptied and she was able to drive down the hill, almost to the exit, to make her walk into town as quick as possible. The wind had been building all day and when she tried to open the car door, she had quite a struggle. She could hear the pounding of the sea far below her and her hair was blowing into her face as she fumbled to lock the car. Suddenly she heard a commotion behind her.

'Shut him up!' A harsh voice commanded.

Her eyes adjusted to the dark. Three men were walking across the car park, a few yards ahead of her. That was not strictly true – two men were walking, the third was being dragged between them and he was shouting. The party halted, there was the sound of a sickening blow, the shouting stopped and Felicity saw the man in the middle fall to his knees. She cried out but no one seemed to hear her, she started forward but her legs seemed incapable of movement. Lights flashed as the doors were unlocked remotely on a car further up the car park.

'Put him in there, put him in there,' that voice again, There was more shouting, more protests, then someone began to scream. Felicity could not see clearly what was happening but suddenly two of the men were running back towards her. She cowered against her car. There was a whooshing sound and in an instant, the whole car park was lit with flames. The two men climbed into a now familiar Range Rover. Backlit by the flames there was no mistaking the identity of the driver. The Range Rover pulled away without lights. Instead of heading for the exit of the car park, Smithson drove up past the burning wreck to the entrance, slowly, without any sign of panic. Felicity was amazed at his apparent calm – this was clearly not the first time he had left a crime scene. As she stood there, gazing helplessly at the blazing car, the wind suddenly returned and caught at her coat. She grabbed at it to pull it around her and when she looked up again, the burning car had vanished. She turned her back and ran from the car park. When she reached the narrow steps leading down into town, she paused to catch her breath and then shakily began her descent to the safety and comfort of Cormorant Cottage.

Buffeted by the wind and frozen to the bone, Felicity burst through the front door of Cormorant Cottage. She realised immediately that something was different. Annie, an early riser, always retired by nine but tonight the lights were blazing, there was talk and laughter coming from what Annie called the parlour ... and there was something distinctly familiar about the laugh. Felicity, still shaken from her experience, cautiously pushed open the door of the parlour, took in the sight of three women grouped around a merry little fire, recognised Gilla and Ellie, and promptly burst into tears. Gilla was beside her in seconds, an arm around her drawing her towards the fire.

'Fizzy, whatever is the matter? You look like you've seen a ghost and you're freezing.'

'I have,' said Felicity, between sobs. 'Oh, Gilla, it's so good to see you, and you too, Ellie.'

Annie patted the chair beside the fire. 'Sit down, my girl, before you fall down. What on earth have you been up to?'

Felicity lowered herself gingerly into the chair. Already the warmth from the fire and being surrounded by people who cared about her, was thawing the horror which had gripped her.

'You've just had one of your turns, haven't you?' said Gilla. Felicity looked up at her, grateful to be with someone who knew her so well. She nodded.

'What did you see this time?' Annie asked.

Despite the circumstances, Felicity could not help but be amused. It sounded as though Annie was asking for a report on a trip to the cinema. She noted Gilla looking at Annie sharply, obviously surprised that Felicity had confided in her landlady. She took a deep breath. 'It was horrible,' she said, 'I saw them bundling the "Skunk" into the car, he was screaming and very much alive when he went into the boot. Then, the next moment, the car was a ball of flame. They burnt him alive, Annie.'

'Who's the "Skunk"?' asked Gilla, 'What on earth is going on, Fizzy? I don't think you should be listening to this, Ellie, you should go to bed.'

'Oh Mum, for heaven's sake,' said Ellie, morosely.

Felicity looked properly at her god-daughter for the first time. Ellie was slumped in a chair on the other side of the fire. She was wearing an ancient-looking black tweed coat. On her feet were scuffed, black leather, lace-up, biker's boots, her face was deathly pale and her eyelids and lips had been extravagantly painted in dark plum. Her beautiful red hair had been dyed black. The total effect was completed by a nose ring. She noted though, that despite Ellie's rather alarming appearance, Annie was looking at her fondly.

'I'll go and make you a nice cup of cocoa, my dearie, and get something a wee bit stronger for the other two. Fizzy!' she said as she left the room, 'what sort of name is that?'

'What a funny old girl,' said Gilla, in a stage whisper when the door had closed.

'She's been a true friend,' said Felicity, 'I don't know what I would have done without her in the last few weeks.'

'You have true friends in Oxford,' said Gilla, with a decided edge to her voice. 'Would it be asking too much, Fizzy, for you to tell us what on earth has been going on?'

Felicity looked from mother to daughter. Ellie, normally sulky and feigning disinterest, for once appeared positively animated. 'Alright,' she said, 'I'll go back to the beginning – my flight from Oxford and take it from there.'

By the time she had finished her story, Annie was back with drinks – the promised hot chocolate for Ellie, plus a bottle of wine and two glasses.

'Aren't you going to join us, Annie?' Felicity asked.

'No, my bird, it's past my bedtime and besides, you two need to talk. God bless you, I'll see you in the morning and don't you go having any nightmares now.'

Ellie followed Annie upstairs ten minutes later, leaving Felicity and Gilla alone. The wine had been a good idea.

'So what happens now?' Gilla asked.

Felicity shook her head. 'I've absolutely no idea, but I do know now that there is no question of me letting the thing drop.'

'Are you sure?' said Gilla. 'I mean, what else can you possibly do? You've told your pet policeman everything you know.'

'Not everything,' said Felicity, in a small voice. 'I haven't told Keith Penrose why I know the "Skunk" killed Charlie, and now, how I know Ralph Smithson killed the "Skunk".'

'Forgive me for saying this,' said Gilla, 'I don't mean to be disparaging, but Policeman Penrose is probably not going to be overly impressed by one of your little turns.'

'I know,' said Felicity, 'but that's hardly the point, is it, Gilla? I believe in them and I know what I saw happened, really happened. I'm now carrying the burden of knowing how Charlie died and the man who killed him. It places a huge responsibility on me to find a way of convincing the police of what I know to be true.'

'And get yourself killed in the process,' said Gilla. 'That's a stunningly good idea, Fizzy.'

'Why should I do that?' Felicity asked.

'Oh, for heaven's sake, Fizzy, wise up and start thinking straight. I know you've had a shock, but you've got to pull yourself together. For some reason, this chap you call the "Skunk" upset Ralph Smithson and look what happened to him. If Ralph gets wind of the fact that you're sniffing around whatever nasty business he's into, he'll dispatch you in exactly the same way. Fizzy, this is a police matter; you've really got to leave it to them now.'

Felicity smiled at her old friend. 'You are a bossy moo, Gilla,' she said with a smile. 'I hear what you say and I promise to be careful, but I'm sorry, I can't drop it.'

'Well, at least I have the whole weekend to try to talk you out of it,' said Gilla, picking up on the change of mood.

'This is awful,' said Felicity, 'here I am, playing the drama queen, and I haven't even said thank you for coming to see me. How long are you here?'

'Until Monday,' said Gilla.

'So we have two clear days together, wonderful. It's good you bought Ellie.'

'I don't think Ellie would agree with you,' said Gilla. 'She moaned the entire journey and I have to tell you that five hours of teenage moaning is not an enjoyable experience.'

'Well, let's see if we can cheer her up tomorrow,' said Felicity.

Felicity and Ellie breakfasted alone the following morning, Gilla being notoriously bad at getting out of bed. Despite Felicity's best efforts at cheerful conversation, Ellie was still morose and uncommunicative – at this rate, it was not going to be a particularly jolly weekend for any of them, she thought in despair. They were lingering over a last cup of coffee, when the doorbell rang. Moments later Annie appeared and showed Martin Tregonning into the room.

Felicity was pleased to see him; he had been much on her mind since their meeting. His offer of help felt like a much-needed lifeline. They shook hands rather formally and Felicity introduced Ellie who managed the ghost of a smile. By magic, Annie appeared with a fresh pot of coffee and another cup. Felicity introduced her as well and Annie lingered, clearly anxious to miss nothing.

'Well,' said Martin, appearing slightly self-conscious at having an audience. 'I've nothing very much to report – just a couple of possible points of interest.'

'If you have anything of interest to report, then you're ahead of me,' said Felicity. 'I had to wait hours to see D.I. Keith Penrose yesterday, who is my police contact in Truro, and when I did finally catch up with him, he didn't seem very impressed on hearing it was Ralph Smithson who the "Skunk" had met in the Sloop. I may be doing the man an injustice but once he knew it was Ralph Smithson of Boswithey, he seemed to have already decided such an illustrious person couldn't possibly be involved.'

'That's where he could be wrong,' said Martin, helping himself to the coffee. 'I did a spot of research myself yesterday. Firstly, I talked to some coastguard colleagues at Penzance. They have had absolutely no success in catching any drug smugglers on the coast for some months now. There was a small haul of cannabis, which they intercepted at a cove up near the Lizard, as a result of a tip-off. That was about eight months ago, but since then – nothing, which apparently is quite unusual. It suggests that a new location has been found for bringing the stuff into the country, which of course, may not be in Cornwall at all.' He paused to drink his coffee. Ellie, Felicity noticed, was suddenly decidedly more animated and listening intently to what Martin had to say. His good looks were clearly not lost on her god-daughter. 'Anyway, I got to thinking about the cove at Boswithey. I don't know whether any of you know it.'

'I've seen it,' said Annie, 'when I went to the gardens, but we didn't go down there. I can't remember why.'

'Because you can't,' said Martin, 'it's a rope beach.'

'What on earth's a rope beach?' Felicity asked.

'Just what it sounds,' said Martin with a smile. 'The only access to Boswithey Cove, apart from by sea, is to go down a very sheer piece of cliff. Foot holds have been hammered into the granite, where possible, and then there is simply a rope, secured at the top of the cliff, to hold onto while you climb up and down. Certainly, it is not a thing for visitors to the garden to undertake. It's a shame – there was once a beautiful pathway running all the way down to the cove apparently, but it's been eroded now.'

'It doesn't sound an ideal place for smuggling, if that's what you're meaning.' said Felicity.

'Well, no, it isn't,' said Martin, with a triumphant smile, 'but there have been developments.'

'Go on,' said Felicity.

'The head gardener at Boswithey is a nice old

boy, Michael his name is, Michael Scott. He has spent most of his working life at Boswithey and when I worked there, he and his wife used to come to supper sometimes.' He hesitated, his expression clouded. Something awful has happened to this man, Felicity thought, something's tearing him apart. 'Anyway,' Martin continued, clearing his throat. 'I had a drink with Michael last night. It's probably nothing, just a coincidence, but shortly after I left Boswithey, Smithson asked Michael to improve access to the cove – put in more foot holds, stake the rope to the cliff face that sort of thing. Michael thought it was pretty odd because at this time of year they normally haul up the rope with the gales coming. In fact, hardly anybody ever goes down there – the only time is if the beach gets particularly messy.'

'How do you mean?' Felicity asked, with a frown.

'You can see down to the cove from pretty much every angle of the gardens so it is important that it looks good for visitors. If the wind is in a certain quarter, debris from the boats in Mount's Bay can end up being blown ashore – bits of plastic, that sort of thing. In the season, if the cove looks scruffy, Michael sends one of his boys down to collect a couple of bin bags of rubbish. Out of season, though, no one would bother to do that – certainly not at this time of year, with the equinox gales on their way. It would be a full-time job picking up rubbish, and pointless, too. Michael wouldn't normally send someone down there again until Easter.'

'It can't be easy, though,' said Annie, who had been listening intently, 'bringing anything up by rope, I mean.'

'It's not a difficult climb for anyone reasonably fit,' said Martin, 'and remember what they're smuggling – it's light and easy to carry, not like barrels of brandy – now that would be a challenge!'

'Do you really have smugglers around here?' Ellie asked, clearly intrigued.

Martin smiled at Ellie. 'We certainly do.'

'Martin is a coastguard,' Felicity explained.

'It's not as exciting as it sounds; most of my time is spent on fairly mundane stuff – rescuing the odd stray dog or tourist who has been stupid enough to venture off the cliff path. Then there are the usual bunch of people who insist on ignoring all the warnings and manage to get themselves cut off by the tide. So, a bit of smuggling would be quite exciting, but we don't get a chance to be involved in the action anymore. We're not like the excise men used to be. Once we've spotted anything dodgy, we simply hand the matter over to the police.' He turned back to Felicity. 'There was one other thing I learnt from Michael last night – in fact it's awful.'

'What's that?' Felicity asked.

'Michael's daughter, Polly, is housekeeper up at the big house. She told her dad that Ralph has been particularly violent to his wife, Amelia, recently. Polly hears things, of course, as she lives in, and over the years apparently, Amelia has had a number of injuries which she usually blames on riding accidents – she keeps a horse. The beatings have been getting worse and more frequent. A couple of weeks back, Amelia had black eyes and a great big bruise on the temple. It certainly confirms that he is a man capable of anything.'

'Poor woman, I wonder why on earth she puts up with it,' Felicity said, 'you'd think she'd just leave him.'

Annie was busy clearing the table. 'Some women like to put themselves in the position of victim. Odd really, but you see it over and over.' She stopped clearing, put her hands on her hips and fixed Martin with one of her bright bird-like stares. 'Now, my boy, would you like a bit of breakfast?'

'No, thank you,' said Martin, smiling, 'I must be off.' He stood up. 'I've asked Michael to keep a look out,' he said to Felicity, 'just to be a little diligent and check whether there are any comings and goings down at the cove. He hates Ralph Smithson, too. He'd love to see him nailed.'

'It wouldn't be very good for his job prospects, poor man,' Felicity said.

'Michael's near retirement and he's never been happy at Boswithey since Ralph bought the estate, so I don't know what the future holds for him.'

'How long ago was that?' Felicity asked.

'About ten years ago. I think he bought it as soon as he arrived from South Africa,' said Martin. 'It used to belong to a chap called Brigadier Hawkesworth, the estate had been in his family for generations. Michael's a wicked old boy; he never misses the opportunity of praising up the Brigadier in front of Ralph. Must be off, keep me posted.'

'I will,' said Felicity, 'and thanks, Martin.'

As he left there were sounds of a commotion in the hall and Gilla's unmistakable voice sounding extremely animated. Seconds later she was through the dining room door. 'Wow!' she said, 'who is he, where on earth did you find him, Fizzy? He's absolutely gorgeous!'

'Oh, for heaven's sake, Mum, stop being so embarrassing.' Ellie pushed back her chair and slouched out of the room, slamming the door behind her.

Felicity grinned at her friend. 'Ellie is quite right, you're very embarrassing, and don't even think about him being your next victim. That was Martin Tregonning, who I told you about last night. He has only recently married and I am absolutely certain he would not be susceptible to even your charms, Gilla, so forget it.'

'Poor man,' said Gilla, dreamily, 'so good-looking and tied down to married life. Perhaps he needs a reminder of what freedom was like.'

'Stop it!' said Felicity, laughing. 'Sit down and have some coffee. Do you want any breakfast?'

'What are you two ladies planning for today?' Annie asked.

Felicity looked across at Gilla. 'I haven't really thought, I've been so preoccupied with everything. I suppose I'll take them around town and then we'll have lunch somewhere.'

'Only I was thinking,' said Annie, 'Ellie isn't going to find it very interesting trailing round the Tate and the Barbara Hepworth Museum with you

118

two. I thought I might ask my grandson to take her out and show her around.'

Gilla looked up sharply. 'That's so kind of you but she'll never agree to go.'

'He's a nice boy, my grandson,' Annie said. 'You needn't worry about him. He's eighteen and he is a sensible lad, she will be in good hands.'

'I'm sure she will,' said Gilla, hastily, 'it's just that at the moment she's not interested in doing anything or going anywhere.'

'She's shy,' said Annie, 'leave her to me. I'll talk her into it.'

Gilla waited until Annie had left the room. 'Ellie won't get anywhere, Annie's wasting her time.' she said.

Felicity smiled. 'I have the benefit of having known Annie for nearly a month now. I can assure you, Gilla that if Annie Trethewey has decided on a course of action, even Ellie, in the biggest of grumps, won't be any match for her.'

Three hours later, the two women collapsed in the Seafood Café with a bottle of Pinot Grigio. They had walked for miles, visited the galleries, shopped and gossiped.

At the Barbara Hepworth Museum they had sat in the garden, the peace and tranquillity silencing even Gilla.

'I've always admired her,' Gilla said, 'a really feisty lady. She had an awful death though, didn't she? Burnt alive in her bed, they think she dropped a cigarette.'

119

'Like the "Skunk",' said Felicity.

'Fizzy, we're not talking about any of that stuff today.'

'Sorry, sorry,' said Felicity.

They walked to Porthminster beach and had coffee there. Obligingly the sun came out from behind the clouds and Gilla was dumbstruck by the beauty of the beach.

'It's like the Maldives,' she said, 'all this white sand and blue-green sea and the water is so clear. I can understand why North Oxford is losing its charm.'

They shopped in Fore Street. In the first shop Fizzy bought some surfing tee shirts and a pair of baggy cargo pants for Ellie.

'They look like boys' trousers,' Gilla said critically, 'they're completely shapeless and why black?'

'Because,' Felicity said patiently, 'in case you hadn't noticed, black is the only colour your daughter will wear at the moment.'

'Well, that's no reason to pander to her.'

'Oh stop being such an old misery, Gilla, I bet she'll like them and they are really trendy amongst the young at the moment.'

By the time they reached the Seafood Café Gilla had got over her huff and Felicity felt more like her normal self than she had done in weeks. She was pleased at being able to find something for Ellie and even more pleased that Ellie had proved no match for Annie. Her grandson Jago, a nice-looking boy with floppy fair hair, had turned up to collect Ellie and she had gone without protest. She had made no concessions for her 'date' and wore the same awful black coat and biker boots. However, Jago had seemed very impressed with this demonstration of urban chic and they had gone off together happily enough. Gilla was astounded.

Lunch was fun. They ate too much and drank too much, and it was only after coffee that Gilla raised the thorny subject of what Felicity was going to do next. 'I really think it's time you came back to Oxford,' she said. 'You've done everything you can down here. As I said last night, the matter is with the police now. Just leave it, Fizzy, and come home. It's time to let go.'

'I can't,' Felicity answered. 'I have to see this through. I have to see it through for Charlie's sake.'

'For Charlie's sake or for yours?' Gilla queried.

'I don't know,' Felicity admitted, 'but does it matter?'

Just at that moment her mobile phone rang. 'Saved by the bell,' said Gilla, sagely.

'Mrs Paradise?' Felicity recognised the voice immediately.

'Inspector Penrose?'

'Yes, I'm in St Ives and I was wondering whether we could have a quick chat?'

'Yes, of course,' said Felicity, flustered. 'Where would you like us to meet?'

'I'm having a coffee at the Tate Gallery. Would that be convenient? It's quite quiet up here at the moment.'

'Yes, that's no problem,' said Felicity. 'I'll be

with you in ten minutes.'

'Goodness,' said Gilla. 'So you're wanted by the police now, Fizzy.' She giggled. 'I'm starting to realise why you don't want to come back to Oxford with men pursuing you all over St Ives.'

'Stop it, Gilla, give it a rest,' Felicity said, smiling. 'Would you mind if I went, he's waiting for me up at the Tate? Something must have happened, I normally have an awful job getting hold of him. As he's contacted me, it must mean something's up.'

Keith Penrose stood up as Felicity came into the café. The place was indeed very quiet with just one other couple seated some distance from their table. Coffee ordered, Keith and Felicity regarded one another in silence for a moment. Away from his office, Keith suddenly seemed much more approachable.

'You've discovered something?' said Felicity, 'you must have done to want to see me.'

Keith sighed. 'Not precisely, Mrs Paradise, no. I've interviewed Ralph Smithson, who was very co-operative. He has an alibi for the night in question.'

'Don't tell me,' said Felicity, 'provided by his wife.'

Keith looked up, surprised. 'Well, yes.'

'He beats his wife, Inspector Penrose, she would say anything.'

'You seem to know an awful lot about this man. Have you met him?'

'No, never,' said Felicity, 'but I do have my sources.'

'So it would appear,' said Keith, with a smile.

'The trouble is, unless you can give me anything more by way of evidence "from your sources", I can't take the matter any further.'

'But what about his meeting the "Skunk" in the Sloop?' Felicity asked.

'He denies it. He says you must have mistaken him for someone else.'

'I didn't,' said Felicity, weak with frustration, 'and it's not just me who saw him. There's an old boy called Billy, who regularly props up the bar, he saw Ralph Smithson with the "Skunk", too.'

'Does Billy know Mr Smithson personally?'

'No, of course not.'

'Then I'm sorry – your word and Billy's against his – it wouldn't stick.'

'I know he's guilty, Inspector.' Even to her own ears, Felicity sounded desperate.

'Then you had better tell me whatever it is you have been keeping from me,' said Keith, evenly.

Felicity hesitated. How had the wretched man seen through her so easily? To hold back would lose his trust, to tell him. Oh, what the hell, she thought. 'Supposing I told you I saw Ralph Smithson murder the "Skunk",' she said quietly, willing him to believe her.

Keith stared at her in amazement. 'What on earth are you saying, Mrs Paradise? Did you witness him setting fire to the car? Why haven't you told me this before? Withholding information of this kind is a very serious matter.'

Felicity hung her head, seeking for some sort of inspiration as to how to appeal to the logical mind of a policeman. 'I know this is going to sound strange to you,' she began, 'but I have second sight.'

Animated with hope of a breakthrough a moment before, Keith's spirits plummeted. He had started to like Mrs Paradise, started to want to help her. Now it was looking as if his initial instincts were right. She was building up a story surrounding her husband's death as her method of coping with it.

'It's something I inherited,' Felicity continued, gamely, 'from my grandmother. It is not something I can control, it just happens, or it doesn't.' Keith said nothing but his expression was not encouraging. Felicity pressed on. 'When I got back from seeing you the other night, I parked in Barnoon car park. It was a very windy night, so windy I had difficulty getting out of my car. I was just locking it when suddenly the wind disappeared. It became a calm, starlit night and then I saw them. Two men dragging a third across the car park. He was screaming. At one point they stopped and hit him but he still wasn't unconscious. They put him in the boot of a car, I couldn't really see what was happening but he was still shouting and protesting and then the two men were running back towards me. Suddenly, the car exploded into flames, it was horrible.' Keith still said nothing. 'It was then,' said Felicity, 'I saw who they were, at least I saw Ralph Smithson. They got into his Range Rover. I knew it was his because it had Boswithey Gardens on the side and when they drove out of the car park, I caught sight of his face. It was definitely him.'

'And then what happened?' Keith asked, dryly.

'The wind came back,' Felicity said simply. 'First the wind and then I looked up and the burnt-out car had gone. The fact remains, Baxter was very, very conscious when they forced him into that boot, Inspector Penrose. Can you imagine?'

'Yes I can,' said Keith, 'and I can also see that you have something of a rich imagination, too, Mrs Paradise. Do you remember that when we met last, I told you that Ronald Baxter was alive when the car was set alight? I regretted telling you; it was a slip of the tongue. It was information that you could have well done without. It sounds to me as if it was preying on your mind and when you got back to the scene of the crime, it was very understandable that you should relive it.'

'Was it a still, starry night that night, the night Baxter died?' Felicity asked.

'Yes, it was,' Keith admitted, 'along with many other such nights. We're given to starry nights down here.'

Her credibility was so completely blown, Felicity could see no harm in continuing. 'I saw my husband die, too. In fact twice and on the second occasion, I concentrated on the driver. It was Ronald Baxter who drove at my husband, Inspector; I saw the white streak of his hair quite clearly.'

'I'm sorry, Mrs Paradise, this really isn't helping,' said Keith.

'Which is why I haven't told you before,' said Felicity. 'I knew that once I told you about my second sight, you would stop taking me seriously.' Her words were such an accurate reflection of his feelings that Keith could think of absolutely nothing to say. 'My landlady here in St Ives, Annie Trethewey her name is, she believed me straight away, and do you know why?' Keith shook his head. 'Because she's Cornish, a Celt, and therefore she is able to acknowledge that some people do have the sight. You're Cornish, too, Inspector Penrose.'

'I'll hold my hands up to that charge, Mrs Paradise. What with my name and my accent, I would be hard pressed to be anything else, wouldn't I?'

'Then can't you accept that such a thing is possible, like Annie Trethewey?'

'I'm a policeman, Mrs Paradise, a boring old Inspector Plod. I spend my life sifting through evidence, resifting it, looking at it from a different angle and turning it on its head. It is an exercise in logic and it takes me a while, but I usually get there in the end. There is absolutely no room for second sight in my investigations. I'm sorry.'

'I don't enjoy it,' said Felicity, desperate now. 'It's just something that happens. It doesn't normally revolve around such violence, though I admit strong feelings are usually associated with what I see.' She looked at him candidly. 'I've lost you now completely, haven't I?'

'Not completely,' Keith replied, tactfully, 'but without more evidence, proper evidence, I'm afraid I can't take this particular line of enquiry any further.' He stood up and Felicity did so, too. They shook hands. 'I can promise you, Mrs Paradise that if I am able to shed any further light on your husband's death, I will let you know.' He started across the restaurant and then stopped. 'Oh, one thing ...' he walked back to her side. 'I was going through the Ben Carver file last night and there was one enclosure with the file which didn't make any sense.'

'What was that?' Felicity asked, hope flaring.

'There was a cutting from a newspaper, the *Johannesburg Times*; it was concerning the whereabouts of a man called Jack du Plessey. A nasty piece of work by all accounts, wanted for everything under the sun – drug running, prostitution, extortion, money lending – even murder.'

'So what has that got to do with Ben Carver?' Felicity asked.

'No idea at the moment, said Keith Penrose.

'Well there is a link, Inspector, if this man du Plessey is South African, as it sounds,' said Felicity. 'Ralph Smthson is also a South African, and so was my husband Charlie.'

8

The words echoed again and again in her head as Felicity walked slowly along Porthmeor Beach. The tide was way out and she walked as close to the sea as she could – she needed to be alone. Her trainers were soaked through but she was too lost in thought to mind, or even notice. There had to be a connection, a South African connection, there were just too many coincidences.

Charlie Paradise had been fatherless for most of his childhood. His mother, Elizabeth Nicholls, was the only child of an impoverished, but well-connected, family from Derbyshire, who had lived in decaying splendour in the family ancestral home. She had been a timid girl, whose only big adventure had been when she was sent to Paris to a young ladies' finishing school. However, the experience had been a disaster – she had been so homesick that she was brought back to England after only a month. Undoubtedly Elizabeth would have spent a dreary spinsterhood caring for her elderly parents in their collapsing home, had it not been for her father,

Antony. Sir Antony Nicholls enjoyed the friendship of a man named Crispen St John Brookes, who shortly after Elizabeth's abortive trip to Paris had been appointed as Master of one of the more illustrious Oxford colleges. The two men had been to prep school together.

Less out of a sense of compassion and rather more because he hated driving, Antony took his daughter along with him to celebrate his old friend's new appointment. It was during one of the many celebrations and receptions to which father and daughter found themselves invited, that Elizabeth was introduced to a young man named James Paradise, a South African who had come to Oxford to read law. James was in his final year. Years later, Charlie was to confide to Felicity that he was suspicious of the motives which had prompted his father to marry his mother, for, despite his devotion to her, Charlie could see that her plain looks and timid nature were not obviously attractive to a potential suitor, certainly not to a flamboyant young man such as James Paradise.

From a son's point of view, however, Elizabeth was a wonderful woman – kind, devoted and full of ambition for her son. Although during most of Charlie's boyhood they lived alone together, Elizabeth never held him back, had never been possessive. Instead, she encouraged him in every way she could, desperate (Charlie believed) that he should not suffer from the same shyness with which she herself was plagued. As to his father's motives for the marriage, over the years Charlie came to suspect that the promise of an only daughter and an ancestral home, including eight hundred acres of Derbyshire, was probably the true reason he so relentlessly pursued Elizabeth, for two people less suited to be together it would be hard to find. In contrast to the timid, upper class, English girl James had married, he was brash, loud, over-confident and concerned about no one in the world except himself. Within months, the marriage barely existed. James spent most of his time in South Africa. Although he returned, briefly, when his son was born, he was soon back in South Africa again while Elizabeth struggled to raise the boy alone, in genteel poverty. The Derbyshire estate collapsed in bankruptcy, never realising its potential because it was discovered, on Sir Antony's death, that it had been pledged to the bank years before.

According to Charlie, Elizabeth had repeatedly suggested to James that they should go and join him in South Africa but he had always refused saying it was no place for a woman. As Charlie was fond of saying, that couldn't be quite right since presumably there had to be some women in South Africa for there to be a population at all.

When Charlie was ten, James died. He had apparently drowned. There was talk of suicide and even of murder but nothing was ever proved. He was buried in South Africa; there was no money forthcoming from his estate and so Elizabeth and Charlie had struggled on alone. Luckily Charlie was so clever that he won a full scholarship to Eton.

Felicity searched her memory for details as she

strode on, trying to avoid the pools left behind by the tide. After Oxford, Charlie began working for corporate lawyers in Lincoln's Inn. It was during this time, she was fairly confident, that he had visited South Africa, something connected with a case on which his firm was working. He had volunteered to go because he wanted to see his father's homeland. He had found the grave, he had told her, a sorry sight apparently, neglected and shabby. There were no grandparents to visit, no uncles, aunts or cousins. On his return from South Africa, Charlie had decided that corporate law was not for him and that he missed Oxford. He began his Articles again, this time in a local Oxford firm of which, ultimately, he and Josh Buchanan had become sole partners. It was shortly after his return to Oxford that he had met Felicity at a college May ball.

Ralph Smithson was South African. Charlie's father was South African. Charlie had a newspaper cutting in the Ben Carver file about a missing South African and Martin Tregonning had visited South Africa. Not for the first time, Felicity wished that her second sight could be ordered about. She turned her back to the wind and began slowly climbing the steps to the Island. Despite her frustration, the thought of her so-called gift brought a sudden smile when she remembered the expression on Keith Penrose's face as she had told him about it. She had definitely blown her relationship with him – he would now have her firmly filed away under 'N' for 'Nutter' – that is if he ever did any filing.

The rest of the weekend with Gilla and Ellie

proved to be a success. Ellie returned to Cormorant Cottage briefly on Saturday evening to say she was meeting Jago and some of his mates at the Isobar. Annie provided her with a key and it was certainly in the early hours before she returned. Sunday morning breakfast was very different from the day before. Ellie was a changed girl. She still wore her mad clothes but the sea air had bought colour to her cheeks and above all, she looked happy. When she was happy and smiling, Felicity realised, she was actually very pretty.

Neither mother nor daughter wanted to leave on Monday morning. During the weekend, there had been protracted negotiations between Felicity and Ellie on one side and Gilla on the other. The subject was Orlando, who could no longer be expected to live alone in Oxford, being fed by a neighbour. Finally, Gilla relented and agreed that the cat could live with her and Ellie temporarily. But for the prospect of having a cat to stay, Felicity doubted whether they would ever have been able to extract Ellie from St Ives.

'Your family certainly have a talent for making people feel better about themselves,' Felicity said to Annie as they stood by the door, waving at the departing car. 'I haven't seen Ellie look this happy in years, if ever. I suppose she is hopelessly in love with Jago.'

'I don't think so,' said Annie, 'I think she was just having a good time. It is all very relaxed down here, not so much pressure on the youngsters. She's promised to come and stay with me next summer, bless her, as my guest, of course.'

'That's really kind of you, Annie,' said Felicity.

'Not kind,' said Annie, briskly, 'it'll be a bit of company. Talking of which, my girl, I suppose you're staying on a while?'

They went inside and shut the door. 'Yes please, if I may, anyway for another week,' said Felicity.

Annie cocked her head on one side and studied Felicity in silence for a moment. 'I'd like you to stay forever, you know that, but I wonder if your friend, that Gilla, isn't right. You're chasing your tail at the moment, getting nowhere, trying to make something of nothing. Wouldn't you be better off going back home to your friends and your job and trying to start a new life without your husband? It's hard, I know, I've been there, but you have to face it sometime.'

'But Annie,' said Felicity, genuinely distressed at her words, 'I'm not making something out of nothing. You say you believe in my gift of second sight. If you do, then you know I saw the "Skunk" kill Charlie and Ralph Smithson kill the "Skunk". That's two murders, one of whom happens to be my husband. I can't simply leave it there, can I?'

'But what are you going to do?' Annie persisted.

'I'm going to ring Martin Tregonning,' Felicity said, suddenly decisive. 'Inspector Penrose says that the case is going nowhere so we're just going to have to make something happen to prove him wrong.'

A sort of fanatical energy overtook Felicity in the hours immediately after Gilla's departure. During the previous night she had lain awake for some time debating what she should do next. At that dreadful hour of three in the morning, when everything always seems black and hopeless, she had been very tempted to take Gilla's advice and return home. However, having resisted the temptation to do so, she now found the decision seemed to have inspired her with a rush of enthusiasm and decisiveness.

Firstly, she rang the school and explained that she was still unable to return to work, citing delayed shock following her husband's death as the reason. There was no problem. A temporary supply teacher was filling her job and was happy to do so until Christmas, if necessary. The headmistress was very understanding and wished her well. Momentarily she felt depressed, thinking of her little art department, which she had loved for so long. It was supremely uncomfortable to recognise the ease with which it seemed possible for her years of dedication to be so easily replaced.

Next she rang Martin and asked if they could meet for lunch. 'I've nothing else to tell you,' Martin said. He sounded low and less than enthusiastic about meeting.

'Just a quick lunch,' Felicity heard herself pleading, 'on me. Let's meet at the Sloop, one o'clock.'

'Alright,' said Martin, with what sounded like unflattering resignation.

Felicity's third call was to Josh Buchanan. 'So, did Gilla cheer you up?' he asked.

'I think it was more the other way round,' Felicity replied, with a touch of self-satisfaction.

'Certainly St Ives has done wonders for Ellie. She arrived very sullen and miserable and I've sent her home decidedly cheerful.'

'Well that is nothing short of a miracle' said Josh. 'How are you, Fizzy? We're missing you up here.'

'And I'm missing you,' said Fizzy, 'but I can't come home until I've resolved things. That's why I'm ringing actually; you could help me to speed things up.'

'I'll do anything I can,' said Josh, 'particularly after the bollocking I received from your policeman chum.'

Felicity was amazed. 'What sort of bollocking?'

'It appears he felt I should have done more to help you, more to investigate your theory that Charlie's death was murder.'

'Good Heavens,' said Fizzy. 'Are you saying that Inspector Penrose actually believes there's more to Charlie's death than meets the eye?'

Josh hesitated, obviously giving her enquiry serious consideration. 'Yes, Fizzy, I rather think he does.'

'Damn,' said Fizzy, 'and now I've blown it. Blast – I bet he's lost faith in me now.'

'Why's that?' asked Josh.

'Too long a story to tell you now, Josh. Can I ask you a couple of questions?'

'Fire away,' he said.

'Did you notice a press cutting from the *Johannesburg Times* in the Ben Carver file? Stupidly I forgot to ask the date of it, but there was only one,

I understand.'

'I remember seeing it and deciding it had no relevance. I'm sorry, I can't help you with the date. I imagined it had been misfiled, to be honest.' He sounded decidedly cagey, Felicity thought.

'I haven't seen it,' said Felicity, 'but according to, as you put it, "my policeman chum", it was about a man called Jack du Plessey who was wanted for just about every possible crime against humanity. Does the name mean anything to you, Josh?'

'Absolutely nothing at all, I'm afraid,' said Josh. Again, he sounded oddly uncomfortable.

'No matter. The other thing is, do you know anything about the law firm Charlie worked for before coming back to Oxford?'

'It was all before my time, Fizzy.'

'And mine too,' Felicity said, 'I don't even remember their name.'

'I can help you there. They're very big in international corporate law, their name is Derwent Strange.'

'Are they still in existence?' Felicity asked.

'Yes, of course, they're one of the absolute top flight firms.'

'During the time Charlie worked for them, Josh, he went to South Africa – with one of the partners, I think. I just wondered if we could find out what he did out there.'

'That's a pretty tall order, Fizzy,' said Josh, 'we're talking about thirty years ago. Any partner would be long retired or dead, I imagine.'

'Well, we're not going to know for certain

unless we ask, are we?' said Felicity, exasperated, 'and they're far more likely to talk to you than to me. However, if you won't help, I'll just have to do it myself.'

'No, no,' said Josh, hurriedly. 'As it happens I do have a pal in the firm who handles intellectual property. I'll have a word with him and see if he can do some digging for me. What exactly are you looking for?'

'I wish I could tell you,' said Felicity. 'Anything really. I just want to know why Charlie went to South Africa, what case it was they were working on. Somehow I feel there's a link.'

'Another one of your turns?' Josh said. There was a trace of sarcasm in his voice, which irritated Felicity enormously.

'No, not one of my turns, Josh. My chief suspect in this whole business happens to be South African, Charlie was half-South African and there is a South African newspaper cutting in Ben Carver's file. One doesn't have to be a brain surgeon to work out that there has to be a connection.'

'Or just a coincidence. I can't really see the relevance of a case Charlie worked on thirty years ago.'

'Oh, for heaven's sake, Josh, are you going to help me or not?'

'Yes, yes, of course,' Josh said. 'I'm sorry, Fizzy. I'll get back to you.'

Felicity replaced the receiver thoughtfully. Why did she feel Josh was holding out on her, why did she feel he had something to hide?

Keeping faith with herself and her instincts was the hardest thing, Felicity mused, as she walked along the Wharf towards the Sloop. It was so exhausting fighting all the time to keep the case alive. She stopped and stared out across the water, towards the lighthouse, marvelling at the colours. It was another beautiful, golden day, the water a wonderful combination of deep azure blue and bright leafy green.What would Charlie think of her now, she wondered? Here she was struggling to prove he had been right all along when she had been so critical of him in the last few weeks before his death. Was this the true cause of what was rapidly becoming an obsession? Was she trying to atone, after his death, for what she had failed to do in life – trust his judgement? If only he had just shared with her his true reasons for taking the case, it would have made all the difference. Clearly, he had a hidden agenda which in itself was so out of character. Normally, Charlie Paradise was an open book. A small cloud blotted out the sun momentarily and Felicity shivered. Suddenly she wondered whether she actually wanted to discover the truth, whether she was afraid of what she might find. Abruptly, she began walking again. She needed to get a grip – her husband had been murdered and she could not rest until she had found out why.

Martin Tregonning was not in the Sloop when she arrived. Felicity ordered a glass of wine and went to join Billy Jenkin in his corner of the bar. He was delighted to see her. 'So how's your detective work going?' he asked.

'Not too bad, Billy. In fact I'm following up one of my leads right now, I'm meeting him here. You were so helpful the other day.'

'My pleasure,' said Billy. 'He was in again yesterday, that fellow you're after.'

'Really,' said Felicity, 'and who was he meeting this time?'

'Same bloke as before, looked like a fisherman.'

'He *is* a fisherman, or rather, he has a fishing boat,' said Felicity. 'Blast, that's something I should have told Inspector Penrose.'

'What would that be, then?' Billy asked.

'The name of the boat the fisherman left in after his meeting with Ralph Smithson. Damn, that really might have been worth following up. I don't think I'm actually a very good detective, Billy.'

Billy grinned at her. 'Well, I don't know whether you're any good, girl, but you're certainly enthusiastic.' He squinted at her through a plume of smoke. 'There's a young man over the other side of the bar, trying to attract your attention. He's very slightly better-looking than me and just a tad younger. I'd go and join him if I were you.'

Felicity's heart sank as she and Martin ordered sandwiches and collected his drink. He was both monosyllabic and miserable. 'You seem very down?' Felicity ventured, once they were settled at their table.

'I am a bit low.' Martin hesitated. 'Look, we hardly know each other but you've trusted me enough to tell me your story. I think perhaps, it's time

I told you mine.'

'If you think it would be helpful, I really would be so grateful,' said Felicity, humbly, aware suddenly, for no reason she could identify, that she was treading on eggshells.

'God, I just don't know where to start ... with my name, I suppose.' Martin hesitated and then seemed to steel himself. 'With a name like Tregonning, you no doubt realise I am Cornish, born and bred, I grew up on the Lizard, in a village just outside St Keverne. My father farmed there, but farming today, particularly on a small scale and particularly down here, is a mug's game. It broke his health and his spirit – he died about ten years ago. I loved the farm and wanted to take it over but my father saw the writing on the wall while I was still a boy, and so after school I went to Cirencester Agricultural College and learnt about forestry.' Martin smiled. 'My father's philosophy was that without trees our planet is doomed and sooner or later everybody is going to recognise it. So, as he saw it, if you will forgive the pun, I would be in a growth industry. He has been proved right, really. I've never been out of work – well, until now – and I've worked all over the world. I loved growing up in Cornwall but it is insular and I had a tremendous thirst to travel. I had a long spell in Canada and in South Africa too. I also spent some years in Scotland.'

'I can see that West Cornwall isn't the ideal place to practise forestry, it's not exactly overburdened with trees,' said Felicity, smiling.

'You're right there,' said Martin. His expression

suddenly changed and became very solemn. 'It was while I was working in Scotland that I met a girl. I don't know what was wrong with me, arrested development or something, I suppose, but I was getting on for forty before I found the right girl. Her name was Helen and she was fifteen years younger than me.' Felicity immediately noticed the use of the past tense, but said nothing. 'I don't really know whose idea it was, hers or mine,' Martin continued, 'but we decided we would like to settle in Cornwall and quite by chance, I saw a job advertised at Boswithey. Over the years I had developed an interest in sub-tropical plants and had a number of projects under my belt. Boswithey combined forestry and gardening. The post was to manage and care for the entire estate, not running the commercial side of it, you understand, just the maintenance and development of the flora and fauna. It was a gift of a job, fabulous really.'

'When was this?' Felicity asked. 'When did you apply to work for Ralph Smithson?'

'The February before last,' Martin replied, 'and I worked for him up until July of this year.'

'Heavens,' said Felicity. 'So recently! Sorry, I didn't mean to interrupt.'

'That's OK,' said Martin, as their sandwiches arrived. 'I've got to the difficult bit now.' He paused for a moment and gazed out of the window across the harbour. Felicity sensed that she should keep very quiet if this man was to tell her anymore. 'I got the job,' said Martin. 'There were a great many candidates after it, people younger than me, much more qualified than me. It was odd in a way.'

'In what way?' Felicity prompted.

'Well, I immediately didn't like the man and I suspected he didn't like me either. He's a bully, very up himself, and I realised as soon as I saw him that I had met him before when I was working in South Africa. Well, I say "met" him. That isn't really the right expression. South Africa was the first place I went to after college and it took a while for me to find a job. While I was hunting around, I worked in rather a smart bar and fish restaurant on the Cape, near Constantia. There was this group of local young people who came in a lot – mostly young men but with a few girls in tow. Ralph Smithson was one of them. They were loud, ordered bucket-loads of champagne and arrived in expensive sports cars. They were spoilt and rich, and treated me like dirt – I couldn't stand them. I never knew his name, I didn't know any of their names, but over the weeks, while I worked at the bar, I saw them fairly frequently, and came to dread their visits.'

'Did you tell him you recognised him?' Felicity asked, intrigued.

'Well, I did, yes, and I think it's why he gave me the job. He questioned me for some while about what I was doing in South Africa and whether I had applied for the job because I knew him. It was all a bit strange. He was quite intense about it. Anyway, I got the job. It came with a fantastic cottage on the estate. Helen and I were married by then and we moved in straight away. Although I wasn't mad about Ralph, I didn't see him that much and I loved

Boswithey.'

'So what went wrong?'

The tension that had been building in Martin seemed to freeze and darken his features. 'In May of this year, Helen and I decided to take a couple of weeks' leave. I had worked for a year without a proper break in order to put the gardens right. I had seen to all the spring preparation work and before the Season really started, it seemed a good opportunity to get away. Helen wanted to go up to Scotland to see her family and we decided to drive there. Helen's family live in Argyll, just north of Oban. We took a couple of days to get there and were just a few miles from her home, winding our way through the lanes ... it was dusk,' he hesitated and cleared his throat, '... a tractor just came out of a field in front of us, just drove straight onto the lane. I didn't even have time to brake, I drove straight into it. I was OK, just a strained wrist, but my wife was killed outright and so was the baby she was carrying.'

'Oh, my God,' said Felicity, 'how terrible for you.' Instinctively she placed a hand on his arm.

'The tractor driver was charged with manslaughter, but of course I blame myself. I was at the wheel of the car. It should have been me who was killed, not Helen.' He cleared his throat again. 'I'm sorry, I'm not very good at talking about it yet, it's all still too painful, but as you told me about Charlie, confided in me so easily, I felt I should do the same.'

Felicity could think of nothing to say. 'I'm so sorry,' she said again.

'You seem to be a lot braver than me and you

143

lost your husband more recently.'

'I wasn't there though, when it happened,' Felicity began, knowing that in many respects this was not an exactly true statement.

'I just keep thinking about how easily it could have been avoided. We filled up with petrol just as we left Oban. If I had been quicker or slower filling the tank, or if I'd stopped to buy a newspaper or a chocolate bar... It was May Day – somehow that made it worse.'

'May Day?' said Felicity, incredulously. 'The accident happened on the first of May?' Martin nodded. 'How extraordinary!'

'In what way?' Martin asked.

'The student I told you about, the poor boy who died of a heroin overdose, the one who began it all – he died on May Day, too, or at least that was when his body was found. If my theory is right, then Charlie's death can be traced back to the first of May as well.'

They stared at one another in silence for a moment, both lost in thoughts which threatened to overwhelm them. Felicity recovered first. 'So you couldn't face going back to Boswithey after the accident?'

'No, it wasn't that,' said Martin. 'I stayed in Scotland for the funeral and the inquest obviously, but afterwards I couldn't wait to get away. Helen's parents were lovely, so kind, but she was their only child and I'd killed her, and their grandchild.'

'You didn't kill them,' Felicity said, vehemently.

'That's how I saw it, still do.' The way Martin spoke, Felicity knew there was nothing to be gained by arguing with him. 'So I came back to Boswithey and started work. Ralph Smithson had given me compassionate leave and was away when I returned. He was often away on business, which was quite a relief. Anyway, I threw myself into my work and worked every day until I was so exhausted, I couldn't help but sleep. I haven't mentioned much about Ralph's wife, Amelia, have I?'

'No, only that the poor woman is regularly beaten up,' Felicity said.

'Yes, well, they've been married for years, I think. Amelia, like Ralph, is in her early forties. They have a daughter but she seems to be estranged from them in some way, at least she never visits them in England. Her name is Bea, I think, and she lives in San Francisco.'

'That must be sad for them,' Felicity said. 'I wonder why they don't see her.'

'I suspect it's something to do with Ralph, and his brutish behaviour. Anyway, back to Amelia – she is a very timid, nervous, neurotic sort of person, the complete antithesis of him – she was really kind to me when I came back. She would come and find me at work and we would talk about the accident. She seemed to understand that sometimes I needed to talk about it and sometimes not – she would just hang about – she was a great comfort. Often we just talked about horses, which were a mutual passion.'

'She sounds a nice person,' Felicity said.

'She is, I can't think what made her marry Ralph and then stay with him all these years. Anyway,' Martin's face hardened, 'Ralph came back and heard from one of the staff about "secret meetings" with his wife, as he put it. We had a blazing row. He more or less accused me of seducing his wife behind his back. I was so insulted, not for me, I didn't care a damn what he thought of me, but for both Helen and Amelia. Someone less likely to have an affair than Amelia, it would be hard to imagine, and as for me ... I couldn't even look at another woman. Anyway, I was not in the mood to be conciliatory so soon after the accident and I told him to stuff his job there and then.'

'How awful,' said Felicity. 'So in the space of just a few weeks you lost your wife, your baby and your job.'

'And my home,' said Martin. 'It was daft really, I should have kept my temper, I suppose, I so needed to work.'

'So what happened next?' said Felicity, enthralled. She had thought her own life story was dramatic enough.

'I have decided to write a book. I've had the idea in my mind for a long time and Helen was always encouraging me to have a go. It's about sub-tropical gardens. I have a little money saved and I've rented a cottage here in St Ives. I do the odd gardening job and, as I said, I'm a coastguard. In between times, I try to write, but my concentration is fairly poor at the moment.'

'I should imagine it is,' said Felicity. 'How very brave of you.'

'Not brave,' said Martin. 'I'm just running away.'

'Me too,' said Felicity, 'that's exactly what I've been doing, I think.'

'It was the best thing I ever did, that's the

trouble,' said Martin. 'Nothing will ever be able to match it.'

'What was?' Felicity asked gently.

'Marrying Helen, of course. She taught me so much. How to communicate, how to feel and express my feelings. She literally brought me to life. Without her, I'm nothing. God, listen to me, I have life, don't I, while she's dead at only twenty-five – I'm pathetic.' His face was a mask of misery and self-loathing.

'I do have the perfect antidote for your gloom,' Felicity said suddenly, taking the cue from Martin that they should not start wallowing in self-pity.

'Oh really?' said Martin, rewarding her by perking up a little.

'You need plenty to do, that's the answer. You need to be busy and I feel it's absolutely my duty to keep you occupied.' Felicity was aware she was sounding falsely jolly but the enormity of what he had just told her was threatening to overwhelm them both.

'Right,' said Martin, looking brighter by the moment, 'so what exactly do you want me to do now?'

'Do you remember when we met, I asked about the boat leaving the harbour?'

'I vividly remember our first meeting,' said Martin, 'and being placed under immediate interrogation.' He grinned. 'And, yes, I do remember the boat – a fishing boat, wasn't it?'

'Yes,' said Felicity, 'but a slightly strange fishing boat. It seemed to be far too neat and tidy.'

'Something of an expert on fishing boats, are we?' Martin queried, teasing.

'That's better,' said Felicity. 'I'm more than happy for you to be a cheeky sod if you're going to cheer up. No, I don't know anything about fishing boats other than the fact that they're usually appallingly messy and smelly. This one was a positive poem of neatly coiled ropes and well-scrubbed decks.'

'So your point is?' Martin asked.

'My point is, that I would like to find out more about the boat and her owner and it seems to me, in the circumstances, the very best thing to do is ask a coastguard.'

'I suppose you could be right,' said Martin. 'Do you remember the name?'

'Yes, of course I do,' said Felicity. 'It's *Jayne Marie*, Jayne with a "Y", registered in Plymouth.'

'That should be easy enough to track down,' said Martin. 'Anything else?'

'Well, yes actually,' said Felicity, 'but this is the part you're not going to like.'

'Go on,' said Martin, with a theatrical sigh.

'I just wondered if you'd be up for joining me in a bit of nocturnal snooping around Boswithey?'

'Why would we want to do that?' Martin asked.

'I know your chum Michael is going to keep a look out for any odd goings on, but you say he is near retirement age and presumably he doesn't do much wandering around the gardens at night after a hard day's work. I just thought maybe we should spend a few nights checking out the place to see whether anyone is using the cove.'

'Did you read the Famous Five books when you

were a child?' Martin asked.

'I did, as a matter of fact,' Felicity replied, 'I absolutely loved them.'

'So you're going to need a torch, a penknife and a ball of string, and incidentally do you have a dog called Timmy?'

'I'm serious, Martin,' said Felicity. 'I've been told officially by the police that the case is going nowhere. They've interviewed Ralph Smithson, who had a perfect alibi for the night the "Skunk" died. It was provided, of course, by his wife who he would have beaten senseless – according to you – if she hadn't agreed. He absolutely denied ever meeting the "Skunk" in the Sloop and says I must have been mistaken. So far as Inspector Penrose is concerned, Ralph Smithson has been eliminated from his enquiries. I think he's wrong, I think our Inspector may have been taken in by the fact that Ralph Smithson is one of the biggest high-profile landowners in West Cornwall. The only way we're going to get Penrose to reconsider Ralph Smithson is if we can provide him with some sort of proof that he is involved in something he shouldn't be – anything really, to warrant further investigation.'

'It's not a difficult decision,' said Martin. 'All I have to do is to imagine what it would be like if Helen had been killed in a hit and run. I wouldn't rest, not ever, until I'd found out who was responsible ... so, I think that means, yes, I'll be your fellow sleuth because I know exactly where you're coming from.'

9

'Thanks, Jim.' Keith Penrose put down the phone following a lengthy conversation with Jim Brownley, his long-term contact at the Foreign Office. Absentmindedly he took a swig of cold coffee and grimaced, staring down at the newspaper cutting which he had extracted from the Carver file. The article was eleven years old and Keith had just established that Jack du Plessey had never been found; he had simply disappeared off the face of the earth, along with his wife and daughter. An idea was forming in Keith's mind. During his interview with Smithson, he had been told that Boswithey had been purchased just over ten years ago, shortly after his arrival in the United Kingdom. Also, during the interview, Keith had learnt that Smithson had been born and raised in Constantia, a coastal town on the Cape. Jim Brownley had just confirmed that no one named Ralph Smithson had been raised in Constantia during the period Ralph would have been a boy and a young man growing up there. It was interesting the way Mrs Paradise's instincts always seemed to be right.

Josh Buchanan was the first person to react positively to Felicity's morning of frenzied activity. 'I've struck gold,' he said on the telephone, sounding pleased with himself.

Felicity felt her heart begin beating unnecessarily fast. She was standing in Annie's little hallway and grabbed for the back of an envelope and a pen. 'Go on,' she said, breathlessly.

'I decided not to mess about on the telephone with my chum,' said Josh, 'so I arranged to take him out for lunch yesterday.'

'That's good of you,' said Felicity.

'Derwent Strange moved out of the City a few years ago. They are now out on the wastes of Canary Wharf, in an absolutely monstrous pile – all glass and chrome – I felt a real country hick, turning up there, like I should be brushing the mud off my boots. It is hard to believe we are even in the same profession.' Felicity fought her frustration and managed not to interrupt. 'While we went out to lunch, he put his clerk to work in the vaults and, wonder of wonders, when we got back from what I admit was a rather an alcoholic affair, there was this spotty, rather dusty-looking youth clutching a file.' Josh paused for dramatic effect.

'Oh, do get on with it Josh,' Felicity begged.

'The case that Charlie went out to South Africa to assist on was a fraud case, big style, and all rather exotic. Incidentally, he went with Hugh Derwent who was the son of one of the original founding partners. We scrabbled through the file and found that they were there quite a while, about three weeks, I think.

It was all very complicated but to give you a fairly facile explanation, Derwent Strange were representing a UK corporation called Wickham Holdings. Wickham Holdings were under investigation by the Inland Revenue for moving large amounts of cash into their South African-based company. The Revenue reckoned the scam was diamond smuggling, which apparently was very big at the time. Hugh and Charlie's job was to try and pin something on the South African company by conducting an entirely unexpected investigation of their books and records, with the apparent approval of Wickham Holdings.'

'And did they succeed?' Felicity asked.

'No, they came back empty-handed and very frustrated. Hugh Derwent's final report suggested that he still believed there was something fishy going on, but he just couldn't prove it. Of course, the main object of their trip was to try and satisfy the Inland Revenue that the sums of money Wickham Holdings were sending abroad were for legitimate purchases, and in that I suppose they were successful.'

'So he was able to do that?' Felicity asked.

'I think so but whether there was some sort of out of court settlement, I don't know. The file is not forthcoming on what happened next because it relates quite specifically to the South African investigation. However, Wickham Holdings are still clients of Derwent Strange, so they must have survived and certainly no one currently is aware of any massive tax scandal in the past. The thing is, Fizzy, I've saved the best bit till last.' Another dramatic pause. 'Guess the name of the South African company?'

Felicity frowned. 'I've absolutely no idea, Josh.'

'Du Plessey,' said Josh, triumphantly.

Felicity took a moment to react. 'Du Plessey, as in the newspaper cutting from the Carver file?'

'The same,' said Josh. 'The Managing Director at the time of the investigation was a Thomas du Plessey. Despite the high-tech chrome and glass world of Derwent Strange, when they want someone tracked down they still use the services of a private investigator. My chum contacted him yesterday and he has just rung me this morning with the results.'

'Go on,' said Felicity.

'Thomas du Plessey had two children, firstly a girl named Susan and then a son called Jack.'

'I suppose there could be two Jack du Plesseys,' said Felicity.

'Oh yes, easily,' said Josh. 'Apparently du Plessey is not an uncommon name in South Africa, but I think it's hardly likely. I suspect Charlie came across a newspaper article about du Plessey and clipped it out of interest, bearing in mind his time out in South Africa. I still believe it was a piece of misfiling.'

Felicity ignored him. 'What year did Charlie visit South Africa?'

'1972,' said Josh.

'I wish I knew the date of the newspaper article,' Felicity said. 'You really can't remember, can you?'

'I barely glanced at it,' said Josh, 'but your Mr Plod still has it. You could ask him, I suppose.'

'I certainly will,' said Felicity. 'I'm going to take this information to him straight away.'

'But why?' said Josh, sounding suddenly very concerned.

'Why do you think? It's another piece in the jigsaw.'

'But surely the article is of no significance to the Carver case, or Charlie's death? Charlie will have been interested in it because it proved Hugh Derwent's instincts were right, that the du Plesseys were a rotten lot, but there can have been no other reason. You're trying to make something out of nothing, Fizzy. Just forget it. Charlie clipped the article out of a sense of morbid curiosity, nothing more.'

'Josh, why won't you admit the connection?' Felicity said, exasperated.

'Because I don't believe there is one,' said Josh firmly.

Felicity put down the phone with mixed emotions. As always, it seemed that her investigations led to one step forward and one back. On the face of it, the du Plessey connection had to be important, so why was Josh so adamant about its insignificance? There was something about Josh, about his manner that troubled her. It was as if he was feeding her information – just enough, or so he thought, to shut her up. Well, there he was mistaken.

Before leaving for Truro, Felicity rang Martin Tregonning's mobile. 'Bad moment?' she asked.

'No, perfect. I'm gazing out of the window pretending to write, any diversion is greatly appreciated.'

'What year were you in South Africa, Martin, when you first met Ralph Smithson?'

'Let me think,' said Martin. 'I left college when I was twenty, and I had my twenty-first down here in Cornwall and I then went off to South Africa, so ... that was nineteen years ago.'

'1983?' Felicity said.

'Yes, must have been. Where on earth did all those years go? Are you going to tell me what this is all about?'

'I am,' she said, 'but not now.'

'Truro again?' said Annie. 'I don't know why you don't stay in a "B & B" there, my bird. It would be a lot easier for you than all this toing and froing.'

'Because I wouldn't find a landlady as wonderful as you,' said Felicity, hopefully. She was rewarded with the threatening shake of a feather duster.

Keith Penrose saw her almost immediately.

'If we are going to keep meeting like this, Mrs Paradise, I really ought to book a permanent interview room for you ... and perhaps your own car parking space.' Despite his words, his manner was friendly and more relaxed than usual. 'What can I do for you today?'

'What is the date on that newspaper cutting, the one about Jack du Plessey?' Felicity asked, without preamble. Much to her surprise, the file appeared to be already open in front of him. He leafed through some papers and then handed the cutting to her.

'14th July, 1991,' she read. 'Eleven years ago.' She looked up at Inspector Penrose. 'My husband's partner, Josh Buchanan, has been doing some digging. When my husband, Charlie, was a young man he was articled to a law firm called Derwent Strange. In 1972, he was sent out to South Africa to assist in a fraud investigation, the company in question was called du Plessey. The Managing Director at the time was a man called Thomas du Plessey who had two children, one of whom was named Jack.'

'That's very intriguing, Mrs Paradise, but I honestly can't see how it relates to the Carver case, but for the fact, of course, that the press cutting was in the Carver file?'

Felicity let out a deep sigh. 'Surely you can see the link, Inspector Penrose?'

'I can't,' he said, 'but I have the feeling you're going to tell me.'

'Ralph Smithson is Jack du Plessey,' she said, triumphantly. She had expected a look of amazement on his face and was disappointed when he appeared unmoved.

'It's a novel idea,' he said, 'but what brings you to that conclusion?'

'It's obvious isn't it?' she said. 'Charlie told me very little about the Carver case, but what he did say was that he believed Ben Carver was just a very small minnow in a very large pond. He believed there was a "Mr Big" behind the drugs racket. I think Charlie died because he was on to Ralph Smithson and somehow he had linked him to the du Plessey family. Maybe Charlie met him when he was out in South Africa – I don't know, but there is a connection, I'm sure of it.'

'Jack du Plessey would have been only a boy in 1972,' said Inspector Penrose. 'That was the year you said your husband went to South Africa?' Felicity nodded. 'So, Mrs Paradise, let us suppose you are right and they are one and the same person, Jack alias Ralph would only have been about twelve.'

'Nonetheless,' said Felicity, doggedly, 'there has to be a connection.'

Inspector Penrose regarded her in silence for a moment. 'It is standard police procedure to tell witnesses as little as possible about what is going on.'

'I had noticed,' said Felicity, dryly.

'So,' said Inspector Penrose, with the appearance of a genuine smile, 'I'm going to break the rules and tell you that was an excellent piece of research, Mrs Paradise, and I believe that your theory could be right.'

Felicity sat back in her chair, smiling too. 'I do believe, Inspector Penrose, that you've just made my day.'

'I'm glad to hear it,' he said. 'Would you like to celebrate with a cup of truly dreadful coffee, with the compliments of Devon and Cornwall Constabulary?'

'I'd like that very much,' she said.

'I think your apparent enthusiasm might be

going a little far in the circumstances, Mrs Paradise.'

He returned moments later with two polystyrene cups of brown liquid, which certainly did not smell of coffee. Felicity didn't mind. She was well aware of the importance of the gesture – this was a true turning point; he was starting to take the case seriously – at last.

He went behind his desk and sat down. 'Ah, while I think of it, Mrs Paradise, I have something for you.'

There was some ineffectual scrabbling on his desk for a moment or two and then a triumphant. 'Got it!' He solemnly handed her a brown envelope.

Felicity took it. 'Do I open it?' she asked.

'As you wish,' Keith replied.

Felicity shook out the contents. Inside were a dozen or so sheets of silver paper, all carefully smoothed out. 'Inspector, that is very kind of you, thank you so much.' She was genuinely touched. Inspector Penrose took a hasty gulp of his coffee and looked embarrassed. Aware of his awkwardness, she quickly added, 'though what your Chief Superintendent is doing to his lungs, I hate to think.' They exchanged a smile; the moment of difficulty passed.

'There was something I forgot to mention to you when we met last,' said Felicity. 'The man Ralph Smithson met the second time I saw him at the Sloop – I don't know his name but I did follow him along the harbour. He went off in a fishing boat. The name of the boat was *Jayne Marie* and it was registered in Plymouth.'

'Did you note the boat's registration number?' said Inspector Penrose, looking stern.

'Well, no, I didn't,' Felicity stammered. 'I suppose I should have done.'

'Should really,' he said, with a grin.

'You're not being very kind, Inspector,' said Felicity. 'I didn't get the number but I did notice something unusual about the boat.'

'What was that?'

'It was too clean for a fishing boat, too tidy. Whatever he was using it for, it wasn't fishing. I have asked a friend of mine, a coastguard, to try and find out where the boat is now.'

Inspector Penrose took another gulp of coffee and winced, then he regarded Felicity in silence for a moment. 'I think I might take early retirement, Mrs Paradise, and just hand the whole case over to you.'

10

Martin Tregonning telephoned Felicity while she was still at the breakfast table the following morning. 'There've been a few developments,' he said. 'Shall we talk on the phone or meet?'

'Do you fancy a coffee at Annie's?'

'I'll be straight around,' he said.

There were two other couples at breakfast so Annie showed them into her parlour to give them some privacy. It was clear Annie had developed a soft spot for Martin – coffee and a couple of warm saffron buns were placed in front of him in seconds.

'You eat up now,' she instructed, 'you look a touch peaky to me. I hope you're looking after yourself,' and with that she was gone.

Felicity studied Martin in silence for a moment. There were dark circles under his eyes and he needed a shave. Maybe Annie's preoccupation with ensuring everybody was well-fed and cared for was rubbing off on her, but it seemed to Felicity that even in the short time she had known him, Martin had lost weight.

'And are you?' she asked.

'What?'

'Looking after yourself.'

'After a fashion,' he said, defensively.

'I'm so lucky to be living with Annie at the moment,' Felicity confided. 'She bullies me unmercifully, but if you're living alone, I can imagine how easy it must be to just stop bothering. I had a period a week or two back when ...' She stopped.

'Go on,' said Martin.

Felicity shrugged. 'Everything seemed so pointless. I just felt so exhausted all the time. I didn't want to do anything, go anywhere. Annie saw me through it and, ironically, since I've been concentrating on Ralph Smithson and his evil ways, I've felt better – still miserable, still lonely and all that, but back in charge, at least for the moment.'

'I spoke to my sister last night,' said Martin, 'she says I'm suffering from depression and I ought to go to the doctor about it, but I don't want to, I don't want to dull the pain with chemicals. I probably sound like some sort of pathetic martyr, but I feel I owe my wife and child proper grieving time, and to hide from it wouldn't be right.' He hesitated. 'It is awful isn't it, just for that second in the morning? When you first wake up, you're free of it, and then you remember and the whole thing overwhelms you again.'

They sat in silence for a moment, listening to the crackling of Annie's fire.

'Cheerful couple, aren't we?' said Martin.

'It's good for us to share how we're feeling,' said Felicity. 'However kind and caring one's friends and family, unless you've been there ...' she hesitated. 'Charlie and I had a row that last morning, I can't get it out of my head, I never will. I told him he was a selfish pig.' Her voice cracked; she picked up the paper napkin Annie had thoughtfully placed by the saffron buns and pressed it into her eyes.

'And was he?' Martin asked gently.

'A selfish pig? I don't know, Martin, but I suppose that's exactly what I'm trying to find out, what he was keeping from me, and why.'

'I found the name of the owner of the boat for you.'

'Really? That's good.' She made an effort to pull herself together.

'His name's Harold Blundy. I have his address, or rather the address he used to register his boat. He comes from Plymouth, I've written it down for you.' He passed her a piece of paper. 'I thought your policeman might like it.'

'I don't know why everyone calls him "*my* policeman".' Felicity grumbled. She stared at the address in silence for a moment. 'The "Skunk" came from Plymouth, too.'

'So do a lot of other people,' said Martin, with more than a hint of sarcasm.

Felicity closed her eyes for a moment. 'Why is it so hard to convince anyone that there is something fishy going on? Nobody believes me. I think everybody views it as an exercise I'm putting myself through in order to cope with the grief of losing my husband, but it's not that, Martin, it's really not, something's going on, I know it.' Again she pressed the napkin to her eyes.

Martin leant across and put a hand on her arm, rubbing it gently. 'I'm sorry, the last thing I want to do is upset you Felicity, but equally I don't want to give you false hopes, either.'

'Are you still willing to have a snoop around Boswithey?' Felicity said.

Martin drew back and considered her in silence for a moment. 'That's the other piece of news I have for you. Amelia Smithson is back in hospital. Michael rang yesterday to tell me.'

'Another riding accident?' Felicity asked, sarcastically.

'This time, she apparently fell down the stairs, broke her collarbone and fractured a couple of ribs, one of which punctured her lung – hence why she's been hospitalised. She's in Truro.'

'Poor woman, I hope Ralph's at her bedside.'

'No, according to Michael, he called an ambulance, saw her bundled into it, then he announced he was going off on a business trip and he'd be away several days.'

'That man is all heart,' said Felicity, excitement suddenly rising. 'Well, this gives us our chance, doesn't it, Martin?'

'To take a look around, you mean?'

Felicity nodded. 'With both the Smithsons out of the way, even if one of the staff caught us snooping, I don't expect there would be a row, would there?'

'No, probably not,' said Martin. 'I've got a pretty good relationship with most of them.'

'Shall we do it then?' said Felicity.

'Would I be right in thinking I'll have absolutely no peace until I agree?'

'You'd be absolutely right,' said Felicity.

Felicity left a message for Inspector Penrose with the identity of the boat owner. She imagined it was information he would already have, but within half an hour of her call, he returned it. 'Thank you for the information, Mrs Paradise, most helpful.'

'So both Harold Blundy and Ronald Baxter are from Plymouth,' Felicity said.

'That point hadn't escaped me,' Keith said.

'I'm sorry if I'm being irritating, Inspector.'

'Not at all,' he replied. 'I'm quite happy to have you check up on me.' There was a pause. 'The reason I'm ringing, Mrs Paradise, is I wonder whether your husband's diary might be around somewhere.'

'Diary?' said Felicity. 'We just had a wall chart in the kitchen.'

'No, I mean his office diary. I assume he kept one, or would he have used his laptop?'

'Good heavens, no,' said Felicity, 'not Charlie, it definitely would have been a conventional diary.'

'And written in ink rather than biro, I suspect, a man after my own heart,' said Keith Penrose. 'I'd very much like to have a look at it, if that would be possible?'

'Why don't you ring Josh Buchanan?' Felicity asked.

'I thought it a little insensitive, Mrs Paradise. Although an office diary is, strictly speaking, an office matter, I didn't like the idea of asking to see something of your husband's without at least telling you first.'

'That's very thougtful of you, Inspector. I'll give Josh a ring right away and if it hasn't been thrown out I'll make sure he sends it to you.' She hesitated. 'Are you looking for anything specific?'

'No,' said Keith, 'not really. It's what my Chief Super would describe as one of my fishing expeditions.'

They decided to lie to Annie, which Felicity wasn't very happy about. Their story was that they were going to the cinema in Truro and would have supper afterwards. Somehow, Felicity had the feeling that Annie did not believe them.

She handed Felicity the front door key and looked her up and down. 'You're not dressing up much for him, are you? Jeans, boots, big scruffy old coat – you could have made a bit of an effort, Felicity.'

'It's not a date,' said Felicity, defensively. 'Anything like that would be far too soon for either of us. Anyway, he's younger than me.'

'Nothing wrong with a bit of cradle snatching,' said Annie, smiling, but her eyes were sceptical.

'We should have told Annie what we're up to,' Felicity said as she climbed into Martin's car.

'No, I'm sure we've made the right decision, to keep quiet,' said Martin. 'Trespassing is an offence.

The less she knows the better, just in case anything goes wrong. She's a sweet old girl and she needs protecting – ignorance is bliss in this case.'

'You're making it all sound very scary,' said Felicity.

'Then perhaps this is the moment I should remind you whose idea it was,' said Martin, as he slipped the car into gear.

Twenty minutes later they were on the south coast and Felicity caught a glimpse of the great sweep of Mount's Bay, just as the light began to fail. The familiar, yet extraordinary sight of St Michael's Mount – that great mound of rock – reared out of the sea below them, the castle clinging to it like a limpet. A few lights burned high in the turrets; beyond the Mount were the lights of boats moored in the bay and beyond that the lights of Penzance. It was a magnificent sight.

'It's so beautiful, but it's getting dark awfully early,' she said a little wistfully, thinking suddenly that this would lead to her first winter without Charlie.

'Just as well,' said Martin, 'I'm not very keen on the world and his wife being witness to our trespassing.'

'Look, if you're not happy about this,' said Felicity, 'we really don't have to go ahead. It's not that I think we're going to catch anyone red-handed, it's more that if we are going to nail Ralph Smithson, it would be so helpful to see where he lives and get the lie of the land.'

'I've said I'm happy to take you,' said Martin, 'it just seems a slightly odd thing to be doing, and certainly trespassing is not anything I've ever done before.'

'Nor me,' said Felicity. 'I just have this feeling I'm looking for something, the problem is I don't know what it is.'

'Oh, terrific,' said Martin, with a grin, 'that's very reassuring.'

They parked Martin's jeep on a muddy verge by the entrance into a field, which created a small lay-by. 'It's only a five-minute walk from here,' he assured Felicity.

The entrance to Boswithey was impressive. The huge wrought iron gates were closed now for the day, but they sported a large sign outlining the wonders of the estate and quoting public opening times and entrance fees.

'You see the lodge, just the other side of the gate that's where Michael lives. He and his wife Katie have been there forever. I just hope that when Michael retires, Ralph is going to let him stay on. It's the only home they've ever known.'

'How are we getting in?' Felicity asked. 'Are you going to call Michael?'

'No,' said Martin. 'I feel about Michael like I feel about Annie, it's best he's not involved. We're going to climb over the wall just a few yards further on, then we can walk along in the shelter of a hedge until we reach the house, which is still about a quarter of a mile away.'

'It's so exposed,' Felicity said. 'I thought you said there were trees.'

'There are,' said Martin, 'but all the other side of the house. The sub-tropical gardens are all south-west facing, they sort of tuck sideways into the cliff. You'll see in a minute.'

The wall surrounding the estate was only about five-feet high and with Martin's help Felicity had no trouble climbing over it. They dropped down the other side and Martin indicated the hedge immediately ahead of them.

'You'd think that if Ralph was really up to something,' Felicity whispered, 'he'd have more security. If I can make it, middle-aged old biddy that I am, anyone could climb over that wall.'

'If he started employing high security measures around these parts, he'd draw an awful lot of attention to himself – it's just not the way people live down here.'

'I suppose not,' Felicity agreed.

The ground was soft underfoot and heavy going after recent rain. It seemed a long time before, ahead of them, they saw the shape of the house. The last of the light had left the sky now and it was necessary to use torches. They kept them pointing downwards to create the minimum of light.

'We'll skirt round the house to the left,' said Martin, in a whisper, 'that's the quickest way to get to the gardens.'

'What about the dogs?' Felicity whispered back.

'They don't have any,' Martin said over his shoulder.

'Bit odd, isn't it, a place like this not having dogs?'

'Just be thankful they don't. I suppose it's because Ralph's not here a lot of the time, and Amelia has her horses. Knowing you, though, I'm sure you're reading some sinister motive into their lack of canine companionship.'

Felicity did not trust herself to reply.

It was difficult to make out any details of the house as they walked silently past it and around the side. The back windows were all shuttered. It was painted white, tall and impressive, with strange castellations around the roofing.

'How old is the house?' Felicity whispered.

'I think there's been a house here for centuries,' Martin said, stopping for a moment. 'The main part of this house was built in the seventeen hundreds but the tackroom and estate office, which is where we are now, are considerably older. If you see, they are built in a different style, much simpler, cottage-like. It is generally recognised that these formed part of the original dwelling and the main house was built onto them. It's not a particularly beautiful property; it's the gardens which make it special.'

'I like it,' she said. 'It's unusual, a bit quirky. What a waste for the Smithsons to live here.'

'Michael's daughter, Polly, has a flat on the other side of the house,' Martin whispered, 'so when we come round to the front, we'll have to leg it across the lawn to reach the gate that takes us into the public area. We'll be completely exposed but there's no other way, so just keep very quiet. If you hold my hand, I should be able to lead you across.'

Felicity did as she was told, took his hand and they began tiptoeing across the grass. Once again Felicity wondered what on earth Charlie would think if he could see her now. What an extraordinary chain of events that had begun with Oliver Colhoun's tragic death and had bought her to the point where she was tiptoeing across a stranger's lawn, holding hands with a coastguard, in the midst of some serious trespassing. She stifled a giggle.

'What is it?' Martin whispered back furtively. 'Do be quiet, Felicity.'

'Sorry,' she murmured.

They reached the far side of the lawn without incident. There they found all the paraphernalia normally associated with opening a property to the public – a kiosk, a turnstile and a stout oak door proclaiming it was the garden entrance.

'How do we get through there?' Felicity asked. Like a magician producing a rabbit out of a hat, Martin took a key from his pocket.

'In the rather undignified rush of me being sacked,' Martin said, 'I overlooked giving back this key. I returned the keys of the cottage but I only found this some days later in one of my jacket pockets. I've been meaning to return it and then when you created all this fuss about Boswithey, I thought I better hang onto it.'

'Brilliant,' said Felicity.

Martin inserted the key into the lock and it turned with a well-oiled clunk. They slipped through the door and he shut it behind him.

'Are you going to lock it again?' Felicity asked.

'No need, there'll be nobody around, honest.'

They had walked into wonderland. Even in the dark Felicity could make out the shapes of shrubs and trees. 'What's that I can smell?' she asked.

'Jasmine,' said Martin. 'It climbs everywhere, like a weed.'

'It's wonderful.'

'Come on, we'll take this path, it goes straight to the cliff edge. Follow me.'

The path led downhill through dense vegetation, sometimes forming a canopy under which they walked. 'I'd love to see this in daylight,' Felicity said.

'It is magical, isn't it?' Martin said. 'I do miss it dreadfully.'

'I didn't like to ask near the house but where was your cottage?'

'The other side of the house from where we were and further up the drive, sort of midway between Michael's lodge and the main house.'

'Is someone living there now?' Felicity asked.

'I don't think so.' Martin's voice was bleak.

'I'm sorry,' said Felicity, 'not a very tactful thing to ask.'

There was silence between them as they picked their way. The path was well kept but such was the density of the vegetation that great roots protruded above ground, making walking difficult. 'This must be a bit of a nightmare for people in wheelchairs and babies in buggies.'

'This isn't the main path,' Martin said. 'This is

open to the more intrepid public but there's a warning to say it's rough going. I'm taking you this way because it's the quickest.'

They had been walking for six to seven minutes when, as abruptly as it had begun, the trees and shrubs disappeared and ahead of them was the sea.

'How extraordinary,' said Felicity.

'Originally the gardens went much further down the cliff,' Martin said, 'but, sadly, erosion has caused them to fall into the sea.'

'And is the erosion still going on?' Felicity asked.

'Oh, yes, very much so. There will come a time when the gardens are no longer safe but they should be good for at least another fifty years. Now, follow me along this path, carefully – are you alright with heights?'

'Yes,' she said, her thoughts distracted by the slow destruction of the gardens – nature turning on itself.

'Do be careful.' Martin sensed he needed to emphasise the danger as Felicity was clearly so over-awed by her surroundings. 'We're right on the cliff edge here – just follow me closely and I'll take you to where the rope is fixed.'

There was a light onshore wind but even so Felicity suddenly felt quite vulnerable as she stumbled along in the dark behind Martin, aware that to her left was a drop of several hundred feet into the sea. After about five minutes Martin stopped. 'Here we are, the problem is it's high tide so you can barely see the cove. However, if we just sit here for a moment while our eyes get accustomed to the dark, you should be able to pick out the line of surf, and here's the rope, look.'

A set of metal steps, not unlike those normally associated with a swimming pool, was fastened to the side of the cliff and beside the steps a stout rope was anchored.

'It looks terrifying,' said Felicity. She flashed her torch about – it looked like the drop into an abyss.

'It's certainly not something to do in the dark, but it's actually much easier than it looks. There are good foot holds and with the rope to hold onto, it's pretty hard to go wrong. Sit here by the steps, the grass isn't too wet, and in a moment you'll start to see the cove.'

He was right. Gradually, as her eyes accustomed themselves to the dark, she could pick out details of the little cove below. The tide was indeed very high, the waves already striking the base of the cliffs. 'Does the cove disappear completely at high tide?' She asked.

'Yes,' said Martin, 'in fact, when there's a storm, the spray reaches as high as where we're sitting now, which is why this particular patch around the rope has very little vegetation except headland grass.'

They sat in a companionable silence for a few moments. 'It's beautiful here,' Felicity said, 'and so warm. I can't understand it – the wind, such as it is, is blowing straight at us.'

'It's an odd phenomenon,' Martin agreed, 'it's never cold in these gardens when the prevailing south-westerlies are blowing, but when there's a north-east wind, which comes from behind us and you'd think the gardens would be protected, it's actually freezing – all very odd.'

'It is a lovely place,' said Felicity, 'but something's going on here, I can just feel it.'

'Oh, so you're a white witch are you? You could have told me before, it's very creepy being out at night with a witch.' His manner was teasing.

Felicity took a deep breath; it was a subject she knew she had to raise sometime, if Martin was to understand the whole picture. 'Actually, I do see things, real things that actually happened. It's sort of second sight. You can laugh at me if you wish, it's OK, most people do, but I saw my husband die, and that's why I'm here, I suppose.'

She felt Martin stir beside her. 'You saw your husband die? I don't understand.'

'I went to the place where Charlie was killed and I saw the whole thing happen.' She didn't dare tell him she'd seen it twice, imagining he would think her even more weird.

'God, how awful, no wonder you're on such a mission to find the truth. Come on, let's go back now. There's nothing more to see in this light and we don't want your instincts spooking us, do we?' He took her hand and pulled her to her feet.

Did he believe her? It didn't sound like it. He had changed the subject so quickly. Maybe he was just seeking to avoid hearing any details of Charlie's death. It was hard to tell. Still at least it was out in the open now – no more secrets between them, at least on her side.

They began retracing their steps. 'What do you want to do now you've seen Boswithey?' Martin asked.

'I don't know,' said Felicity. 'I just wanted to have a look around and I suppose I'd hoped we would see something unusual. The trouble is, it's just so dark. We city dwellers aren't used to this amount of dark, you forget that there's a world without street lamps.'

'It's wonderful though, isn't it?' They stopped for a moment and looked up at the sky. He was right. The stars were out now and instead of the odd one or two Felicity was used to seeing in Oxford, the sky was a mass of stars. 'The joys of no light pollution.' Martin said. 'Come on, I'm going to take you back to the car.'

Ten minutes later, they were in the car with the heater going full blast. 'I keep thinking about what you said. Did you really have a sense of something going on in the cove?' Martin asked, as he turned the car round.

'No visions, nothing like that, just a sense of being close to discovering something – not much help I'm afraid.' Felicity was feeling so pathetically grateful that he was not ridiculing her second sight, that she did not want to push her luck by trying to describe the absolute conviction she had felt by the cliff edge that they were close, very close to discovering ... what?

'Only there is something I haven't told you, mainly because I didn't want to fan the flames on your spirit of adventure.'

'What is it?' Felicity turned to him in the dark, hope flaring.

'It's always been rumoured that there was a passageway from the house to the beach – a lot of the houses along this part of the coast had them. Remember Cornwall was a mining county, with plenty of skilled mining labour available. During the main smuggling period – which lasted well over a hundred years – a number of these passages were built. It's only a legend that there was one at Boswithey, because no one has ever found it in recent years. In any event, with the degree of cliff movement and erosion in the last few decades, any such passageway probably would have been destroyed long ago.'

'Are you sure?' said Felicity.

'Pretty sure,' said Martin. 'There's certainly no passageway entrance down to the beach now.'

'But could we just go back tomorrow and have a look?'

'I knew I shouldn't have said anything. Felicity, I've tramped that beach a thousand times. Believe me, there is no passageway.'

'Please,' she said, 'I just can't ignore this feeling, it's important.'

'It's Wednesday tomorrow. I have to admit the gardens are closed to the public on Wednesdays because they are open at weekends. The staff work though, because it's a good day to catch up on the jobs which are difficult to do with visitors around.' He sighed, theatrically. 'If we came back about four thirty, everyone would have packed up and gone, with no visitors to clear out. That would give us an hour of daylight.'

'Then please let's do it,' Felicity pleaded.

'I wonder if it's worth looking carefully at the tackroom,' said Martin, thoughtfully. 'I think I told you it was much older than the rest of the house. It could be where the passageway began?'

'You're starting to believe me,' Felicity said.

They were dropping down into St Ives now. There was a thick mist hanging over the harbour, the shapes of the fishing boats barely visible, but still the harbour lights were warm and welcoming.

'I must be absolutely cracked,' said Martin, with the trace of a smile, 'but actually I think I might be.'

11

The next day dragged for Felicity. She decided it was high time she spoke to her children. It had been nearly two weeks since she had heard from either of them. She put in an abortive call to Melanie's office. She was too busy to speak to her mother, but she promised to call later. Jamie, who largely worked from home, was not there either and Felicity found herself speaking to her daughter-in-law, Trish.

'How are you doing, Fizzy?' Normally the Australian accent delivered at extremely high volume, grated on Felicity, but today she was oddly pleased to speak to Trish.

'I'm fine really. How are Jamie and the boys?'

'All good, missing you though.'

'I'm sorry,' said Felicity. 'I know I've been hopelessly uncommunicative.'

'No worries,' said Trish. 'I keep saying to Jamie, it's just what you need: to get away from it all. I don't know why everybody is making such a fuss about you being in Cornwall. I'm sure that's what I would do if I were you. I couldn't bear to be in that great old house of yours, all on my own.'

An image of her home flashed into Felicity's mind. She thought of Charlie, his study door always propped open with a pile of books, the smell of his evening cigar, his roar of laughter at one of the children's antics.

'Yes, you're right,' she said. 'I think I'm in denial as far as the house is concerned. I was alright for the first few weeks when there was plenty to do but now I have to admit, I am rather dreading going back.'

'Well then, don't,' said Trish. 'Sell up, start again.'

'It would be destroying all our memories.'

'No it wouldn't,' said Trish. 'They're safe in your head. For once, Fizzy, you can think about yourself, rather than everyone else. You go for it, girl.'

Felicity laughed. 'You know, Trish, you're a breath of fresh air.'

'I aim to please,' said Trish. 'Now, no pressure, but when you're back, you will come and see our boys, won't you? They're missing their Granny.'

'I will, love to Jamie and thanks, Trish.'

It was odd, Felicity thought. When Jamie had first introduced her and Charlie to Trish, they had been worried because she was such a dominant person. 'She'll swallow Jamie whole,' Charlie had commented at the time. Yet, where on earth would her shy, hesitant son be now without his wife? She had simply taken over his life and organised it. Jamie was a seriously clever I.T. boffin, who hired out his services as a trouble-shooter when computer systems were causing problems. Trish had completely revolutionised his working life, running Jamie as a business with proper invoices and sensible quotations to reflect the time he spent on each job. Jamie so loved his work, that he would have been happy to do it for nothing, but under the influence of Trish's tender loving care and firm business-like approach, they could now afford to operate from a glorious old farmhouse just outside Chipping Norton. Jamie was so much in demand, he could pick and choose the jobs he wanted to do. He was a happy and successful man. Trish had succeeded in giving Jamie the confidence that both she and Charlie had failed to do, and it was about time she recognised it, she thought.

Her perspective on a lot of things had changed, Felicity mused, as she wandered through the town, in search of a quick snack lunch. Things which had seemed important when Charlie was alive, had lost their significance. The house primarily, but also her job, no longer seemed relevant, nor the expensive trappings which had been an integral part of her life with Charlie – meals out, holidays – none of it seemed to matter now. Without Charlie, the whole structure of her life had simply disintegrated. When this was all over, once she knew why Charlie had died, then Trish was probably right, it was time for a fresh start ... and a much simpler life.

After lunch, Felicity suddenly remembered Inspector Penrose's request for Charlie's business diary. She telephoned Josh.

'I'm sorry Fizzy, I'm afraid I threw it away,' he replied, having listened to her request.

'Threw it away! Why on earth did you do that, Josh?' Felicity asked, exasperated.

'I didn't think it was relevant to anything once the inquest was over.'

'What about returning it to me?' Felicity asked.

'It was a business appointments diary, Fizzy, pretty dry stuff, nothing of any interest, I assure you.'

There was nothing more she could do or say, but the brief conversation left Felicity uneasy. Once again, her instincts told her that Josh was not being entirely frank.

Martin picked her up from Cormorant Cottage at four-thirty sharp. This time, they had been quite unable to keep the truth from Annie. When Felicity had returned the previous evening, Annie had taken one look at the mud on her walking boots and the grass stains on her jacket, raised an eyebrow and said, 'Outdoor cinema, was it? Didn't know they had one of those things in Truro,' and Felicity had been forced to tell her the whole story.

She had expected Annie to disapprove and she was right. 'So what would have happened to you then, if you'd got caught there?' she asked. 'Bundled into the boot of a car and set fire to, like that "Skunk". I don't know what you're playing at. You leave it be, my girl, the police will get there in the end.' When she heard they were returning the following evening, there had been a lot of sighing and disapproval.

'We'll be home by nine,' said Felicity, feeling like a rebellious teenager, '... promise.'

They parked in the same spot and entered the estate by the same circuitous route as the previous evening. Their walk past the house and out onto the cliff seemed much shorter this time.

'That seemed quicker and easier,' Felicity remarked, when they stepped out of the gardens onto the cliff edge.

'It's that much lighter and you've done it before so you knew where you were going.' Martin gazed around him appreciatively. It was another glorious evening.

'The house and grounds seem almost eerily quiet again,' Felicity said.

'With Ralph and poor Amelia both away and no public to worry about, the atmosphere is quite different. We used to love it on Wednesdays, having the place to ourselves.'

The sadness which suddenly descended on Martin made Felicity feel incredibly guilty. Here she was forcing this man to visit a place where he'd been so happy with his now dead wife. She couldn't think of anything comforting to say.

Strangely it was Martin who seemed to recover first. 'Come on then,' he said, 'if you really want to go down to the cove, we're going to have to be quick. I don't fancy doing this climb in the dark and I certainly don't want you to do it. I'll go first, then at least I can break your fall if you do anything silly.'

'I won't do anything silly,' said Felicity, with studied patience.

Martin was right. The descent was much easier than Felicity had imagined. There were plenty of foot holds and although in places the cliff had crumbled slightly, with the stout rope to hold on to, it felt quite secure. About halfway down they stopped for a breather; the cliffs soared up all around them, like a great cathedral, and the sea had turned silver in the evening light.

'It's incredible,' Felicity said.

'Come on,' said Martin, 'you're not here to admire the view, we must keep going.'

'What's that path?' Felicity asked.

They had reached a ledge on the cliff and leading away from the rope towards the centre of the cove, the grass was trampled to a point where a very clear path was in evidence.

'Oh, that'll just be rabbits,' said Martin, dismissively. 'They make all sorts of tracks around these cliffs.'

'Rabbits with very odd habits,' said Felicity. 'Look!' She pointed a few feet ahead of them. There, lying on the path was a cigarette butt.

'I can't think anybody would walk any distance round the cliff at this point, it's madness to leave the rope. It must just have been one of the staff who came down here for a fag break.'

'No,' said Felicity, 'this is a well-worn path, Martin, I'm sure it's too wide and established for rabbits, I think we should investigate.'

'I don't like leaving the rope,' he said. 'I don't want you pitching down the cliff.'

Felicity was exasperated. 'And I don't want you

183

pitching down the cliff either, but if we're careful, it will be fine. Clearly, somebody else has done it, so why not us?'

'I'll go first then,' said Martin, 'but I think it's a waste of time.'

Leaving the safety of the rope, Martin edged cautiously along the path. Felicity followed. The path hugged the edge of the cliff, heading deeper into the cove. There was no problem, or any apparent danger either – as Felicity pointed out, it appeared extremely well used. As abruptly as it had started, the path came to an end at an overhanging outcrop of rock.

'I don't understand it,' said Martin. 'Who on earth would come along here, and why? Just stay there a minute.'

He eased himself around the first rocky outcrop, disappearing from view. Felicity leaned back against the cliff and gazed around her. It was a strange sensation to have gulls flying below her, wheeling and calling, the sound of their cries accentuated by the height of the cliffs. This place doesn't just look like a cathedral, it has the acoustics of one too, Felicity thought. We must be careful not to make too much noise in case anyone is still about. She jumped, hearing a call from Martin. 'Are you alright?' she called back, keeping her voice low.

His head appeared above the rock, his hair tousled, a big grin on his face. For a moment he looked much younger, carefree almost. 'I've found it!' he said, triumphantly.

'Found what?' Felicity asked. 'Don't make so much noise.'

'The passageway, come round, carefully.' She edged her way round the first clump of rocks. 'Look, here!'

At first she could see nothing but by peering into the shadows, she was suddenly able to make out a small, dark entrance directly into the cliff face, camouflaged by the overhang of the rock.

'It's perfect, you see,' said Martin, excitedly. 'You'd never see it from the sea, nor from any angle on the cliff path either. This rock completely protects it, it's brilliant.'

'But why is the entrance here?' said Felicity. 'Why not at the bottom of the cliff? Surely that's where it would have been built, to go all the way down.'

'I've just been thinking about that,' said Martin. 'We're forgetting erosion. The passageway would have travelled up steeply from the beach so, as the cliff eroded, so the entrance would have become higher and higher. It makes perfect sense.'

'So what are you saying?' said Felicity. 'Do you think someone is still using the passage?'

'It certainly looks like it, judging by how worn that path is. Well done for spotting it, incidentally.'

'That sounds a little patronising,' said Felicity.

Martin grinned at her. 'Sorry, you were right, I was wrong, will that do? Now, shall we take a look?'

'Absolutely!' Felicity replied, weak with excitement.

Just for a moment, Martin hesitated by the entrance. 'Annie's right, you know. If Ralph can do what he did to the "Skunk", God knows what he would do to us if he found us.'

'Oh, come on Martin. There's no one here, we know there isn't. The place was absolutely deserted. Let's just take a quick look and then we'll go back to the car and ring Inspector Penrose.'

They eased their way behind the rock and found themselves in the tunnel. Martin switched on his torch. The tunnel was narrow, not much wider than the average person; certainly there was no room to pass somebody else. It was also very low – Felicity could just about stand up but Martin needed to stoop over in order to avoid hitting his head.

'I hope you don't suffer from claustrophobia,' he said. His voice sounded odd, muffled and hollow.

'Let's just get on with it, shall we?' said Felicity, nervously.

They trudged up the passageway. On instructions, Felicity kept her torch switched off to save the battery so only Martin's lighted them. The going was not easy, the path very steep. It was very warm, too. Way behind them, strangely echoing, was the sound of the sea breaking in the cove, and then, after a while, they could no longer hear anything – which was oddly disturbing. They trudged on, higher and higher. Neither spoke. At last, with an oath, Martin came to an abrupt halt. 'Blast, there's a door here.'

'Does it open?' Felicity asked, bumping into the back of him.

'I'm just having a look.' He shone the torch up and down the door and settled the beam on a latch. He clicked it open. The moment they stepped forward, they were in a completely different atmosphere, the dampness had gone, and so had the airlessness. Martin shone his torch around, and flicked on a light switch. The room was immediately flooded with light. Felicity closed the door to the passageway. The room they were in was about twelve feet square and there were shelves around the walls, mostly containing boating paraphernalia, ropes, anchors and a pair of oars. On the lower shelves, there were neatly-stacked cardboard boxes running halfway around the room.

'What is this place?' Felicity asked. 'It's weird, I don't like it.'

'I suspect we're immediately below the house, probably the tackroom, which explains the access to power. Look over there.'

In the far corner of the room, steps had been built leading right up to the ceiling. 'It looks like a trapdoor,' said Felicity, 'shall we see what's up there?'

'Let's have a look around here first,' said Martin. He pulled one of the cardboard boxes off the shelf. The lid was taped down. Very carefully he picked at the tape and pulled just enough back to open one corner. 'Shit!' he said.

Felicity leant over his shoulder. Inside the box there were several plastic bags of what appeared to be white powder. 'What is it?' Felicity leaned in closer, squinting in the brightness of the light.

Martin looked up at her. 'Well, it's not flour, it's not sugar and it's certainly not salt. It looks to me as if we might have found what killed Oliver Calhoun.'

'So are all these boxes the same?' Felicity heard the nervousness in her own voice.

'Have to be,' said Martin, 'and if so, then there must be hundreds of thousands of pounds worth of drugs here. Inspector Penrose is certainly going to take you seriously now.'

'I really don't like it here, Martin,' said Felicity. 'It frightens me. Let's go, while we can. There's too much at stake. This isn't a game anymore, Martin. It's suddenly got very serious.'

'We'll save ourselves a lot of time by going this way,' said Martin, indicating the steps. He climbed them. There was no apparent bolt on the inside of the hatchway. He pushed, nothing happened; he pushed again. 'This is stuck fast,' he said. 'It must be secured from above.'

Felicity looked relieved. 'We'll just have to go back the way we came.'

Martin came down the steps and looked at her thoughtfully for a moment. 'That hatch isn't very thick,' he said. 'It's only made of ply. How would you feel about staying here while I dashed back up to the house? I'll only be five or six minutes. If you sat at the top of the steps and I went into the tackroom, if that is where the passageway comes out, we should be able to hear one another.'

'And what if it isn't? I don't like the idea of you leaving me here,' Felicity said, in sudden alarm.

'Of course I won't leave you, at least only for a few minutes. I'll just try the tackroom and if we can't hear one another, I'll come straight back to get you. Don't try to climb back along that path on your own, it will be getting dark very soon.'

'Why don't we just go together?' said Felicity, 'I really don't like the idea of being left alone here, it gives me the creeps.'

'We can do,' said Martin, 'I just thought it would be helpful to see where this passageway comes out. We know there is no one in the house and even if Michael's daughter did spot me, there would be no trouble, I promise. If I can get that hatch open, it will save you having to climb the cliff in the dark, and go back down the passage. It would also make life easier for Penrose,' he added, grimly.

'OK,' said Felicity. 'I'll sit up on the steps, right at the top. What will you do, call out, bang about?'

Martin smiled at her. 'Both,' he said, 'and remember don't try and leave here on your own. I'll come back for you if I can't open that hatchway.'

'You take care,' Felicity said, as Martin opened the door of the room and slipped into the passageway.

She didn't like being alone; it felt wrong. The room was far less musty and oppressive than the passageway had been, but the thought that she was sitting beside such an enormous cache of drugs made her feel very nervous. She tried to get her mind around what they had discovered. Ralph Smithson was clearly a drug dealer on an epic scale and somehow Charlie must have rumbled him – but how? If Ralph and Jack du Plessey were one and the same person, how had Charlie known that, too? Had they kept in touch after that long-ago trip to South Africa? It seemed most unlikely. A wife-beating drug dealer hardly seemed an appropriate companion for Charlie. She climbed up the steps and sat down close to the ceiling and the hatch. Her back ached and so did her legs and shoulders, now she came to think about it. What was she doing climbing up and down cliffs at her age? It was ridiculous. She smiled to herself, thinking of what her children would say if they could see her now. She suddenly felt very weary – Martin had been right to try and spare her the climb back up the cliff face.

The wait seemed to go on forever. She was almost in despair when she heard a movement above her, slightly to the right of the trapdoor. A footstep. 'Martin,' she called. There was no reply. There was the unmistakable sound of footsteps. 'Martin, Martin. Can you hear me?' She looked around her; there was a boat hook propped in one corner of the room. She ran down the steps, picked it up and returned to her position on the top step. If she bashed the hatchway hard enough with the boat hook, he would be bound to hear her. She was poised to start thumping when she heard a voice. She couldn't make out what was being said, just that it was a man's voice ... and then Felicity froze – there was a second man's voice. Both voices sounded angry. There was a shout, the sound of something falling heavily and a great commotion of voices and footsteps overhead, literally overhead. Felicity shrank back against the steps, expecting any moment for somebody to come hurtling through the hatch. There was more shouting and then, somehow worse than any of the commotion, there was a sudden silence. Felicity sat huddled on the steps, paralysed with shock. Even though the sounds were muffled, it was not difficult to imagine what had happened. Martin had been discovered, and attacked, it sounded like somebody had hit him, he'd fallen and then presumably had been dragged away. She shuddered – to what, the same fate as the 'Skunk'? She tried to calm down and think rationally – could she have misinterpreted the sounds, had he simply met up with Michael? Her heart was racing, she felt alternately hot, then cold and clammy, her hands shook. He had told her to stay where she was, that he would come back for her. Surely that's what he was going to do. The sounds in the tackroom were just him and Michael talking, perhaps they had moved a piece of equipment and it had it fallen. He would be back for her. Five or six minutes he reckoned the journey took between house and cliff, of course he would. She glanced at her watch. It was ten to seven. By seven o'clock, he would be here. Felicity pulled her knees up to her chest remaining seated on the top step and waited. It was the longest ten minutes of her life. Every time she looked at her watch, the hands appeared not to have moved at all. What had been a room with a bad atmosphere now felt like a prison. She kept staring at the rows of innocent-looking cardboard boxes. Had Oliver Colhoun's death sentence sat on these shelves once – Oliver Colhoun's and Charlie's?

When the ten minutes were up, there was still no sign of Martin. It must be completely dark now, Felicity told herself, it would take him longer to climb down the cliff. Fifteen minutes, twenty minutes, still nothing. By now Felicity had come down from the steps and was pacing up and down the little room. What to do? She had forced her mind to accept the unacceptable. Ralph Smithson must have returned home, discovered Martin and kidnapped him. There was no way Martin would have left her here if he'd had any choice in the matter. Felicity thought about the little passageway with dread. Having to find her own way back onto the cliff and then having to find the rope again – and what if, what if, Ralph knew she was here, and was coming for her even now? She stopped pacing. Think, think. She had called out Martin's name twice, but not loudly, and she had never got as far as thumping the hatchway because of the commotion overhead. Was it possible that Ralph, or whoever was up there with Martin, was not aware of her presence? Martin certainly wouldn't tell them. The sooner she got out of here, the sooner Inspector Penrose could start searching for Martin. Staying here could cost Martin his life. The thought propelled her into action. She hurried to the door, turned off the light and stepped into the passageway.

12

Michael and Katie Scott were not having an enjoyable evening. Their supper had been cleared away and they sat either side of the log fire in their cosy little sitting room. To the outsider, they would have appeared a picture of contentment and domestic bliss. In fact their thoughts were in turmoil and emotions were running very high. The cause of their distress was the discussion about their future they'd just had over supper. Michael loved Boswithey. He had been born in the lodge cottage where they now lived. It was also where they had raised their three children. Michael's father, Tom, had come first to Boswithey as a gardener's boy and had risen to be head gardener. Michael had followed in his father's footsteps, he had lived and breathed Boswithey all his life and now he was facing the realisation that they would have to leave. 'If the Brigadier hadn't died so sudden, he'd have looked after we,' Michael said.

'But he did, and he didn't,' Katie replied, firmly. 'It's no good Mike, you just can't go on day after day like this, knowing things aren't right, knowing we should do something about it. We can't just stand by while that bugger beats his wife senseless over and over. Either you, or I, or Polly should go to the police.'

'It's a domestic matter,' said Michael, 'police don't like to get involved in domestics.'

'But it's not just the beatings, is it?' said Katie. 'There is something going on here, something fishy. All these toings and froings, nothing to do with the gardens, and then Ron getting killed like that, burnt to death in the boot of his own car – he didn't put himself there, Mike.'

'The moment we tell the police anything, it will only be a matter of time before we have to leave here. Where do we go? What do I do?'

The note of panic in his voice softened his wife's attitude immediately. She leaned over and patted his knee. 'We'll be alright, love, we've got each other.'

'But no money saved to buy ourselves a little house. We should have saved more but I just never thought we'd have to leave.'

'We did our best,' said Katie, 'we gave our kids a good start. We'll find ourselves a little flat, Helston maybe, and I can get a cleaning job.'

'I don't want to live in a flat in Helston,' Michael burst out. 'I'm a countryman. We've worked hard all our lives, it isn't right. If we can't stay here, we'll just have to find a little cottage somewhere we can rent.'

'Oh, yes,' said Katie, bitterly, 'and where do you suppose you'll find a little cottage we can rent? Any cottage up for rent is a holiday home these days. A thousand pounds a week in season, they say, that's what people are charging now.'

'Never!' said Michael.

'On my life,' said Katie.

'Well, that's it then,' said Michael, 'the Poor House for us.'

As he spoke there was a frantic knocking on the front door of the lodge. The elderly couple looked up at one another in alarm.

'Now what?' Michael said.

'Be careful,' Katie warned.

'Be careful answering my own front door?' Michael said. 'If that's where we've got to then you're probably right, it's time we were off.'

He opened the door impatiently, a scowl on his face, which disappeared immediately, to be replaced by a look of concern. It was raining hard and the woman who was standing before him looked a mess. Her hair was plastered to her head; the boots, jeans and Barbour she was wearing were covered in mud. There were mud streaks on her face and on her hands. She was a pretty woman, thin as a wand, in her late forties he judged. What on earth had she been doing to get herself into that state?

'Are you Michael?' she asked. She appeared to be half-sobbing, half-panting with exertion.

'I am,' he replied.

'Look, I'm a friend of Martin Tregonning. He's in trouble. We need help desperately. I must call the police. Can I come in? I'll take my boots off.'

'Of course you can come in,' Michael said,

opening the door wide. 'What's happened? Where's Martin?'

The woman was busy removing her muddy boots. When she looked up, he recognised immediately the expression on her face – it was terror. She began struggling with her coat and despite having only just met the woman, Michael found himself helping her out of it.

'They've kidnapped him,' she managed, 'at least, I think that's what has happened.'

'Who're they?' Michael asked, gently, guiding her towards the sitting room.

'Ralph Smithson and his mob.'

Katie stood up as they entered the room. 'Who's this then, Mike?'

'I'm sorry, I'm sorry,' the woman said distractedly. 'My name is Felicity Paradise.'

'Some fancy name, that is,' Michael said to his wife.

It had not been a good day for Detective Inspector Keith Penrose either. He hated paperwork and the mass which had been accumulating on his desk, had threatened to overwhelm him. So he had spent the day wading through it and having completed everything that was outstanding, he should be enjoying a feeling of satisfaction – instead of which, he saw the day as a day lost. Somehow he had to find a way to nail Ralph Smithson for he shared Mrs Paradise's views on pretty much every aspect of the case. The question was how? He couldn't simply march into Boswithey and demand a DNA sample.

Besides which, would the South African government even be interested in Jack du Plessey after all these years? Times had changed in South Africa and there was plenty to worry about over there, far more pressing than some piece of low life who had caused trouble over a decade ago.

Keith's other problem was his wife. She had invited some friends to dinner. They were a dreary couple, incomers from London, pleasant enough but people with whom Keith struggled to find anything in common. His wife, by contrast, seemed to think they were wonderful because, he suspected, she considered them to be a step up the social ladder. He sighed at the thought of the weariness of the evening ahead. He always asked his wife not to make any social engagements for him mid-week, but she never took the slightest notice of him. He sighed and was reaching for his coat when the phone rang. He picked it up, almost eagerly, seeing it as a possible lifeline to escape the evening ahead. He was not disappointed.

'Inspector Penrose?' The voice sounded anxious, scared even, and he recognised it immediately.

'Mrs Paradise, what's happened?' He felt an instinctive sense of foreboding.

'I'm in trouble, Inspector, you're going to be very angry but I need your help and I need it now.'

'Calm down, Mrs Paradise. What's the problem?'

'Do you remember Martin Tregonning? I told you about him, the coastguard.'

'Yes,' said Inspector Penrose, slowly.

'He and I have been snooping around Boswithey.'

'Trespassing, you mean?'

'Yes Inspector, trespassing. We discovered a secret passageway up from the beach, well not the beach exactly, from the cliff.' She sounded as if she was crying.

'Go on,' he said.

'We found drugs, masses of them, in a room at the top of the passageway. Martin went to find another way into the room and he's been kidnapped. Oh, Inspector, I'm so frightened. Do you think they'll do to him what they did to the "Skunk"?'

'Where are you now?' Keith asked.

'I'm with Michael Scott, he's the head gardener. He lives in the lodge at Boswithey and he's one of the good guys, Inspector.'

'Right, stay where you are, answer the door to no one and I'm on my way. I'll pick up my sergeant and I'll be with you in ...' he glanced at his watch, 'half an hour, perhaps a little sooner. Have you a pencil? I'll give you my mobile. Call me if you are worried about anything or if there are any developments. I can get the boys out from Penzance, if need be.'

Minutes later, Inspector Penrose screeched to a halt outside a little terraced house opposite the station. His sergeant, Jack Curnow, came out of the house at a run, struggling into his jacket, sandwich in hand. His wife stood in the doorway watching them, a disgruntled expression on her face. Keith had no patience with Mrs Curnow. She shouldn't have married a policeman if she had expected her husband to work regular hours.

'What's up, sir?' Jack said, as he slammed the car door.

'I'm not quite sure yet,' said Keith, 'but I think it could be an interesting evening.'

Michael Scott was already standing at the door of the lodge as Inspector Penrose and his sergeant walked up the path.

'She's inside, she's in a right state,' he said.

At the sight of the familiar figure, Felicity had a strong desire to hug him, despite the very stern expression on his face.

'So what exactly have you been up to, Mrs Paradise?'

As quickly as she could, Felicity told Inspector Penrose everything. About the first trip to Boswithey the previous evening and the discovery of the passageway and what appeared to be a great deal of heroin.

'I've never seen heroin before but it's what Martin thought it was,'

'And Ralph Smithson, where is he now?'

'I don't know,' said Felicity, 'he was away, but I think he must have come back and discovered Martin. That's all I can think.'

'We'd better take a look up at the house.' Keith glanced up at Michael. 'I'd be grateful if you would accompany us, Mr Scott.'

'I'm coming too,' said Felicity. 'I need to show you where the passageway is.'

'Are you expecting there to be anyone in the house?' the Inspector asked as they began walking up the driveway.

'Not unless Mr Smithson has come back,' said Michael. 'Our daughter, Polly, is housekeeper up at the big house, but it's Wednesday, her half-day and she always spends the afternoon and night with her fiancé. He farms out Sennen way.'

There were no cars in the driveway and certainly the house looked deserted.

'We'll start with this tackroom,' said the Inspector. 'Do you have keys, Mr Scott?'

Michael shook his head. 'The tackroom shouldn't be locked, but only Polly has keys to the house.'

'Well, one step at a time.' Keith glanced at Jack. 'If there are the drugs Mrs Paradise describes on the premises, we'll need to call for back-up and at the same time, put out a search for this missing man. Do you want to lead the way, Mrs Paradise?'

Felicity fumbled with the lock of the tackroom; her hands were still icy, and cut and bruised from clambering up the cliff in the dark. She felt disorientated and frightened, above all frightened for Martin. Michael switched on the tackroom light and they looked around the room. It was not difficult to spot the trapdoor. There clearly had been some sort of disturbance, feed buckets were strewn across the floor, a pitchfork lay beside them. A pitchfork – Felicity wondered, with a sickening feeling, whether they'd used it on Martin. In the far corner, beyond a confusion of feed bins, there was the clear outline of a trapdoor in the floor.

'I've never noticed that before,' said Michael.

Inspector Penrose glanced at him. 'Is it normally covered up then?'

'Suppose it must be,' said Michael, 'I don't come in here much and it's always very cluttered.'

'Let's get this trapdoor open, Jack,' said Inspector Penrose.

The trapdoor opened easily, revealing the steps where, it seemed to Felicity a lifetime ago, she had crouched listening to the horrific sounds above.

'Right, Jack, down you go and see what you can see.'

'What the hell's going on here?' A booming voice made them all jump. They turned round and there, standing framed in the doorway, was Ralph Smithson. Felicity began trembling uncontrollably. She could feel the power of the man and his anger. Inspector Penrose stepped forward. Even in the midst of her fear, Felicity felt an instant admiration for him. He was a head and shoulders shorter than Ralph Smithson and at least ten years older, but he exuded authority and calm.

'We've had a report, sir, that there are some illegal substances on your premises and a man is missing. I'm here to question you about both but first we'd like to take a look in your cellar.' He turned to his sergeant. 'Right, off you go, lad.'

'I resent this intrusion, Inspector. Do you have a search warrant?'

'No, I don't,' Inspector Penrose replied, 'and nor do I need one. The gravity of the report I've

201

received is sufficient in itself.'

'Nothing down here, sir, that I can see,' Jack Curnow's voice drifted up through the hatchway.

Ralph Smithson raised an eyebrow, his large ruddy face taking on a supercilious expression. 'If you had simply asked me, Inspector, I could have told you there was nothing there.'

'There must be!' Felicity broke away from the group and before anyone could stop her, was clambering down the steps into the room. It was exactly as she had left it, except that all the cardboard boxes had disappeared.

Trembling from head to foot, Felicity climbed slowly back up the steps. She could not meet Inspector Penrose's eyes. 'He's right, there's nothing there now,' she murmured.

'*Now*! Nothing there *now*!' bellowed Ralph. 'Who is this damn woman and what's she doing in my house?'

Felicity would not have believed it possible to feel this humiliated and this terrified, all at the same time. 'Where's Martin?' she stammered, 'what have you done with him?'

Ralph loomed over her, his face now purple with rage. 'How dare you question me! I'm the one asking the questions. Who the hell are you?'

'My name's Felicity Paradise,' Felicity began, her voice cracking in terror at the hatred and venom coming from this man.

Just for a second, she saw a flicker of recognition in his eyes. Then she felt a reassuring hand on the elbow. 'Mrs Paradise, go with my sergeant to the car and wait there, while I speak to Mr Smithson,' said Inspector Penrose, gently but firmly. She was not about to argue.

Fifteen minutes later, Felicity was sitting in Keith Penrose's car, Jack Curnow having been relegated to the back seat. Privately, Keith Penrose was thanking God that his instincts had told him not to call for support until he had checked out Mrs Paradise's story. He would have looked a right idiot. 'So what am I going to do with you now, Mrs Paradise?'

The last few minutes with Ralph Smithson had been uncomfortable. With no evidence to support Felicity's allegations and with complete denial from Ralph Smithson as to Martin Tregonning's whereabouts, there was little he could do but to apologise and retire. Ralph had expressed fury at the intrusion and informed Inspector Penrose that he would be consulting his lawyer about trespass. He had also accused him of wasting police time.

'The car,' Felicity said suddenly, 'Martin's car.'

'What about it?' Keith asked.

'Well, presumably it will still be where we left it. Then perhaps you'll believe me.'

They drove out onto the road and up to the entrance in the field where hours before they had left the car. It was nowhere to be seen. 'God, they're good at this,' said Felicity. She climbed out of the car. 'You can see the tyre tracks.'

Keith joined her and looked at her quizzically. 'Along with everyone else's. This has to be a favourite spot for pulling off the road, look at the view.'

Mount's Bay lay below them, the lights of Newlyn and Penzance to their right. There was a large ship moored off, lights ablaze. The sea was calm and glassy, more like a lake and a beautiful shaft of moonlight cut a path across the water towards Newlyn. 'Inspector, don't you see what's happened. Ralph discovered Martin in the tackroom; he kidnapped him, removed evidence of him ever having been here and then shifted the heroin in case Martin had told anyone about it. What he hadn't bargained on was me. He didn't realise I was there. We can't just walk away from this, Inspector, we just can't, and what about Martin?'

'I'll file a missing person's report and I'll put Boswithey under surveillance. When tempers have simmered down, I'll go back and interview Ralph Smithson again, but apart from that, Mrs Paradise, there is very little I can do. It's your word against his.'

'Great,' said Felicity, 'and who do you think is the most reliable?'

'Getting angry with me isn't going to help. Now I think the best thing I can do is drive you home. You're still staying in St Ives?'

Felicity nodded.

Felicity barely spoke on the journey back to St Ives. She was suddenly exhausted, aching all over, and the fight had gone out of her. She desperately wanted to help Martin but couldn't think what else to do. This thing was beyond her, had become too big, too scary – meeting Ralph face to face for the first time had been a terrifying experience. She had, after all, witnessed the man in action when he'd dragged the 'Skunk' across the car park to his death, and now this brute of a man had Martin, somewhere. In desperation, she turned to Inspector Penrose. They were just dropping down into St Ives.

'Please believe me,' she begged. 'Ralph Smithson recognised my name, I'm sure of it.'

Keith, too, had seen the split second of recognition before Ralph had regained control of himself. Telling Mrs Paradise wasn't going to help her at this moment. 'I do believe you, Mrs Paradise,' he said soothingly. 'It's just that there is absolutely no evidence to support you, or help either of us.'

'But just imagine how we're going to feel if Martin's body turns up somewhere,' she shuddered. 'We should be doing something.'

'We are doing something,' said Inspector Penrose. He stopped the car on the wharf at the bottom of the lane leading up to Cormorant Cottage. 'Now, I want you to promise me, and I mean absolutely promise me, that there will be no more expeditions into other people's houses.'

'I promise.'

'Now, could you direct me to Martin Tregonning's cottage? We'll just have a look around, and make sure he hasn't gone home.'

'He wouldn't have left me, Inspector.'

'Nonetheless ...' he hesitated.'I don't suppose you have a key to his cottage, do you, Mrs Paradise?'

Felicity blushed at the insinuation. 'No, of course not, I've only known him a week or two. It's not that sort of relationship at all, Inspector. We've both recently lost our respective spouses, that's all we have in common.'

Keith ignored the reprimand. 'If you would just tell us the whereabouts of his cottage – even after all these years, I still get lost in St Ives.' His attempt to lighten the mood was lost on Felicity – she continued to glare at him as she gave directions. 'Right then, Jack will see you to your door, Mrs Paradise. Try to get a good night's sleep.'

He watched as Jack Curnow escorted Felicity up the cobbled street towards Cormorant Cottage. She was still caked in mud, which certainly lent authenticity to her story. Did he believe her? Yes, of course he did. Just then his mobile phone rang; wearily he reached for it and his own home number flashed up. He had completely forgotten the dinner party.

The following morning Felicity felt as if she was under house arrest. Having picked at breakfast, she went to her room to fetch her coat and on her return found Annie, bristling with rage, standing between her and the front door.

'And where do you think you're going, my bird?'

'I'm going for a walk,' said Felicity, 'just to try to clear my head.'

'And why should I believe a word you say?'

'Oh, Annie, please. We went through all this last night. I've been lectured by Inspector Penrose and by you. It's all such a mess – Penrose is threatening to charge me with trespass, Martin is God knows where and nobody seems to be taking his disappearance seriously enough.'

'I'm taking it seriously enough,' said Annie, 'which is why I want to know exactly what you're going to do next. You're not going back to Boswithey, are you?'

It was amazing, Felicity thought, how a woman of such small stature and tiny frame could be so intimidating. Felicity shook her head. 'I promise you, I'll be back within an hour or so. I'm just going to walk around the Island. If I stay here, I'll go mad.'

Annie reluctantly stood aside. 'I've been in this trade for forty years and you are by far the most troublesome guest I've ever had.' Despite her words, a small smile was fighting to make an appearance.

Impulsively, Felicity swept her into a hug. 'How weird,' she said, holding Annie at arm's length, 'when you're quite the best landlady I've ever had.'

'No more than an hour, now,' Annie said, clearly not in the mood to be charmed.

It was a crisp, clear autumn morning and one of those days that, in normal circumstances, Felicity would have loved. The light was golden, warming the old stone cottages and the rocky shoreline, throwing long shadows across the sand where the pools left behind by the tide also reflected the golden light. It was magical, but this morning's beauty was lost on her. Her head ached and her limbs still felt sore and heavy from her frantic climb in the dark, back up the cliff face, after Martin's disappearance. It had been a terrifying ordeal, made worse by the fact that, at every turn, she expected somebody to be lying in wait for her. The idea of going straight to Michael had been inspirational, but in the end, despite all her best efforts, she had not been able to save Martin. She trudged up the Digey and at the Tate, climbed down onto Porthmeor beach. For once, there was no wind, the tide was way out. She slowed her pace and began walking across the sands to the Island. She was very tempted to go to Martin's cottage. It was ridiculous to expect him to be there, she knew that. In any event, instinct told her there were bound to be police officers about. They might think it odd her going to the cottage – as if she knew something she was not telling them, or even, worse still, making up his disappearance. This thought made her wonder about Keith Penrose. There had been moments, the previous evening, when she had got the impression he thought she was fabricating the whole story.

Halfway round the island, Felicity's strength seemed to leave her and she sat down on a bench and stared out across the sea towards Godrevy lighthouse. If Martin had been injured, or even killed, it would be entirely her fault. She had talked him into coming to Boswithey with her, not only once but twice, and he had been reluctant to do so on both occasions, but especially the second time. In her arrogance, she had ignored advice from everyone and refused to accept that the police were doing their job in their own good time. Her actions would probably rebound on poor old Michael Scott as well. Ralph had seen him with her and the police and as a result, he would almost certainly lose his job, and his home.

Her meddling was messing up people's lives and was she really any nearer to understanding why Charlie had died? The answer, of course, was no, and why did it even matter anyway? An eye for an eye – the man who had killed Charlie was dead, too, now – wasn't that enough?

Her feet seemed to be made of lead as she climbed the steps by the coastguard's lookout. She arrived at the top of the island, puffing and panting, feeling old beyond her years. She gazed out across the town. 'Where are you, Martin?' she whispered. She felt too tired and drained to walk back through town and decided to take a shortcut across Porthgwidden car park. When she reached home, she decided, she would ring Inspector Penrose and ask whether he had made any progress. The one concession he had made the previous evening had been to give her his mobile number. She was halfway across the car park when she saw it – parked, she realised, in his reserved car parking space. With a pounding heart, she walked up and peered through the windows of the car. There was absolutely no mistaking it – it was Martin's battered old Volvo.

'I mustn't make a fool of myself again,' she thought, 'I must be absolutely sure I'm right.' She walked around it a couple of times. Her heart gave a lurch, when she recognised his old fleece on the back seat. There was definitely no mistake. With a trembling hand she dialled Keith Penrose's mobile number.

'Penrose.' He sounded terse and decidedly unfriendly.

'Inspector Penrose, it's Felicity Paradise. I've found Martin's car.'

There was a pause. 'I thought we agreed you'd stay in town, Mrs Paradise. Where are you and where is the car?'

'I have stayed in town, Inspector Penrose. It's parked in his reserved car parking space in Porthgwidden. It's as if we never went to Boswithey.'

'I'll be with you in five minutes. Porthgwidden, you say?'

'Five minutes, that's quick.'

'Yes, I'm at Martin Tregonning's cottage at the moment.'

'Have you found anything, have you heard anything?'

'I'm afraid not, Mrs Paradise. Just wait by the car for me, would you?'

Good as his word, within five minutes Felicity saw Keith and his sergeant drive into the top end of the car park.

'Are you absolutely certain that this is Martin Tregonning's car?' Keith Penrose asked as he and Jack Curnow joined her.

'Absolutely,' said Felicity, 'I double-checked before I rang you. There is no doubt about it and it's parked correctly in his reserved parking space. How could it have ended up here, Inspector?'

'There are a number of explanations. Whoever is holding Martin Tregonning thought that the best way to dispose of his car was to simply put it where it belonged. Alternatively, Mr Tregonning could have driven it here himself, or,' at this point Inspector

Penrose had the grace to avoid eye contact, 'the car could have been here all the time.'

'You think I'm making up the story about us going to Boswithey?' She felt a sense of dread creeping over her.

Keith Penrose forced himself to look Felicity in the eye. 'We have to consider all possibilities, Mrs Paradise.'

Felicity was so angry and upset she could think of absolutely nothing to say. Keith circled the car for a moment, or two, then murmured something to his sergeant. Moments later Jack returned from the police car with a set of keys which he began inserting in the boot lock. Standing either side of the car watching him, Keith's eyes met Felicity's. Two emotions assailed her, one after the other – firstly, the look of sympathy and kindness on Keith's face made her realise that he was just going through the motions, that he did believe her, that he did understand what she was going through; and secondly, this momentary relief was overcome by the sudden realisation of what he was asking his sergeant to do – he was checking to see if Martin's body was in the boot of his own car. At the same moment as the realisation struck her, Jack said 'Got ya!' and the boot sprang open. Together, Felicity and Keith stepped forward and peered in. The boot was empty.

'Call forensics and stay with the vehicle until they arrive,' Keith said to Jack. 'Where are you going now, Mrs Paradise?'

'I was going back to Cormorant Cottage,' said Felicity. She felt sick and faint. Distractedly, she ran a hand through her hair and could feel her hand trembling as she did so.

'Then, would you mind if I walked with you?'

'No,' said Felicity, 'I'd like it.'

We must look an odd couple, she thought, trying desperately to calm her shattered nerves by focusing on the trivial. Inspector Penrose was looking particularly dapper in a dark suit and sombre tie in contrast to her jeans, still muddy boots and ancient Puffa jacket.

'How well do you know Martin Tregonning?' Inspector Penrose asked, cutting through any chance she might have had to recover herself.

'I thought we went through all this last night,' said Felicity, 'I don't know him that well at all.'

'How did you meet?'

'I bumped into him on the pier, when I was pursuing one of the contacts Ralph Smithson had made when he was in the Sloop. I asked for Martin's help in identifying the boat, the fishing boat I mentioned to you, *Jayne Marie*, and then we had a coffee and talked. We … ' she felt tears well into her eyes, 'we have quite a lot in common. His wife was killed in a car crash in Scotland last May.' Her voice trailed away.

'You know he worked for Ralph Smithson?'

'Yes, of course,' said Felicity.

'And was sacked, according to Smithson, because he was having an affair with Smithson's wife.'

'Not an affair,' Felicity said hotly. 'Amelia was just kind to him in the weeks immediately after his wife's death.'

'And who told you that?'

'Well, Martin of course.'

'I'd like you to consider the possibility, Mrs Paradise, that Martin Tregonning could be involved in all this.'

Felicity stopped dead in her tracks. 'You are absolutely wrong about that, Inspector Penrose.'

'And what makes you so sure?'

'If he was still working for Ralph Smithson, say, helping him with his drugs scam, he would never have agreed to take me to Boswithey. Think about it, would he have allowed me to find the passageway and the huge drugs haul? Of course he wouldn't. All he had to do was to have refused to take me and I would have been quite incapable of discovering anything on my own. Besides which, Inspector, he's a decent honourable man, I'm sure of it.'

'Based on what, three weeks' acquaintance?'

'I'm not a child, Inspector. I think I'm a reasonably good judge of character.' Even as she spoke the words, she began to wonder if they were true. Why was his car back here in St Ives, why had he abandoned her when he had promised to come back? She felt her mind being sucked down into some dark whirlpool of confusion, caused by the insidious undermining of her confidence. Keith Penrose's methods were certainly very effective. She shook her head, as if to clear it. 'I truly believe he's been kidnapped, Inspector Penrose, and I also believe that if you don't find him soon, he will be killed.'

'We've been trying to locate this drugs haul you allege you saw. How many boxes are we talking about and what sort of size?' Inspector Penrose was becoming increasingly business-like and impersonal.

Felicity tried to match his mood. She stopped walking for a moment and leaned on the stone wall by the museum, gazing out across the bay. She closed her eyes and tried to focus on the little underground cellar below the tackroom. 'There were about three dozen boxes I should think, could be a few more. They were square, about twelve inches by twelve and quite deep, six or eight inches.'

'Ordinary brown cardboard?' Inspector Penrose asked.

'Yes.'

'No labels?'

'No.'

'Difficult for someone to remove and hide all those boxes in such a short space of time,' Keith suggested.

'It wasn't really such a short space of time,' Felicity corrected. 'After I heard the noises above me in the tackroom, I waited – for at least quarter of an hour, probably twenty minutes – before I decided Martin wasn't coming back. Then it took me ages to go back down the passage and then to climb back up the cliff in the dark.'

'Ages?' Keith asked. He was certainly far from sympathetic about her ordeal.

'Half an hour,' said Felicity, 'and then I had to creep through the grounds and find Michael's lodge. That probably took another fifteen minutes. Then I had to wait for you to arrive and tell you what was going on. It must have been nearly two hours from the time I first heard the scuffle overhead to when we opened the trapdoor in the tackroom. Plenty of time, Inspector, to move a few dozen boxes and hide them, they weren't even particularly heavy. Have you searched the house?'

Inspector Penrose had joined her, leaning too on the harbour wall. 'Are you trying to teach me my job again, Mrs Paradise.'

'No, but I am concerned you're not taking Martin's disappearance seriously enough, that you are wasting precious time doubting my story, when you should be trying to find Martin before it's too late.'

Keith turned and regarded her in silence for a moment. 'Would it help if I told you that we have made a thorough search of Boswithey, the main house, the outbuildings, even those open to the public, the passageway and the cliffs and beach area? There is no sign of either the infamous cardboard boxes or Mr Tregonning.'

'I bet Ralph was happy with you doing that.'

Inspector Penrose allowed himself a small smile. 'It was necessary to get a search warrant,' he admitted.

'So what happens now?' Felicity asked.

'We keep looking. Tell me, did Mr Tregonning have a mobile?'

'Yes, he did,' said Felicity, 'and I've been ringing it ever since. Would you like the number?'

'Please.' Keith began patting his pockets

looking for a pencil and paper.

'Just put it straight on your mobile, Inspector.' Felicity said.

Keith looked embarrassed. 'I've no idea how to do that, Mrs Paradise, that's the truth of it.'

'Here, let me teach you.'

Keith watched in silence while Felicity tapped in the number. 'I've put it under Martin T,' she said.

'I'm not very good with gadgets,' Inspector Penrose admitted.

'Certainly your office would be a lot tidier if you learnt to use a laptop.'

They exchanged a smile. 'You're starting to sound like my wife,' he said.

Felicity was allowed out of Cormorant Cottage at lunchtime – partly for good behaviour and partly because Annie had to go and see one of her husband's surviving sisters, who was not well.

'I'm sorry I can't give you a bit of lunch here,' said Annie, 'I've just had such a busy morning, cleaning up after the guests. There'll be no one until half term now, except you, of course. I can't get rid of you. Can I trust you out and about, my girl, no running off?'

'I'm so sorry,' said Felicity, 'I should have helped you, and yes, you can trust me.'

'Alright, my girl, I'll see you later.'

Felicity settled on the Caffé Pasta for lunch. She ordered a glass of wine and a salad but could work up no enthusiasm for either. How could she be sitting here enjoying lunch when Martin ... her mind recoiled from what he could be going through. She forced her mind once more to consider the insinuations that Inspector Penrose had made, that perhaps Martin was still working for Ralph Smithson in some capacity. It was an idea she simply could not entertain, but it was an unsettling idea nonetheless. She recognised that in the months since Charlie's death, there had been times when her behaviour was somewhat irrational and her thoughts out of control. Was it possible that she had been taken in by Martin's good looks and tragic story? Was it possible that she was such a poor judge of character that he had made a complete fool of her?

She picked through her meal, paid the bill and was just leaving the restaurant, when her mobile phone rang. It was Michael. 'Just thought I'd check up on you and see how you're feeling, my dear?'

'Oh Michael, that's so kind of you. I suppose you haven't heard any news, have you?'

'Not a thing, but there have been police crawling all over Boswithey most of the morning. Mr Smithson is beside himself with fury, they say. I've just kept well clear of him but Polly has had a rough morning.'

'And they've found nothing?'

'Don't think so,' said Michael, 'certainly nothing they're prepared to share with anyone.'

'You do believe me, don't you,' Felicity asked, 'about Martin disappearing and the drugs and all that?'

'Course I do,' said Michael, 'and so does the wife. Now, don't you fret, he's a big strong lad, well capable of looking after himself. Oh, one piece of news – Mrs Smithson's home, she arrived back by taxi early this afternoon. She's still very frail, Polly says.'

'I'm sure her husband was delighted to see her,' said Felicity, sarcastically.

'Oh, he'd already left by the time his wife got back from hospital. No change there.'

'Where's he gone?' Felicity asked.

'I don't know,' said Michael, 'he didn't say. Said he would be away tonight and that the police knew of his whereabouts, that's all he told Polly.'

'So he's leaving his wife alone on her first night back from hospital?'

'She's got Polly and after what he's done to her over the years, I should think Mrs Smithson's grateful he's not around, particularly in the mood he's in at the moment with the police swarming all over the place.'

'I'll call you if I hear anything, Michael.'

'Thanks my dear and I'll do the same.'

Even as she switched off her phone, an idea was forming in Felicity's mind. Amelia was on her own in the house, she was recovering from a violent attack made on her by her husband who had not even had the good manners' never mind the compassion, to welcome her home or see to her welfare in any way. Amelia clearly had been fond of Martin. She had tried to help him through the worst of his grief, even though she must have known that she would incur her husband's wrath if he ever found out that she had been entertaining his estate manager. Maybe, just maybe, this would be the moment when Amelia Smithson would be prepared to talk.

13

Annie's obsession with *Neighbours* was total. Nothing was allowed to interrupt her viewing schedule, which happened twice a day. Felicity could not understand why it was necessary for her to see the repeats, given that the plot could be grasped first time round by any averagely intelligent person over the age of eighteen months. Annie's excuse was that her youngest son lived in Australia and watching *Neighbours* helped her feel more in touch with him. Having teased Annie constantly over her dedicated interest in the goings on in Ramsey Street, at this particular moment, Felicity thanked God for it.

All afternoon the conviction that she should go and confront Amelia had been growing and with Annie glued to the television, she knew she could slip out without being seen. This meant she could be at Boswithey by six, which seemed a good time to visit somebody who had just come out of hospital. She knew what she was doing was a risk, possibly dangerous – very dangerous – but she had to do something. She had checked her mobile phone a hundred times during the day in the hopes of a call from Keith Penrose. There had been none. Martin, if he was still alive – she shuddered at the thought – had clearly not been found and every hour that he was missing put his life at greater danger.

It was a cold, clear evening, as she climbed the hill to Barnoon car park. The wind was icy; she bowed her head and struggled on and when she reached the shelter of the car, she sat for a few moments at the wheel, going over again in her mind what she was doing, and why. She wondered if she should tell someone where she was going in case she too disappeared, but who? Keith Penrose was out of the question for he would forbid her to go. Annie would undoubtedly shop her to the police if she tried to go back to Boswithey. Suddenly she thought of Gilla. She reached for her mobile and began to text her oldest friend.

'Getting near to solving the problem,' she texted. 'If I go missing and anyone asks you where I am, say I went to Boswithey to see Amelia Smithson. Lots of love. Be home soon. Fizzy xx.' She pressed Send, took a deep breath and started the engine.

Felicity was still driving through Carbis Bay when the door bell began ringing repeatedly at Cormorant Cottage. For a while, Annie didn't hear it. She had the television volume up very loud – she was getting a little deaf, although she wasn't prepared to admit it. It was only when the sound of hammering on the door reached her that she turned the volume down and, cursing the interruption, went to investigate the commotion. She opened the front door, cautiously. A burly young man in a fisherman's jersey stood on the step outside.

'Hello, my lover,' she said, 'what can I do for you?'

'I've come to see Felicity Paradise. Is she in?'

'I think so,' said Annie, 'I'll call her.' Annie called up the stairs. There was no response. 'That's odd,' she said, 'she was here a moment ago. I'll go up and check.'

'Don't bother, I'll go myself,' he said, roughly.

'No, you won't.' Annie stood her ground in front of the stairs. With a vicious swipe of his arm, the young thug hurled her aside. Annie's head cracked painfully against the open door of the parlour. She slumped to the floor, dazed. 'You leave her alone,' she managed.

'Shut up, you silly old bitch, which room is she in?'

'I'm not telling you,' Annie began.

He leaned forward, almost casually, and delivered a powerful blow to the side of Annie's head. She fell sideways, silently, a thin line of blood escaping from the corner of her mouth. The man stood over her for a moment. Silly old cow was out cold, no point wasting time with her. He gave the fragile body a vicious kick and bounded up the stairs.

With Ralph away, Felicity decided there was nothing to be gained by creeping into Boswithey by Martin's circuitous route. The simplest thing to do was to go up the driveway and park in front of the house. It was dusk by the time she arrived. The house looked deserted except for one light in a room at the front of the house on the ground floor, and at the top of the house on the third floor, to the extreme left. There were no other cars in the drive and the lights suggested that Polly had probably gone up to her quarters and that Amelia was in some downstairs sitting room, hopefully alone, hopefully without Ralph. At the thought of seeing Ralph Smithson again, Felicity felt her stomach lurch. Was she mad to be back here? Yes, of course she was, but she really felt there was no other alternative.

Cold and scared, she got out of the car. She decided to leave it unlocked, thinking it would be easier to make a quick get away if she needed to. She had also turned it round so it faced the driveway, for the same reason. She slipped the car key into her jeans pocket so that it would be easy to reach if she was separated from her handbag. What else could she do to help herself? Nothing. She rang the doorbell.

There was a moment's silence and then the porch light snapped on. The door swung open and there, standing before her, was a woman of about her own age or a few years younger who could be no one but Amelia Smithson. Felicity's carefully-prepared speech died on her lips. Even now, Amelia wasn't simply good-looking or pretty, she was beautiful. Her hair was pure white, her cheekbones were high, giving her face a sculpted look and the dominant features of her face were two huge, china blue eyes. She had a petite, perfect little nose and a full mouth. All that marred her otherwise exquisite appearance was the clouded look in her eyes and her hesitant, nervous manner.

'Can I help you?' she asked. She leaned heavily on the door, one arm in a sling; clearly standing up was painful.

'I'm terribly sorry to trouble you,' Felicity began, 'but are you Mrs Smithson, Mrs Amelia Smithson?'

The expression on Amelia's face turned to alarm. 'Yes, I am,' she stammered. 'Why do you want to know?'

'I'm terribly sorry to trouble you,' said Felicity. 'I rang earlier in the day,' she lied, 'and was told that you were just coming out of hospital. I appreciate that this is not a good time, but I wondered if I could just talk to you for a few minutes.'

Some of the tension seemed to leave her. 'May I ask why?' There was no trace of a South African accent in her voice, as there was in Ralph's. She spoke perfect, upper class, BBC English.

Felicity had prepared carefully for this question. 'When my husband was in South Africa, he met your husband. My husband sadly died recently and I am trying to gather some information about his past for my children and grandchildren. I was just hoping you might be able to help.' Felicity had suspected the loaded question would shock Amelia and she was not disappointed. The big blue eyes widened in terror, there was a trembling around the mouth.

'We don't have any friends from our South African days,' she began, 'we haven't lived there for a long time.'

'Oh, really?' said Felicity. 'I thought you'd only

been in this country for ten years.'

'That's true.' Amelia's voice trailed away. She frowned in concentration. Felicity suddenly suspected that although there was no disputing Amelia's glorious looks, she was probably not terribly bright. She could almost see her mind working. 'How could this woman's husband have known Ralph in South Africa when he was living under a different name? What should I do? What should I say?' Felicity seized the moment while Amelia dithered on the doorstep.

'Would it be possible to come in for just a few moments? It's absolutely freezing and you look like you should be sitting down.'

The drawing room of Boswithey was charming. It appeared to be Queen Anne in proportions with a beautiful old fireplace. It was furnished sympathetically in a colour scheme of pale green and dove grey. It was a restful room and Felicity judged it to be far more in Amelia's taste than Ralph's. Once inside the sanctuary of her drawing room, Amelia recovered a little.

'Would you care for a drink?' she asked.

'No, I'm fine,' Felicity replied. 'I really don't want to intrude on your time for more than a few minutes.'

'Well, sit down, at least,' said Amelia, 'I'm afraid I'll have to. As you must have heard, I had a little accident – so silly of me and I'm still rather sore.'

'How are you feeling now?' Felicity asked.

Amelia winced as she lowered herself into the

chair. 'Not too bad. It's my ribs which cause all the pain. Everyone said it would be my collarbone that hurt most but it's not the case. I'm sorry. I don't even know your name.'

'My name is Felicity Paradise.' Felicity watched Amelia's expression carefully, but there appeared to be no hint of recognition. She took a deep breath. 'I lied,' she continued, without preamble. 'I lied to get in here in order to talk to you. I'm actually a friend of Martin Tregonning and I'm worried sick because he's disappeared, as you probably know. I believe your husband has something to do with his disappearance.'

'Are you something to do with what happened yesterday?' Amelia asked, at once agitated again. 'Polly told me that my husband found Martin and a woman friend of his trespassing in the tackroom. The police were called, I understand, in fact they were still here when I came back from hospital but they kindly said they wouldn't interview me until tomorrow, so that I had time to settle in.' She paused. 'I can't think what they want to interview me about.' Her voice trailed away.

'Yes, I was the woman who was here with Martin yesterday,' Felicity said. 'We've become friends in recent weeks.'

Amelia looked at her properly for the first time. 'I'm glad Martin's got someone in his life, he's a very nice man and he was so devastated by the loss of his wife and baby.'

'I'm not in his life,' said Felicity, 'I am simply what I said, a friend. I lost my husband too, just a few months ago, and that's all Martin and I have in common.'

'Oh,' said Amelia, with apparently genuine concern. 'I'm so sorry about your husband.'

'So you should be,' said Felicity, with a venom she could no longer control.

Amelia started at her words, reacting almost as though she had been slapped, recoiling back into her chair. 'I don't understand!' she said. 'I don't even know your husband.'

'And neither will anyone else now,' said Felicity. The anger and frustration that had been building in her all day had reached boiling point. She knew she should be tactful with this fragile, nervous, broken woman but the clock was ticking away and, instinctively, Felicity knew another life would be lost if she didn't act quickly. 'I'm going to tell you a story,' she said, 'and I want you to listen very carefully.'

Felicity began at the beginning, with her concerns about Charlie taking the Carver case, right through to the horrific disappearance of Martin the previous day. By the time she had finished, Amelia seemed to have shrunk. The already tiny woman looked pale and suddenly much older. Her beauty was still there, but, like everything else about her, it was diminished.

'So,' said Felicity, 'are you going to help me?'

'I'm sorry,' Amelia stammered, 'I really don't know anything about my husband's business colleagues. Men come and go, some of them I know don't work here on the estate, but I really couldn't identify any of them, even the one you call – the "Skunk" – I don't remember him at all.'

She was lying and she making a very poor job of it. There was absolutely no point in being subtle. 'Maybe you can't confirm details of your husband's business contacts, and I'm not even asking you whether you know of his involvement in the drugs trade, all I want to do is to find Martin. Please tell me if you have even the slightest idea where your husband might be holding him. Any delay could cost Martin his life. It's not fair that he should have become involved in all this; he was only trying to help me. Despite being sacked by your husband, he had no desire for revenge; he's a gentle man and a very damaged one too, at the moment. I know you are fond of him and I know he thinks the world of you. Please help him.'

There was a long tense silence.

'You're right about Martin,' Amelia said at last. 'I certainly wouldn't want anything to happen to him. The poor man has been through enough.' She glanced up nervously at Felicity. 'He was very kind to me. We used to talk a lot in the gardens. I was trying to help him in those first dreadful weeks after the crash but, in a strange way, I think he ended up helping me more than I, him.'

Felicity drove home her advantage. 'Whatever you tell me now, it may already be too late. He could well be dead, so please, please, no more delays.'

Amelia gasped. 'Please don't say that, please don't. I've got nothing to tell you, nothing at all. I have absolutely no involvement with my husband's business.'

'Just stop it,' said Felicity, jumping to her feet. 'I don't want to hear any more of this. I just can't understand why you're protecting your husband. Look at the state you're in, he could have killed you.'

'These injuries were the result of my stupidly falling down the stairs,' said Amelia. There were tears in her eyes and for the first time, Felicity realised she had a nervous tick on the left hand side of her face, an uncontrollable spasm. It should have made her feel compassionate; instead it had the reverse effect. Something about this woman's ineffectualness, her total inability to face up to the truth, finally pricked the bubble that had been building in Felicity all day. She strode across the room, stopping within inches of Amelia's chair.

'Stop it!' she shouted, 'I can't stand any more of this rubbish! Why deny it? It's pointless – everyone knows your husband beats you! Every minute we sit here, your precious husband – who you seem so anxious to protect – could be killing Martin who, as you say, doesn't deserve to die. Your silence was responsible for my husband's death.' She leant towards Amelia. 'Is another man going to die because of your cowardice?'

Amelia shrank back into the chair and Felicity realised, with a shock, that she had assumed Felicity was going to hit her. So used was she to being struck that, clearly, the reaction was entirely instinctive. The gesture drained the anger from Felicity, but she did not draw away from the chair, sensing that, like a cornered animal, it was just possible this was the moment Amelia would give up. There was a long agonising silence and finally Amelia managed in a strangled voice. 'Ralph sometimes has meetings on his boat.'

'The *Jayne Marie*?'

Amelia looked startled. 'You know the boat?'

'Yes, I do,' said Felicity. 'Where is it at the moment?'

'I don't know,' Amelia whispered. 'I've been in hospital. I've been out of touch.'

'Think,' said Felicity, leaning in closer. In a moment it seemed as if Amelia would disappear in to the upholstery.

'Before my accident I think he said he was taking her round to moor off Newlyn.'

Felicity let out a sigh. 'OK,' she said, patiently, 'so let me get this straight. If Ralph hasn't killed Martin already, then you think it's likely he will be holding him prisoner on the *Jayne Marie*?' Amelia nodded, she was crying now, quietly, hopelessly. She had finally cracked. Time to try for just one more piece of information. 'Who are you?' Felicity asked. 'Who are you really?'

'I don't know what you mean!' Amelia said, glancing up but avoiding Felicity's eyes.

Felicity decided on the spur of the moment that there was nothing to be lost. 'I know who your husband really is. I know his real name is Jack du Plessey.'

Amelia's eyes widened for a moment, then she looked down at her hands, which she was twisting in her lap. 'I've nothing else to tell you.'

'I think you owe me, of all people, some sort of explanation,' Felicity said, her voice dangerously calm now.

'What do you mean?' Amelia asked.

'If you hadn't protected Ralph all these years and provided him with a respectable front for his crimes, my husband would probably be alive. No, not probably, Charlie would *certainly* be alive. Your silence, Amelia, has been as damaging to my family as if you had driven the car yourself.'

'What car? I don't understand,' Amelia sobbed.

There was nothing more to be gained here, Felicity realised that. 'I'd better go,' she said, standing up.

'Where are you going?' Amelia stammered.

'To Newlyn.'

'Will you tell the police?'

'Of course,' said Felicity, 'and if you want to do anything to try and put matters right, then the least you can do is to tell them everything you know. The charade that's been going on at Boswithey all these years, it's over, Amelia. The drugs Martin and I found were a massive haul. I know they've been moved, I know that we've no proof to show the police, but we both saw them. Just think for a moment of the human misery that's been meted out by your husband; the young people, their lives cut short by drug dependency and in some cases, like poor Oliver Colhoun, death. I just don't know how you can sleep at night.'

Amelia tried to speak, tried to stand up, too, but she was so distressed, she slumped back in the chair.

231

Without another word Felicity walked to the drawing room door.

'Felicity,' Amelia managed to call after her. 'You asked who I am. The clue is in the boat, you see. It's my name, Jayne Marie, Jayne Marie du Plessey.'

Felicity ran down the steps of the house, jumped into her car and started the engine. She had a plan. She would drive to the lodge and use Michael's telephone, that way she could inform Inspector Penrose where Martin was likely to be. With a bit of luck Michael might come with her to Newlyn. She wondered where Inspector Penrose was, hoping he was still in St Ives and not in Truro. She slipped her car into third gear as she drove as fast as she dared down the drive. Just at the final bend before Michael's lodge, a car came out of the woods that bordered the drive, right in front of her. She slammed on the brakes, skidded, hitting her head on the steering wheel. She stopped just short of colliding with the car. With a sinking heart she recognised it immediately. It was the Boswithey Range Rover. Still dazed, she tried to move but before she could, two men were bundling her out of her car. She began to protest, to scream, hoping her shouts would reach Michael. She felt a prick in her arm and then nothing.

14

Inspector Keith Penrose watched the ambulance pull away, cursing his stupidity. Of course, whoever had taken Martin Tregonning would want Mrs Paradise as well. What Martin had seen, she had seen. He should have kept her under police protection; instead of which, she was missing and a sweet little old lady had been battered half to death. As they loaded her into the ambulance, although semi-conscious, the old girl had been absolutely adamant about one thing. The man who had attacked her hadn't got Felicity. It was Felicity who he had wanted but she had not been there. 'She must have crept out,' Annie slurred, 'while I was watching *Neighbours*, the minx.'

Jack was at his side. 'Where to now then, sir?'

'Just give me five minutes, would you?' Keith walked briskly down the hill to the Wharf and stood gazing out across the harbour. Think, think, what would you do if you were her, what madcap scheme would she get up to now? Once again, he felt he had handled Felicity Paradise badly. Insinuating that Martin Tregonning might have been in on the scam – that was stupid. It must have driven her to take the law into her own hands because she now sees me as the enemy. So where would she go?

His frustration and concern was such that he began pacing up and down the Wharf. Suddenly he stopped in his tracks. The wretched woman would have gone back to Boswithey; she'd have broken in again and tried to mount a search. Martin Tregonning wasn't there, he was sure of it, but Felicity Paradise didn't know that. 'Damn!' He turned on his heel and began running up towards his car. 'Jack,' he roared, 'come on. We're going to Boswithey.'

They were just dropping down through Gulval when they took the call. There had been an incident at Boswithey. A Michael Scott had telephoned to speak to Inspector Penrose. Could he go there straight away? There had also been a telephone call from a friend of Mrs Paradise's, saying she had texted her to say she was going to Boswithey, and that it sounded dangerous.

'Bugger,' said Keith. 'What the hell has happened? Put your foot down, Jack. If something has happened to that woman, I'll never forgive myself. It's all my fault.'

'I don't think so, sir, she's not easy to control, that one.'

'Shut up, Jack, and just drive. You concentrate on what you're doing and just ignore me, I'm thinking aloud.'

'Sorry, sir.'

The police car slewed through the gates of Boswithey. Michael Scott was standing outside his lodge.

'Just go on up the drive there, Inspector,' he said. 'That's her car. There's a letter addressed to her on the seat.'

'Mrs Paradise's?' Inspector Penrose shouted, beside himself with tension.

'Yes,'

'Is she in it, is she hurt?'

Michael shook his head. 'Nowhere to be seen, I'm afraid.'

Jack drove the few yards down the drive and there, sure enough, was Felicity's car. It had obviously been in a near collision, there were skid marks, and the driver's door was hanging open. Michael arrived, panting, on foot. 'I've put up a note to say the gardens are closed tomorrow morning, sir. I hope I did the right thing, only I didn't think you'd want to move the car for a while.'

'You did absolutely the right thing, thank you,' said Penrose. 'Jack, call for back-up and forensics, we'd better get this checked out. Where had she come from, Michael, had she been to see you?'

Michael shook his head. 'No sir, she must have been coming from the big house.'

'From the house, but surely she would never have driven up there, not after what happened yesterday?'

'I've been thinking the same, sir,' said Michael, 'been going over it in my mind. I think it is all my fault.'

'How do you mean?'

'I told her Mrs Smithson was out of hospital and

235

Mr Smithson was away. I reckon she went to visit Mrs Smithson to see if she knew where Martin has fetched up.'

Inspector Penrose stared at Michael. 'Why the hell didn't I think of that? I think you're right. Jack!' They were back in the car, mounting the verge to get past Felicity's car and in moments, screeching to a halt outside the front door. Before the car had properly stopped, Inspector Penrose was out of it and thundering up the steps.

'Steady on, sir,' called Jack.

Inspector Penrose ignored him. He rang the bell and then began thumping on the door. In a matter of seconds a frail, white-haired woman opened the door.

'Mrs Smithson?'

A younger woman came bounding down the stairs behind her.

'What's going on?' she called.

'Ah,' said Inspector Penrose, 'you must be Polly, Michael's girl.'

'Yes, that's right, but what's happened?'

Keith ignored her. 'Mrs Smithson, has Felicity Paradise been to see you this evening?'

'Yes.'

Inspector Penrose studied the woman properly for the first time. Her face was tear-stained; she looked on the very edge. He must go easy, take it slowly or he could mess this up. 'Did she – did she, tell you where she was going next?'

'She was going to telephone the police and then she was going to drive to Newlyn.'

'Newlyn, why ever should she do that?' he

asked gently, desperate with frustration, wanting to shake the truth out of her.

'I told her I thought that's where my husband might have taken Martin Tregonning.'

'Whereabouts in Newlyn?' Inspector Penrose shouted, unable to control his mounting panic.

The poor woman jumped backwards, slumping against the side of the doorframe. Polly stepped forward and put an arm around her. 'She's only just come out of hospital, Inspector.'

'I know that and I'm sorry, but there's no time. Where in Newlyn?'

'To his boat.'

'What, the *Jayne Marie*?'

'Yes.'

'It's moored in Newlyn?' Inspector Penrose thundered.

'I think so.'

'You think so!' he screamed.

'I'm sorry,' said Amelia. 'It's what I told Mrs Paradise. I told her I thought the boat probably would be there. He normally moors up just out of the harbour. That's where Martin will be, if ...' She let the words hang in the air.

'Right, Jack, you stay here with Mrs Smithson, I'll go to Newlyn.'

'You can't go on your own, sir.'

'I'm not going on my own; I'll call for some back-up.'

'But you've already called for back-up here, sir. There's not going to be enough coppers to go round.'

'Leave me to sort that out, lad. You stay here;

don't let her out of your sight.' In a matter of moments, Inspector Penrose hurtled out of the gates of Boswithey and headed for Penzance.

The traffic through Penzance was torturous. Inspector Penrose was seething with frustration. Armed officers were on their way, but they were coming from Truro. Even with all blue lights flashing, by the time they had weaved their way through this lot, they would be another three quarters of an hour. The joys of Cornwall, he thought, there's ordinary miles and then there's Cornish miles.

It was completely dark now. If Smithson had any sense, he would have waited until it was dark and then be under way, moving his prisoners to another port or, perhaps – Inspector Penrose's heart did a flip – dumping them out at sea somewhere. The previous evening he had read up on Jack du Plessey's history of suspected crime. It was like something out of *The Godfather*. If du Plessey and Smithson were one and the same man, then Smithson was capable of anything. He was, to all intents and purposes, a serial killer with apparently no conscience and a great deal of cunning. Penrose drove straight to the Harbour Office. He slammed on the brakes, ran across the yard and erupted through the office door. The young lad inside was heavily involved in making a cup of tea, and barely looked up at Keith's dramatic entrance.

'Stop that!' Keith demanded. 'We've got an emergency. I'm talking life and death here.' He flashed his card. 'The boat, *Jayne Marie*, looks like a fishing boat, is it here?'

The lad looked flustered. 'I don't know,' he said, 'the harbour master would know that.'

'Then where is the harbour master?' said Keith, almost gibbering with rage.

'He's gone home. Stephen will be along later, he's the coastguard on duty. I'm just here to answer the phone. The office is closed really; perhaps you could come back in the morning.'

'Oh, for Christ's sake!' Penrose was beside himself. 'Look, boy, concentrate, in the last half hour has a tender gone out to any of the boats?'

The young man's worried expression cleared. 'Yes, yes about twenty minutes ago.'

'Who was in the tender?'

'Two men and a woman. I noticed because the woman didn't look very well.'

'Yes, yes,' said Penrose, 'and where did the tender go?'

'Oh, I didn't see that bit.' Seeing the expression on Keith's face he made a big effort and hurried to the door. 'He went that way.'

Keith scanned the harbour. 'Could that be the *Jayne Marie*, over there? It's certainly a fishing boat, have you any binoculars?'

'Yes, of course.' The lad was back in seconds, scared by the policeman's obviously pent-up fury.

Keith trained his eyes on the boat. It was too dark and too far away to make out the name. He handed back the binoculars. 'You have a look, you've got younger eyes than me.'

The young man trained the binoculars on the

boat for an agonising length of time. 'I can't make out the name,' he said, 'but it looks like they are preparing to make way, they are hauling the tender on board.' Just at that moment a car rolled down the quay. 'Oh, there's Stephen now,' said the lad, clearly as relieved as Keith.

The contrast in the two men could not have been more different. 'Yes, that's the *Jayne Marie*, been here a few days. Came around from St Ives, apparently,' said Stephen Dexter, who introduced himself with a reassuring confidence.

'Now listen carefully,' said Keith, 'I can't tell you the background to this now, there isn't time, but we've got to stop her leaving. We have two problems. There is definitely one, but probably two kidnapped victims on board. There are certainly two villains on board, but there could be more – of the two we know about, both have killed and will kill again and they are certainly armed. My back-up team isn't going to be here for another twenty, twenty-five minutes. If we wait that long, the *Jayne Marie* will be well away. My fear is that once they're out to sea, they are going to dump their kidnap victims overboard.'

'Shit!' said Stephen, with feeling.

'Could your lad here take me out in a tender?' Stephen looked doubtful. 'It's alright,' said Keith, 'I'm not expecting him to get involved. It's so dark now, if we motor out as near as we dare and then he rows the last few yards, I could probably get aboard without anyone seeing me.'

'And what exactly are you planning to do against two armed men?'

'I'm not sure yet,' said Keith, 'but at least I can buy some time. I see the harbour master's launch is moored up. Could you have it primed and ready? The moment my boys arrive, load them on and just go for it, straight to the *Jayne Marie*, all lights blazing, fast as you can. Try to have a doctor on board.'

Stephen nodded. 'Is there any way you and I can communicate?' he asked.

'I've got nothing with me,' said Keith. 'This is a ridiculous situation, I should have anticipated it, the best I can do is use a mobile phone. If you would give me your number … '

The two men exchanged numbers and as they did so, Keith remembered he only knew how to do this because Felicity had taught him. It strengthened his resolve.

Stephen was frowning. 'I don't like this situation very much, Inspector.'

'Please,' said Keith, 'just do as I ask. I accept it's far from ideal but we really have no other option.'

Stephen hesitated and for an agonising moment Keith thought he was going to refuse to co-operate. Then he smiled. 'Don't worry. I'll get one of my lads to the top of the quay to direct your team straight down here. I'll have the engine running and the launch will be with you as quick as we can.'

'And as for this lad here,' said Keith, 'please order him to dump me on the boat and then leave, no matter what happens.'

'You hear what the Inspector says, Bobby?' Bobby nodded enthusiastically. The whole situation was way over his head. He felt frightened and confused.

241

Outside it was starting to rain. Keith swapped his suit jacket for Stephen's anorak, then he climbed gingerly down into the tender and Bobby gunned the engine.

The first sensation Felicity had on coming round was that she was going to be sick, and she was. It was quite dark and she was sitting on the floor. She moved away from the pile of vomit, disgusted with herself, and feeling in her jeans pocket, found a tissue to blow her nose and wipe her mouth. Two further sensations hit her simultaneously. Her head was pounding and the place she was in, was rocking. For a moment, she thought it must be her giddiness and then she realised that she was on a boat. There was an overwhelming smell of fish and this, combined with the rocking, made her retch again. After being sick the second time, she felt slightly better and her eyes were becoming accustomed to the dark. She realised she must be in the fish hold of the boat, there were planks of wood dividing up the space, a pile of fish boxes in the corner and ... a body. Unsteadily, she got to her feet, her heart pounding, and shuffled towards it. The body was hunched on its side. Kneeling down she eased it onto its back. It was Martin, and he was still breathing.

Bobby might have appeared a little on the slow side but he was a good seaman. He cut the engine a few yards short of the *Jayne Marie*. 'There's a ladder right aft which will take you up on deck,' he whispered to Keith. 'I'll drop you there and then if I start the engine and go for'ard, they'll be concentrating on me and what I'm doing and it will give you a chance to get on deck, without being seen.'

'Good idea, Bobby, thanks,' said Keith.

The rungs of the ladder were slippery and Keith's shoes highly unsuitable for climbing but he made it up onto the deck. He was grateful for Bobby's idea. The boy had let the tender fall with the tide well away from the boat and then started the motor. As he motored past the *Jayne Marie*, the two men on deck – one of whom in the light from the wheelhouse, Penrose could identify as Smithson – momentarily stopped what they were doing and watched the tender going by.

'What the hell's he up to?' Smithson said to his companion.

'Oh, don't take any notice of him, Ralph, he's the thick one.'

There was nothing for it, nothing else to do. Keith squared his shoulders and stepped out from behind the wheelhouse. 'Mr Smithson, you're under arrest. You do not have to say anything but anything you … '

Before he got any further Smithson wheeled round, looked at the Inspector and burst into laughter. 'Inspector Penrose,' he said, 'welcome aboard, so you've come to arrest me – you and whose army?'

'Half a dozen police marksmen,' Keith replied with as much confidence as he could muster.

'Oh, yes, then why aren't they with you? Get your hands up, Penrose.' Smithson was suddenly holding a

243

gun, which apparently had come from nowhere.

Penrose did as he was told. 'I'm unarmed,' he said.

'I bet you are, too, you English are unbelievable.' He nodded to his companion. 'Tell Ted we have an unexpected visitor. We'll just have to take the good Inspector along as a travelling companion.'

Ted, blast, thought Keith, so there is a third man on board. What chance had he of stopping them now? – not a chance in hell.

Felicity could hear voices above. She had no idea whose they were, but she had to get help for Martin. His breathing was now very shallow and he was deeply unconscious. There was blood all over his face and he had some sort of head wound. Instinct told her he was going to die soon if she didn't do something. She wasn't frightened, just very, very angry. She picked up one of the planks that were used for holding the fish. There was a door at the end of the hold, which she had already established was locked. She took a run at it with the plank and much to her surprise the door immediately buckled under the weight of the plank. It made an appalling amount of noise, but she was past caring. She found herself in what appeared to be the crew's sleeping quarters – there were four bunks against the bulkhead and mercifully no one in them.

'Ted, we're getting under way, get up on deck, we need you to take another guest down below.' It was Smithson's voice.

To her horror Felicity saw, on the ladder at the

end of the cabin, a pair of descending sea boots. 'Just coming, Boss. I'll be up in a sec, there's something going on down here, a noise, I'll just check it out first.'

The sea boots continued their relentless descent of the ladder. Felicity dropped her plank, ran forward and seized the man's jeans, just above his sea boots. She pulled, there was a scream and he lost his footing. She jumped aside and he came crashing down the ladder. There was the horrible sound of breaking teeth as his face hit the ladder repeatedly. His head hit the floor with a sickening thump. He lay motionless. For a moment Felicity stood appalled. She had never hurt another human being in her life before. The sensation lasted only a second, then the anger returned and she was scrambling up the ladder.

Three things happened at once and Penrose recognised this was his only chance. Ted, whoever he was, seemed to have disappeared, temporarily, with an apparent shriek and clatter, which caused Smithson's other companion to go towards the wheelhouse to investigate what had happened. Smithson was distracted by what was going on and was only half concentrating on covering him with the gun. Then, mercifully, a passing boat kicked up a wash, the *Jayne Marie* began rocking violently, and in that moment, Penrose launched himself on Smithson. Head down, he charged him like a bull, and caught him full in the ribs. The gun went flying across the deck, unfortunately towards the wheelhouse. Keith was struggling and although

Smithson was not as fit as Keith, he was a big and powerful man. They were rolling over and over on the deck ... if he could just get to the gun.

'Ralph, I've got the gun, hold him still.'

'Bugger,' thought Keith; the guy from the wheelhouse had picked up the gun. If Keith could just keep moving then he wouldn't be able to aim properly. There was a sound of a shot as Keith rolled on his back pulling Ralph on top of him. Keith felt Ralph's body stiffen and slump.

'Fuck!' Keith heard the guy say.

Ralph was a dead weight on top of him now. Keith began to struggle to get out from underneath when a second shot rang out. He felt the bullet sickeningly penetrate his shoulder. He let out a cry of pain.

This was it then, the end. With his job, he knew it would probably end like this one day. Most of his body was pinned down by the weight of Ralph and his shoulder and right arm were now useless. Keith suddenly had an image of his children. He remembered a day they had been making a sandcastle at Kennack Sands. It had been one of those perfect Cornish days; blue, blue sky and sea, golden sand and just enough of a breeze to make it comfortable. They had laboured all day on the sandcastle; it was magnificent, and now they had to leave it. The tide would be in soon and he didn't want the children to see the way the sea would destroy their handiwork so relentlessly. Happy days. He braced himself for the second shot.

Felicity had reached the wheelhouse. She stared in

horror at the scene on the deck. The light from the wheelhouse was not enough to make out who was who, but there were two bodies on the deck and a man was standing in front of them, firing a pistol at them. She had to assume that this was not a good guy. She acted instinctively. Looking desperately around her, she saw a fire extinguisher clipped to the bulkhead. She wrenched it free and charged out of the wheelhouse. She ran towards the gunman, he started to swing round, but she was already on top of him. The fire extinguisher made contact with his head and he was down. He made a grunt as he fell, the gun falling from his hand onto the deck. She dropped the fire extinguisher and picked up the gun, pointing it at the figure slumped at her feet, but there was no need, he was out for the count. God, supposing I've killed him, she thought. Then she turned her attention to the two bodies on the deck, one of whom appeared to be squirming about. 'Mrs Paradise, is that you?'

Felicity went weak with relief at the sound of his voice. 'Yes, Inspector, are you hurt?'

'Just get this body off me, would you? It's Ralph Smithson. I think he might be dead.' Felicity shuddered. 'Oh, and Mrs Paradise, please put that gun down, would you, you're making me nervous.'

Felicity heaved Ralph Smithson's body off Keith, who grimaced, and stood up, one hand swinging uselessly at his side. He picked up the gun and studied the two bodies for a moment.

'Well, I don't think we're going to have much trouble with these two. Where's the third?'

'I pulled him down the ladder,' Felicity said. 'I think I've knocked all his teeth out.'

Keith smiled. 'You're quite a force to be reckoned with, aren't you, Mrs Paradise? Can you just get the mobile phone out of my jacket pocket? If you just ring the number it's set to, we'll get some help.' Felicity did as she was asked. 'Is Mr Tregonning on board?'

'Yes, he's alive, and he's breathing.'

'You go down to him, if you like, I'm alright here. I'll wait for my back-up.'

'I don't think you're going to have to wait very long,' said Felicity. 'There's a boat bearing down on us with all lights blazing and positively bristling with people. They are the good guys, aren't they, Inspector Penrose?'

Keith glanced over his shoulder and grinned. 'They certainly are. That's the harbour master's launch. They'll have medical help on board.'

'I'll go below then,' said Felicity. She started for the wheelhouse.

'Mrs Paradise.'

Felicity stopped. 'Yes?'

'Thanks,' said Keith, 'you saved my life.' He smiled. 'I think, traditionally it's supposed to be the other way around. I think, as a policeman, I'm supposed to save yours. Anyway, you were great.'

'My pleasure,' said Felicity. 'I can't believe I did it, I'm such a non-violent person.' She glanced around the deck. 'It looks like the last scene of *Hamlet*. I'm frightened I might have killed that guy.'

Keith walked over to the body, and knelt down,

feeling his pulse.

'He's fine; he's just going to have a headache. You really did very well.'

'Not bad for an old widow lady?' Felicity asked.

'Not bad at all,' said Keith.

The casualty department of the Royal Cornwall Hospital had an almost festive air.

'Just as well it isn't Saturday night, Inspector,' the registrar grumbled at Keith.

'You should be grateful for the custom,' Keith said. Despite his jocular manner, he looked pale and drawn, Felicity noted, as she sat by his trolley.

'You must have lost a lot of blood,' she said.

'Don't fuss,' said Keith, 'I'll have enough of that when the wife arrives.'

The roll call of casualties was considerable. Ralph Smithson was not dead: the bullet had clipped his lung and he was in intensive care but expected to make it. Felicity had mixed feelings about that. Keith was being kept in overnight but it appeared that the bullet had not shattered any bones in his shoulder – it was purely a flesh wound. Annie was being discharged the following day. She was conscious, perky and apparently giving the nurses a very hard time, and Martin – Martin, too, was going to make a full recovery. He was suffering from the drugs Ralph Smithson's mob had pumped into him and the various beatings to which he had been subjected. His right ankle was fractured where he had been thrown down the fish hold and he was likely to remain in hospital for a few days. Felicity was weak with relief.

Keith interrupted her thoughts. 'There's a police car outside waiting to take you back to St Ives. You won't have your car for a couple of days, I'm afraid. We need to let the forensic boys play with it first. I'll come and see you tomorrow; I'll need a statement, of course. I think things will be a little clearer for both of us in the morning, don't you?'

'It's my view,' said Felicity, 'that you should have the day off tomorrow, Inspector.'

'You tell that to my Super.'

'I would be delighted to do so,' said Felicity, 'and give him a lecture on his smoking habits while I'm at it.'

'I was joking,' said Keith, genuinely nervous, 'don't you dare. You go home and have a good rest, Mrs Paradise. You've earned it. Incidentally, I'm fairly certain that your reign of terror has immobilised all Ralph Smithson's henchmen, but in case you've missed anyone, there'll be a policeman outside your door tonight to ensure you sleep well.'

Much to her amazement, Felicity did sleep well that night. Alone in the house, and despite the police guard, she expected to feel nervous – instead she felt completely relaxed. She wondered what had happened to Amelia, whether she knew about her husband being in hospital, and in custody – if she cared, if it was a relief. It was so hard to guess at what she really felt about anything.

15

The following morning was a beautiful Cornish day. Felicity made herself a coffee and took it down to the harbour, remembering a similar day, less than a month before, when she'd done the same thing, before everything had happened. What an extraordinary period of her life this had been. Her mobile phone rang. She set down her coffee to answer it. It was Josh.

'I've had a call from your policeman, Fizzy. My dear girl, what have you been up to? You seem to have been impossibly brave. Penrose says he owes you his life. Gilla is having hysterics, she says she had a text from you – she thinks it's all due to her that you're safe. Typical! How are you feeling?'

'I feel fine,' said Felicity, 'I'm probably still in shock. There are a lot of loose ends to sort out yet but it does look as though we've got Charlie's "Mr Big". So, not only do we know who ordered Charlie to be killed, we now have the man who killed Oliver Colhoun.'

'I have got some loose ends I need to go through with you, too,' said Josh. His voice was oddly hesitant, embarrassed almost.

'Fire away then,' said Felicity.

'No, it's all rather complicated. I'd really like to come down and see you, when you've recovered.'

'Josh, I'm absolutely fine and I've got all the time in the world right now. I'm going to pick up Annie this afternoon, but I've nothing on until then. Whatever it is, just tell me.'

'I'd rather talk it through with you, face to face,' said Josh. 'I thought I'd get the sleeper and pick up a cab from Penzance. I can be with you by about half past eight to nine tomorrow morning. Will that be alright?'

'Yes, of course,' said Felicity, 'but you're being very mysterious. Should I be worried?'

'No, no, of course not,' said Josh. 'It's just that I can probably fill in a few of the gaps for you.'

Felicity felt oddly disquieted by her telephone conversation with Josh. For the first time since Charlie's death, she had begun to feel a sense of closure. Now, it seemed, there were still things she didn't know. Somehow the pleasure had gone from her day. She began wandering back up the street towards Cormorant Cottage and was cheered to see a couple of familiar figures standing outside.

'Inspector Penrose, how are you?'

'I'm fine,' he said, 'and you?'

'Good,' she said.

He did indeed look fine. His arm was in a sling but the exhausted pallor of the night before had gone. The sergeant, who was a tall lanky man, towered over them both. 'I'm not letting either of you out of

252

my sight ever again,' he said, 'you could have been killed, both of you.'

'But we weren't,' said Felicity. 'Would you like some coffee? I'm sorry I wasn't here, I wasn't expecting you yet.'

'I couldn't sleep,' said Keith. 'I discharged myself last night and had a couple of hours on the sofa. Then felt I needed to sort everything out while it was fresh in my mind.'

Felicity settled them at the kitchen table while she made a cafetière of coffee. 'Will you have any difficulty proving Ralph Smithson is Jack du Plessey, because you know, Amelia confessed it to me?'

'And me,' said Jack, 'she told me everything, about their escape from South Africa and their starting again here.'

'We're matching DNA now,' said Keith, 'just in case Ralph tries to deny it. One of the people he murdered in South Africa was a young woman. He raped her first, before he killed her.' Felicity shuddered. 'So we have DNA evidence on Jack du Plessey. It's not the sort of thing a policeman should say without the evidence, but I am absolutely confident that they are one and the same person.'

'It's why, of course, he was so nervous about Martin Tregonning,' said Felicity. 'Ralph gave him the job so that he could keep an eye on him and make sure that Martin didn't know his real name. He needn't have worried, Martin had no idea. So far as he was concerned, Ralph was just one of a group of badly-behaved young people who came into the bar where he worked and took the piss out of him.'

'For Martin's sake it was just as well he didn't know Ralph's true identity, because if he had, without any doubt, Ralph would have killed him,' Keith said, grimly.

'Will he go back to South Africa for trial?'

'I don't know yet,' said Keith, 'that's up to the powers that be. My job is to ensure the DPP have a bullet-proof set of evidence for trial here and then the British and South African governments can fight over him. I imagine he may be tried here and then sent back to South Africa to serve his sentence while he's being tried over there. That would be logical anyway.'

'And Amelia?' Felicity asked.

'Amelia is certainly going to be charged with perverting the course of justice but it's a question of whether she can demonstrate to us that she knew nothing about the drugs or the murders. My own view is that she will go down for a long stretch.'

'Really?' said Felicity. 'But you don't believe that she had anything to do with what Ralph's ghastly crimes?'

'No, I don't,' said Keith, 'but she must have known what he was doing. They have a daughter, you know, she lives in California. The moment she was eighteen, she left England and refuses to have any contact with her parents. There is a conclusion to be drawn from that. It looks as if the daughter knew what was going on – in which case, so did the wife. Just think how many lives Amelia could have saved if she had shopped her husband; including your husband's, Mrs Paradise.'

'I thought about that last night,' said Felicity. 'I was feeling sorry for her, still do in a way, but then I thought how she could have saved Charlie. I just can't understand why she protected Ralph, it makes no sense. I don't want to sound bitchy, Inspector, but although she is very beautiful, I don't think she's very bright. Maybe she just couldn't work out how to escape.'

'Possibly,' said Keith, 'maybe we will find an explanation, but more likely not, in my judgement. On the face of it, it appears she couldn't imagine life without him and was prepared to put up with both his criminal activities and his beatings. She obviously had some sort of self-destruct button she kept pressing every time she was tempted to bail out, and he had found a formula for controlling her – absolutely.'

They spent a couple of hours preparing Felicity's statement. When at last they'd finished, Felicity found it had proved to be an almost cleansing process. She felt better, easier, freer – except for one thing. As she made yet another pot of coffee, she steeled herself to ask the question. 'What exactly is Ralph Smithson going to be charged with, Inspector?'

'Kidnap, threatening a policeman with a firearm, assault and if we can find those drugs, drug running.'

'What about Charlie's murder and Ronald Baxter's?'

Keith let out a sigh, stood up and walked over to

the window. With his back towards her, Felicity could not see the expression on his face, but from the despondent set of his shoulders and the sadness in his voice, she knew he minded telling her what, in her heart, she knew was inevitable. 'The only evidence we have linking Ronald Baxter to your husband's death, and Ralph Smithson to Ronald Baxter's death, is your moments of second sight. I don't disagree with your conclusions, Mrs Paradise. I am perfectly prepared to believe that you saw exactly what happened, but without a miracle, I can see no way we will ever prove it.' He turned around, his eyes full of sorrow. 'Ralph Smithson will never be a free man again, you can be sure of that, but I'm afraid the official verdict on your husband's death will be that he was knocked down accidentally in a hit and run incident.'

'Because he was drunk,' Felicity finished, in a small voice, tears welling into her eyes.

'But we got him,' Keith said gently, 'we got your husband's "Mr Big".'

It was decided that Annie should go and stay with her daughter up in Bodmin for a few days in order to recuperate. There were no visitors booked into Cormorant Cottage.

'Do you mind looking after the cottage for me, my bird?'

'I think it's the least I can do,' said Felicity, sitting by Annie's bedside.

'It'll make a nice change, going up Bodmin. I don't see my daughter very often; she's too busy with all those children. Still with me to help her, she can have a bit of rest for a few days.'

'Annie,' said Felicity, in despair. 'I don't think you've grasped the purpose of the visit. You're going up there to recuperate, after being bashed over the head.'

'Don't fuss,' said Annie, and Felicity knew better than to argue.

Martin, too, was looking a lot better. He was just finishing his statement to Keith and Jack, when Felicity arrived at his bedside. Keith stood up as Felicity approached Martin's bed.

'He's making a lot more sense today,' he said, smiling. 'I've finished with him, he's all yours.'

'Inspector Penrose,' said Felicity, 'since this morning, I've been thinking about those drugs, they can't have been moved very far. I take it they weren't on the boat?'

'I have to admit that's where I thought they would be,' said Keith, 'but there's no sign of them. I thought Smithson's "lovely assistants"– who incidentally, have recovered from your various assaults on them – would be happy to tell us the whereabouts, but for some reason, they're not talking.'

'Felicity's clearly not a woman to be trifled with, is she?' said Martin, his voice still hoarse.

'I should say not,' Keith agreed.

Felicity was not going to be sidetracked. 'You said you've searched the house and the outbuildings at Boswithey?'

'We searched everywhere,' said Keith, 'and

Michael helped us. We went through every garden shed and I even had the boys sorting through the coal bunker, which was popular, as you can imagine.'

'What about my cottage?' Martin said, suddenly.

Both Keith and Felicity stared at him. 'Your cottage?' said Keith.

'Yes, Ralph hasn't found anyone to take over my job, so I presume the cottage is empty.'

'Bugger,' said Keith, 'why the hell didn't I think of that?'

'It's worth a look,' said Martin.

'It certainly is.'

Felicity's second night alone at Cormorant Cottage was not as peaceful as the first. The adrenalin which had carried her through the immediate aftermath of the events on the *Jayne Marie* had worn off. She was tired, but restless and irritable. She knew the cause of her problem – she was worried about Josh's visit and what he might have to tell her. She had bacon sizzling and coffee brewing when Josh arrived. As he was always a man keen on a big breakfast, Felicity was surprised when he refused and just asked for coffee.

'I have a kind of confession to make, Fizzy, something I have to tell you. Do you mind if we go straight to it? I just really need to tell you everything and tell you now.'

He looked terrible, Felicity noted, as though he hadn't slept at all. Her heart was beating unnaturally fast. Whatever it was Josh Buchanan was about to tell her, she knew she wasn't going to like it. 'Sit down, Josh, I'll pour the coffee.'

'Did you notice a change in Charlie in the last few weeks of his life?' Josh began.

'Yes, of course,' said Felicity, 'from the moment he took on the wretched Carver case.'

'To start with,' said Josh, 'I wondered if you and he were having difficulties. He became very morose and monosyllabic in the office, he wouldn't discuss the case, he was working all the hours God gave, he wouldn't go to the pub but he was drinking a lot in the office, after hours. One night, I got home and remembered I'd left a file behind so I came back to the office. I'd left Charlie working and he was still at his desk when I returned, and he was on the telephone. He put the phone down very quickly when I came into the office. He was white as a sheet, Fizzy, so unlike him, and he invited me to stay and share a Scotch with him. It was a cry for help, I could see that. I wanted to go home really because I had some work to do and I was tired, but he'd been so good to me in my times of trouble, I felt I had to accept. Anyway, you know how it is. We had a few drinks and then a few more and when the bottle ran out, I suggested we went to the pub. Much to my amazement, he agreed. We went to the Eagle and Child and sat in the snug at the back. We were both pretty drunk by then and I asked him point blank who he had been talking to on the phone, because whoever it was had clearly upset him ... and, Fizzy, he told me. It was Ralph Smithson, alias Jack du Plessey, and he was blackmailing him.'

Fizzy stared at Josh. 'Jack du Plessey was blackmailing Charlie?' Josh nodded. 'But Josh, why, what on earth could that horrible man have on Charlie?'

'That,' said Josh, heavily, 'is what I am about to tell you. What you have to understand before I start, Fizzy, is that Charlie made me swear, both that night when we were drunk, and again the following morning, when we were sober, that I would never tell a living soul what he had told me – and especially not you. He was deeply ashamed, you see.'

'Oh, for heaven's sake, Josh, please just get on with it.' Felicity stood up and began pacing the kitchen.

'Stop it,' said Josh, 'come here and sit down, hold my hand.' She did as she was asked. 'What you have to remember about Charlie is that he had a very difficult childhood.'

'I know all about Charlie's childhood,' said Fizzy, impatiently, 'if you remember, I was his wife!'

'OK, OK. I'm just reminding you. As you know, he did well at Oxford and was offered prestigious articles at Derwent Strange. He was very bright, and also had that other magical gift – charisma, charm, everyone liked him. He was good-looking and attractive to women, yes, but men liked him too. He was tipped for the very top, which is why Hugh Derwent singled him out from all the other clerks to accompany him on the trip to South Africa. The man they were going to investigate, as you know, was Thomas du Plessey. What you don't know is that Thomas du Plessey knew immediately who Charlie was, because James, Charlie's father, had been a mate of his.'

Felicity looked appalled. 'Charlie's father was friends with Ralph's father?'

Josh nodded. 'I think they had some business dealings together. I'm not suggesting for a moment that James did anything violent or terrible, in fact, I'm not sure he even did anything illegal. However, his death, by all accounts, was somewhat mysterious – he drowned. He was a strong swimmer, with no reason to kill himself, so there is a suggestion that he may have been murdered, but there was no evidence to back the theory. I'm digressing – the point is, that as far as I know, there was nothing especially sinister in the relationship between James and Thomas and, certainly, although Thomas was undoubtedly up to his eyes in fraud, there was no suggestion that he was a violent man either. It's his son who is the really evil bastard.' Josh paused to have a sip of coffee. The hand that held the cup trembled, Felicity noticed.

'Please go on, Josh,' she said, her voice almost a whisper.

'Thomas took Charlie under his wing as soon as he arrived in South Africa. He explained to Charlie that he had known his father, and Charlie quickly realised that Thomas knew his father a great deal better than he did himself. Thomas showed him the house where James had been born and where he had been to school. He also took Charlie to James's grave. Of course, all of this had to be done in a rather clandestine manner. Hugh Derwent would have taken a very dim view of Charlie fraternising with the man they had come to investigate. For Charlie, it was a huge emotional roller coaster. He had idolised his father, having last seen him when he was nine. Thomas fulfilled Charlie's childish dreams about his father. Thomas had a huge house and a swimming pool, a highly successful business, a fleet of cars and lackeys everywhere. It was how Charlie liked to imagine his father, living as he did, in a rented flat with his impoverished mother, while trying to cut some sort of a dash at Eton and Oxford.' Josh cleared his throat. 'I don't know the details, Charlie didn't tell me, but at some point Thomas asked Charlie to suppress some information, some figures presumably, he had discovered which exposed the scam the Inland Revenue in the UK suspected was going on. Thomas du Plessey asked Charlie to do it for his father's sake, to help his father's best buddy out of a hole. He also offered to put a sum of money in a Swiss bank account in Charlie's name. Charlie said he wrapped it all up in such a way that it almost seemed the right thing to do. Thomas said that James Paradise would have wanted him to look after his son and that he should not look on the money as a bribe, but simply as his right, his legacy.'

'But surely Charlie wouldn't have fallen for that?'

'He was twenty-two years old, he was worried sick about his mother and how he was going to support both her and himself, while he finished his Articles.'

'So he suppressed the information?'

Josh nodded and squeezed Felicity's hand

before letting it go. He stood up and walked over to the window. 'I was shocked, too, when I first heard it, but we've all made mistakes, Fizzy, haven't we, over the years, all done things we regret?'

'Not on that scale,' said Felicity.

Josh shrugged. He leaned against the windowsill, hands in his pockets, slightly more relaxed now that he had dropped his bombshell. 'Anyway he came back to London. If Hugh Derwent suspected anything, he didn't say so, but Charlie felt uncomfortable. He realised that he was not suited to life in commercial law. He was worried that if he had been tempted once, he might be tempted again. So he resigned from Derwent Strange, using the excuse of his mother not being well, and moved to Oxford.'

'And the money?' Felicity asked, already knowing the answer.

'He used it to buy the house in Norham Gardens.'

'My home,' said Felicity, brokenly. 'My home was bought with du Plessey money?'

Josh nodded. 'The thing is, Fizzy, I've thought about this a lot, particularly on the train coming down here. That house has provided so much good. Firstly, it was a home for Charlie's mother until she died, the first security she'd had since marrying James Paradise. Then it was a lovely home for you and your children growing up, and it was a haven for the likes of me and Gilla, and all your friends. You made it a very special place; it's nurtured a lot of people.'

'And it was bought with fraudulent money,'

Felicity spat out. 'I can't believe this, Josh. Why didn't you tell me before?'

'Let me finish the story first,' said Josh. 'The phone call I interrupted that night was from Ralph Smithson, alias Jack du Plessey. When Ralph was thrown out of South Africa – shall we call him Ralph, since that's how we know him?'

Felicity nodded. 'He wasn't thrown out, Josh, he had to escape before he was arrested. Inspector Penrose says he's virtually a serial killer. In South Africa, he raped a woman and then murdered her.' She was crying, quietly, tears just pouring down her face.

'Shall I stop for a moment?'

Felicity shook her head. 'No please, please go on.'

'When Ralph first came to England, his father gave him the name of Charlie Paradise. He assumed, I imagine, that he was still working for Derwent Strange and he apparently told Ralph if he needed a favour doing, Charlie was his man. That chap you call the "Skunk" – what was his name?'

'Ronald Baxter,' Felicity said.

'Ronald Baxter got done for drug dealing some years ago now and that is when Ralph first contacted Charlie and asked him to represent Baxter. It must have been shortly after he arrived in the UK, I think. Charlie refused and Ralph told him who he really was and threatened to blackmail him, expose him for having taken a bribe.'

'But surely Ralph wouldn't have done that because Charlie could have countered by exposing

Ralph's position.'

'I guess that's right,' said Josh, 'which is presumably why Ralph did nothing about it for years, but Charlie had to live with the knowledge that at any time Ralph could choose to expose him. Ronald Baxter was put away and was then released about eighteen months ago.'

'Just in time to kill Charlie,' Felicity said, her voice bleak. 'That's rather ironic, isn't it?'

Josh nodded. 'I don't know what made Charlie think that the Ben Carver case was somehow linked to Ralph Smithson, whether the missing link was Ronald Baxter. I presume it was, but I guess we'll never know now. That telephone call from Ralph Smithson was ordering Charlie to drop the Carver case – and if he didn't, his family would be at risk. I think it was the shock of that threat, which made him blurt out the truth to me. If I hadn't gone back to the office for that file, I don't think he would have ever told me.'

'But why didn't he tell me?' said Felicity. 'I was his wife, for heaven's sake, and it was me who was being threatened.'

'Your grandsons, I think,' Josh corrected.

'Oh, my God,' said Felicity, 'you mean he put Ben and Harry at risk and didn't tell anyone?'

'The conversation I'm telling you about – between me and Charlie – happened only two days before Charlie died. I don't know what he was going to do, Fizzy. I don't know whether he was going to tell you, tell the police, pull out of the case and tell no one ... I have honestly no idea. As you can imagine, I begged him to drop the case but he seemed to feel it was dishonourable. He had behaved badly once; he didn't want to do so again.'

Felicity was suddenly very angry. 'This seems to be all about Charlie. What about his grandsons? If they were being threatened, then there shouldn't have even been a discussion about Charlie's reputation or Charlie's behaviour. He should have told me and the police the whole story straight away, and ensured James's family had protection.'

Josh shook his head. 'I suppose he'd internalised it all for so long, carried the burden of what he'd done, he just couldn't offload it.'

'He did to you,' said Felicity, bitterly.

They sat in silence for a few moments, Felicity bleak with shock. Charlie, like everyone, had his good and bad points but truth, honesty and decency were always the elements of him she had loved the most. Now they all seemed to be founded on a lie.

'Are you going to tell Inspector Penrose?'

Josh shook his head. 'I don't intend to tell anyone, ever, provided that's how you feel, too. I know this has come as a big shock to you, Fizzy, but Charlie was a good man. He did one bad thing and he paid a terrible price for it. No one wins by exposing him at this stage and the evidence is all hearsay. Charlie is dead – nothing can be gained by telling anyone.'

'So why did you tell me?' Felicity asked.

'Because you got so near to the truth, I felt it was wrong to keep this from you. Looking at you now, I'm not sure I've made the right decision.'

Felicity took a deep breath and met Josh's gaze. 'You did the right thing, Josh. Thank you. I know it can't have been easy for you but you're right, in my heart I knew something wasn't stacking up. If Charlie hadn't been linked in some way to the du Plesseys, there is no way he would have become involved in a case like Ben Carver's.'

'Do you think your policeman chum suspects there is more to it than meets the eye?'

'I'm not sure,' said Felicity, 'but he's already told me that they won't be re-opening Charlie's case because there's no evidence, and there is plenty of other stuff with which to charge Ralph. They're positively spoilt for choice.'

'I also suspect he knows it could involve opening a can of worms,' said Josh. 'That's another good man, your Inspector.'

Felicity nodded. 'I don't want the children to know.'

'No, of course not,' said Josh.

'Or Gilla.'

'No one, Fizzy, ever. I have to admit that over a slightly alcoholic lunch, I did tell Gilla I had been worried about Charlie's behaviour before his death but no more, I promise.'

'But you didn't tell me anything, Josh. You even confided in Gilla, but not me. Was your investigation at Derwent Strange a complete sham, did it even take place since you already knew all the answers?'

'I told you the truth about my investigations. I had to do it, to stop you contacting them direct. They told me nothing I didn't already know, of course, but it happened, just as I told you.'

'I knew you were holding out on me. I'm not going to find this easy to forgive, Josh.'

Their eyes met and they regarded one another sadly and in silence for a moment or two. Then Josh held out his hand. 'I broke my promise to Charlie by telling you, but that's where it ends. His secret is safe with me, with us, I think.' After a moment's hesitation, Felicity gave him her hand. They shook hands solemnly.

'His secret is safe with us,' she whispered in agreement, but in her heart she knew it would be hard ever to forgive either of them – Charlie or Josh – for deceiving her.

EPILOGUE

1st May 2003, St Ives, Cornwall

Spring always comes late to West Cornwall, but this year, it had been later than usual. But worth waiting for, Felicity thought, as she sat on the first floor balcony of Jericho Cottage, anticipating the arrival of her guest. Orlando lay at her feet, basking in the warmth of the sun. Every time a seagull shrieked, his marmalade tail twitched. He harboured an obsessive and totally unrealistic ambition that one day he would catch a seagull. It had become his raison d'être.

Jericho Cottage had formerly been named 'Harbour View Cottage'. The oddity of the name, combined with the need to bring a little piece of Oxford with her, had produced a good result, she felt. In the end, the decision to move had not been difficult. There was no question of her staying on in Norham Gardens, knowing what she knew now. She had sold the house quickly and having bought Jericho Cottage and retained a few thousand pounds in order to renovate it, she had donated the balance – a not inconsiderable sum – to a drugs rehabilitation centre. This left her with a home, the clothes she stood up in and virtually nothing else. She would have to earn a living and fast. Sometime, she supposed, her children would query what had happened to all the family money. She had talked it through with Josh and they had decided to say that Charlie had made some very poor investments. Now the only thing of value she had was a small painting by Constable, which had belonged to Charlie's mother.

She knew the gesture, however magnificent, could not put right the past. The sum she had donated had to be far in excess of the bribery money Charlie had originally received so long ago, but it could only dull the pain, not heal it. She knew she would never lose the sense of sadness she felt over the fact that Charlie had not felt able to confide in her. For years – eleven years to be precise – he had lived with the knowledge that Ralph Smithson, at any stage, could choose to expose him. In the years preceding that, he had kept secret the fact that he had accepted a bribe. Being the man he was, it would have worried him, gnawed away at him. What did it mean? Did it mean that Charlie didn't trust her, that he believed she didn't love him enough? And if so, was he right? She thought of Amelia who, apparently, had loved Ralph so much, been so under his spell, that she had entirely lost her grip on reality. Could she herself have been that loyal? If she had shared Charlie's guilty secret, would she have persuaded him to drop the Carver case in order to keep them all safe until the next time Ralph Smithson needed a favour? She doubted it.

She would have urged him to defy Ralph, and would the result have been the same – a violent, lonely death on the Woodstock Road?

So lost was she in her thoughts, that she hadn't noticed him walking up the street. It wasn't until there was a knock on the door that, by leaning over the balcony, she could see him below. 'I'll be right down,' she called.

Keith Penrose looked around the kitchen appreciatively. 'This is charming, Mrs Paradise.'

'It is, isn't it?' she said. 'It's very small, just two up, two down. I have a bedroom on each floor. I've chosen to put the sitting room upstairs because of the view. Come up to the balcony, it's such a beautiful day.'

He followed her upstairs. The balcony faced due south with stunning views across the harbour. A bottle of wine stood in a cooler with two glasses and a bowl of olives. 'I know you're not supposed to drink on duty, but I thought we deserved one glass at least.'

'Jack's waiting down on the Wharf in the car. He can drive back, and I agree, I think we've earned it. Let's just get the business out of the way.' He produced a piece of paper from his pocket. 'There's just one final witness statement for you to sign, it's with regard to the drugs haul.'

'But you found it in Martin's cottage.'

'I know, but I just need you to confirm that you saw it first in the room under the tackroom. I don't want the defence trying to say that Martin was the drug runner all along, and had been keeping the stash in his cottage.'

Felicity signed the piece of paper with a flourish. 'Is that it then?'

'Until the hearing. It's been set for the ninth of June. They want to try and push it through before the summer recess.'

Felicity handed him a glass. 'So do we have a toast?'

'I was thinking,' said Keith, 'that boy, Oliver Colhoun, he died a year ago today, didn't he?'

Felicity nodded. 'And it's the anniversary of the death of Martin's wife. I asked him if he wanted me to come and spend the day with him but he said he'd rather be alone. I can understand that.'

'Well,' said Keith, thoughtfully. 'A fair number of people have died, in connection with this case – some good, some bad – but whoever you are and whatever you've done, losing a life prematurely is a dreadful thing. So maybe we should raise our glasses to the future because we – you and I – are lucky enough to have one.'

'The future,' said Felicity. They clinked glasses and drank.

'We really are lucky, aren't we,' Felicity said after a pause. 'You, me, Martin – it could have all turned out very differently.'

'The skipper of the *Jayne Marie*, Harold Blundy, he broke down under interrogation, cried like a baby, admitted everything, including killing Baxter. The plan was to dump you and Martin out at sea, weigh down your bodies – we'd never have found you. It's why they didn't kill Martin straight away. They were using him as bait to get you as well.'

Felicity shuddered. 'It's just as well I had a knight in shining armour to protect me, isn't it, Inspector.'

'It's just as well I was so ably assisted by some crazy artist witch, who would never take no for an answer.'

For some moments they sat in satisfied silence, gazing out across the harbour. Keith asked at last, 'Do you miss Oxford?'

'I miss my friends, and of course, my family, but they'll all come and visit me.'

'I'm sure they will,' Keith agreed, 'with a view like this.'

'The next thing I have to do is to find a job.'

'What are you going to do?' Keith asked.

'Teach art in some capacity, I haven't worked out how yet, but it's the only way I know to earn a living.'

'You're in the right place for it,' Keith said. He smiled slightly and took a sip of his wine. 'I'd wondered whether you'd set yourself up as a clairvoyant, with a crystal ball, tarot cards and all that. You'd be quite popular with the visitors, I imagine.'

'You may mock, Inspector Penrose, but my second sight has proved very useful. Just you remember that now I'm living on your patch, you know where to come if you need any help.'

Inspector Penrose grinned. 'I will bear that in mind, Mrs Paradise.'

Debby Fowler's first short story was published when she was seventeen. Since then, she has had published over six hundred stories for numerous women's magazines. She has also written seven novels and with her husband Alan, a series of small business guide books and various books of non-fiction on subjects as diverse as adoption and money management.

Debby lives in St Ives with her husband and their three younger children.

Letting Go is the first in the Felicity Paradise crime series. The others published so far are *Intensive Care, The Silver Sea, Smoke Damage, Beach Break* and *In a Small Town;* the seventh *Swings and Roundabouts* will be published in 2012.